# ONCE out of RANGE

By
Lucinda Johnson

# ONCE out of RANGE

A Novel

*The seventh Jackson Avery/Charlie Black novel*
By
## Lucinda Johnson

PRUGGUS PUBLISHING, LLC

Paper Book ISBN: #978-0-9900225-3-4

E-Book ISBN: #978-0-9900225-4-1

Library of Congress Control Number: 2015960596

Cover design and book layout
Hoodie Beitz, Custom Graphics, Inc.
www.customgrfx@aol.com

First Printing January 2016

Second Printing March 2018
Printed in USA

*For Pruggus, the one you can always count on.*

**Dedicated to:**
**My dear Black**
Thank you for your persistent arguments.
Thank you for your insistent affection.
**Rest in Peace.**

## Acknowledgements

Thanks to my consultants, especially Tamara, for putting up with my never-ending queries.

Thanks to my friends, real and imaginary.

Thanks to my faithful guardians who have sparked my life.

## CHAPTER 1

After closing the office for the night, and locking the building's outer front door, he tucked his chin against the cold and hurried towards his truck. The thick snow was blowing hard. He dropped his key fob in the snow in the middle of the small parking lot before he'd had a chance to push the unlock button. "Shit!!! Shit shit shit," he cried as he bent over to find the fob.

Not only had he left his hat in his office, he'd left his gloves, too. The snow had piled up at least eight inches in the parking lot and on his truck. His hands were freezing, and he couldn't find the damn fob. It wasn't just his truck key that he'd dropped; all of his keys were clipped to the truck key. He couldn't get back in the office building; he wouldn't be able to get into his house. He was screwed if he didn't find the keys.

"God dammit," he said, as he tried to kick the snow around in hopes of exposing his keys. His shoes, socks, and feet were wet. The snow had gotten into his outer pull-over plastic snow-boots. His situation was getting more uncomfortable by the second.

He looked around the parking lot. The sun had set well over an hour earlier. The outside lights on the office building were subtle down-lights. Not much help in finding keys dropped in the snow. At least he was wearing a coat, he thought. He knelt down on one knee and felt around in the snow where he thought it likely the keys had dropped.

A vehicle turned into the parking lot. The headlights swept across the key search area, and illuminated him still down on one knee. He heard the car engine rev, and then the car swish and slide on the snow as it obtained grip enough to shoot forward. He'd just begun to stand up when the car nailed him. The SUV hit him and threw him further from his keys.

The SUV turned away from him. He rolled in the snow as he fell from the impact with the front left bumper. The vehicle sped out of the parking lot and into the night.

He lay in the snow wondering what had just happened. He didn't try to move. He knew his legs were not in good shape. He thought maybe that was the extent of his injuries until he tasted the blood in his mouth. "Shit. Shit shit shit," he said once again. He instinctively felt in his coat pocket for his cell phone. It wasn't there. His arms worked. Good. He searched all of his pockets. No cell phone.

He heard another car coming. The car turned into the parking lot. The headlights lit up the other end of the lot. The car parked, but kept the engine running. No one got out, but he screamed for help anyway.

He heard the car engine stop. He heard someone get out of the car. He screamed for help again. He heard a woman call back to him, "Someone out here?"

"Yes. I'm over here. Been hit by a car. I think my legs are broken."

She found him lying in the snow. There was blood

on the snow, but she couldn't tell where exactly he was bleeding. "I'll call 911," she said. She went back to her car. He thought she was going to get her cell phone. She got in her car, started it and drove away.

"What the hell? God dammit," he cried out.

He began pulling himself across the parking lot, back to where his keys might be. His legs hurt so badly, he was moving at a proverbial snail's pace. He was so cold. As he got closer to where he'd been when the vehicle had hit him, he earnestly looked in the snow for his keys. At last, he found them. He pushed the button to open his truck. The taillights blinked at him. He kept inching his way, on his belly, towards the truck. It seemed like forever, but he finally reached the truck.

How the hell was he going to get in the truck without the use of his legs? The pain was tearing through him. It crossed his mind that he might just blackout and then freeze to death. How had this happened? He knew. He'd been in a hurry to go to her apartment. Maybe she'd come looking for him. He knew she wouldn't. She'd said he should stop by on his way home. She said she wasn't doing anything tonight. He knew she'd think his wife had something going on that he had to go home for, straight home. She wouldn't think to come to the office parking lot to look for him. She wouldn't think to come to the office to look for him on the ground in the snow by his truck. She'd gone home a couple of hours ago. He hadn't called her to say yay or nay about stopping by. His wife would think he was working late. He always told his wife he was working late. Sometimes he did work late. Sometimes he went to see her at her apartment before going home.

He started to cry. How could a fifty-five year old man, a professional man, have gotten himself into such a situation? He knew he should never have let her rope him into an affair. She'd started it slowly. He'd hired her to be his receptionist. Over the six-months she'd been part of his office staff, she'd insinuated herself more and more into his space. She came in his office and stood close to him, right next to his chair, behind his desk. She touched his arm at first, then his shoulder, then she rubbed his neck. She wasn't pretty. She wasn't smart. She wasn't even his type. She just paid attention to him. She talked to him in a voice that reminded him of when he was a little boy. It suddenly dawned on him, she was like his mother. Oh shit, he'd been having an affair with his mother. He had to put a stop to this.

He tried to reach the door handle of his truck. It wasn't going to happen. He needed help. He had his keys. Maybe he could pull himself back into the office. He looked through the still falling snow at the front door of the office building. The handle on that door was just as out-of-reach as the handle on his truck door. Shit.

Another car turned into the parking lot. The headlights found him. He saw the emergency lights on the car. It was the police. An officer got out and carefully walked through the snow to him. He told him an ambulance was on the way. The ambulance showed up within minutes. He dropped his keys in the snow as they loaded him on the gurney. He was transported to the county hospital.

His wife came to the hospital while he was in x-ray.

She stood by his bed as the hospital personnel put his legs in plaster casts, and then hoisted them into traction position. He was immobilized. He told his wife about the keys and that he'd left his truck unlocked. He was worried about it. She told him she'd take care of it. He unintentionally closed his eyes and passed out.

His wife drove back to the parking lot by his office building. She readily found the keys and locked his truck. Then she let herself into his office building. She crossed the building's common area and let herself into his office space. She turned on the lights. The reception desk had fresh flowers on it. The two staff office doors were closed. His office door was open. His hat and gloves were on his desk. She picked them up. She saw his cell phone on the desk. She picked it up and scrolled through the text messages. One was sent within the past half hour. It was from Duffy, the receptionist. It asked the simple question: where are you? She looked around, saw nothing that seemed unusual to her, so she turned off the lights, and locked the doors as she left.

As she walked to her car, she pulled her own cell phone from her purse. She punched in a familiar number. "Terry's in the hospital. Yeah, he's still alive. Both legs are broken. You should have hit him harder."

## CHAPTER 2

Duffy Dot, Terry Small's receptionist, was as usual the first one to arrive at the office the next morning. The large very late-middle aged, tights and tunic-attired woman strode into the office everyday ready to counter any challenge to her own perceived authority. As Terry's receptionist, she felt in-charge of the office. Except for the personal cell phones, all in-coming phone calls went through her. She was the first to deal with clients who came to the office in-person. She set the tone. It was her domain. This morning, she went through her regular morning routine of turning on the lights, printers, then rebooting the computers and server, and listening to everyone's voice mail. She also made it her business to nose around in everyone's office. Spurred on by her own paranoia and guilt, she wanted to know what others knew and were doing. Not that what she saw in their offices was really helpful to that end, she still did it every morning while she was alone in the office.

Most mornings Duffy Dot beat even Terry to the office. It was a daily goal of hers to be the first one in. It gave her a sense of superiority in some odd way or another. She believed that the first one in the office each morning was the most truly dedicated employee. Well, at least as in the old school office models, that was the thinking. And

Duffy was definitely old school.

Sherry Kroyton, a psychologist employed by Terry, and really the person who did most of the work in the office, was the next to arrive. Sherry had been a licensed, practicing psychologist in Denver, Colorado for thirty some-odd years. When she and her husband, Sherman, moved to Taos, New Mexico the year before, their intention was to retire. She hadn't planned on transferring her license to New Mexico and going to work for another psychologist. Not at all. She and Sherman had been planning their retirement to northern New Mexico for a long time. Sherman put in thirty-five years with a furniture design-build company in Denver. But when the time came to actualize their golden years, their investments were not so golden. Their portfolio had not performed as it'd been predicted to, back when predictions of such were believed to mean something. They now needed additional income to live as they wanted to live. Sherry resumed her licensed psychologist career. Sherman found sales work at an art gallery in Taos. Though he'd always been in sales, he'd never been in retail art sales. He told Sherry it was not unlike trying to sell the emperor's new clothes. But all-in-all, they really liked Taos. They liked the small town aspect and the climate was perfect for them: four distinct seasons and lots of outdoor activities to choose from all year. They were both healthy and fit sixty year olds.

"Morning, Duffy. Where's Terry?" Sherry asked as she looked past Duffy to Terry's darkened office.

"Don't know," Duffy answered in her usual sing-song tone.

Sherry thought better of further useless conversation

with Duffy, so she went straight to her own office and closed the door. She could tell the receptionist had been poking around her desk again. Every morning, the same thing: Duffy consistently moved the keyboard and files on the desk as she snooped, and then never put them back where she'd found them. Duffy didn't take any measures to conceal her snooping. Sherry knew that was a sure sign of a passive-aggressive personality. Duffy had displayed this behavior from the get-go. Sherry had never mentioned Duffy's prying to Terry. Sherry didn't trust Terry. As a long-time psychologist, she was tuned-in to watching and listening to people. She knew there was something a bit off with Terry, but she didn't know exactly what. She really wasn't sure if she wanted to know.

Sherry heard Erlene Vigil arrive. Erlene, recently licensed and excited to be starting her career, was always energetic and happy. Then she heard the attractive young psychologist ask Duffy the same question that she'd asked, "Where's Terry." Sherry also heard the same dead end sing-song response from Duffy.

Erlene knocked and stuck her head in Sherry's office, "Hi. Is Terry coming in today?" she asked.

Sherry replied, "No idea. I haven't heard from him."

Erlene stepped in to Sherry's office, closed the door, and said, "I know he has a court date this morning. But he has to come here first. I have the file he needs."

"What case is it?" Sherry asked.

"That poor old man from Cimarron, you know. Prosecutor says he deliberately pushed his teenaged son out of their boat into the lake over at Eagle Nest last summer.

The son drowned."

"Oh jeez. Yes. Of course, you did the research on that, didn't you?"

Erlene replied, "I did! I did all the work on the entire family's profile. Research, conclusion, everything. Wrote it up. Terry is just going to read in court everything I prepared. Same old same old: I do the work, then he presents it. Usually, he doesn't even look at the file until right before he takes the stand!"

Sherry asked, "Why don't you go to court? You're licensed. You're a damn good psychologist. Do it yourself."

Erlene said, "He won't let me. He says a man has to present in court or the jury won't buy it. He says 87% of the time, if a woman presents the psychological expert witness testimony, the jury ignores it."

Sherry laughed and said, "Bullshit. He's throws out percentages that he simply makes up. Don't ever believe him about anything when he includes a percentage or some statistic as a reason to do or not do something."

"Really?" the younger woman replied. "He makes it sound bone fide."

"It isn't."

"How do you know?" Erlene asked.

"Because he has tried that lame tactic with me. When I began working for him, I noticed how he frequently cited some statistic, or percentage, or something to substantiate his ridiculous statements. At first, I thought he'd really been doing some serious research, and that the stats were real. But, he did it so often, and the percentages were always a little too specific, that I asked him to give me his sources.

He couldn't. He quickly changed the subject and avoided further conversation about whatever the matter had been."

"Wow, really. Now I'll ask for sources."

"Do. He won't have any to give you. He's faking."

"Why?" Erlene asked.

"That, I can't tell you. He's an interesting case."

"Wouldn't he know better? He's a psychologist!" Erlene said.

Sherry added, "He's still an interesting case. Maybe he really bought into someone else's bullshit at some conference or another. It's a pattern that smacks of a business self-help seminar, or a left-over from an Erhard Seminar Training indoctrination kind of nonsense."

Erlene laughed, "I've heard of EST, from the seventies and eighties. Studied that in school. He definitely shows effects of that!"

Duffy open Sherry's office door without knocking, "What are you two gossiping about in here?"

"What do you need, Duffy?" Sherry asked, ignoring Duffy's question.

"I'm wondering if I should call Terry. He has a full schedule today. Not like him to not be here by now."

Erlene asked, "What do you usually do when he's late?"

Duffy screwed her mouth into an odd shape and said in a child-like voice, "I don't know. I can't remember him being late like this. Should we be worried?"

Erlene looked at Sherry and laughed, "Really?"

Sherry suggested to Duffy that she return to her own desk and do whatever she thought best.

Duffy left, leaving the door open.

"Passive-aggressive in-training?" Erlene proposed.

Sherry replied, "The training wheels are long-gone. She's a pro."

Sherry and Erlene heard the front door open again. They expected to hear Terry voice, but were surprised when it was Terry's wife, Gertie Small, who replied to Duffy's greeting and oddly worded inquiry about Terry's whereabouts.

"Duffy, what are you asking?" Gertie Small remarked.

In her insipid sing-song voice, Duffy said, "We were wondering where Terry is. He's always here by now."

Erlene looked at Sherry and said "We?"

Without replying to Duffy's non-question, Gertie walked past Duffy's reception station and looked in Sherry's office. "Oh good, you're both here," Gertie said as she went into Sherry's office and closed the door.

"Hi. What's up?" Sherry asked.

Gertie replied, "Terry had an accident last night. Broke both legs and cracked his pelvis, etcetera. He's in the hospital, in traction."

Erlene asked, "Accident? Where? What happened?"

Gertie said simply, "In the parking lot, here. He was hit by a car as he walked to his truck. He's in the hospital for now. He'll be out of service for a while."

"Sorry to hear that. Anything we can do?" Sherry asked.

"Well, you are both qualified licensed psychologists. I know you are the brains here and that you do the real work for this practice. God knows Terry is not the sharpest tack in the box. If you will just carry on for a while, I'd appreciate it," Gertie said. "I hope to get this worked out soon."

Sherry and Erlene looked at each other, a little surprised at what they'd just heard. Sherry said, "Sure. We will...umm...keep everything moving here. Tell him not worry about anything."

Gertie said flatly, "No problem there! He only knows how to worry about himself."

Erlene asked, "Should we go see him? Can he have visitors?"

Terry's wife replied, "He's pretty drugged up right now. The breaks were seriously painful I'm told. They told me he'll need extensive therapy just to walk again. So he's kind of out-of-it for the time-being. Don't bother. He won't know you're there. Just tell the Duff to send him a plant or something."

"Okay. Anything we can do for you?" Erlene asked.

"No. I'm fine. Thanks. The kids are probably going to come visit him. No emergency. He's not going anywhere. Both legs in traction. Bad break for him," Gertie said with a small laugh. "Okay then. Thanks a lot. Call me if you need anything!"

Sherry and Erlene said goodbye to Gertie. They heard her tell Duffy in the most off-handed way that Terry would be out of the office for an indeterminate period of time because he had broken both legs and would be hospitalized for some time. They heard Duffy's exaggeratedly high-pitched squeal of horror in response to the news.

"Oh nooo. Oh my God! Where is he? What hospital?"

Duffy asked through sudden tears.

Gertie said as she left, "Well since there is only one hospital in the county, maybe that's where he is."

Sherry said to Erlene, "Better get ready for court. You are the expert witness this morning!"

Erlene smiled and said, "Hope that infamous 87% of the jury doesn't harbor gender bias for expert witnesses."

Sherry laughed, "You'll be great."

## CHAPTER 3

After Duffy Dot completed her drama-fest reaction to the news of Terry's accident, she announced to Sherry and Erlene that she was going to personally deliver flowers to Terry at the hospital.

"Fine idea. Take the day off. You're too upset to work today," Sherry suggested sarcastically.

Duffy not even noticing the sarcasm said, "I think I should. I'll see you tomorrow...if I feel better."

After Duffy had gone, Erlene and Sherry concluded that yes their long-held suspicions of Terry and Duffy's amorous liaison was true. They also concluded that Gertie was well aware of it.

Erlene said, "You'll be here alone. I'm off to the courthouse."

Sherry said, "Ah yes. The Duff, as Gertie calls her, is out of the office. Wonderful day ahead for both of us. I should call Sherman and let him know about Terry."

"Does he know Terry?" Erlene asked.

"No, they aren't friends or anything. Does Terry have any friends? Just want to let him know. It's a small town, you know."

"You're right, Terry doesn't have any friends that I know about. Except the Duff. He has the Duff!" Erlene quipped. They both laughed.

Sherry phoned her husband at the gallery, "Sherman, hi. Today's big news is that Terry is in the hospital with both legs broken and a cracked pelvis. He was in some kind of car accident in the office parking lot last night."

Sherman exclaimed, "Oww. That had to hurt. Both legs?"

"That's what Gertie said. Both legs are in traction."

"He gonna have any surgery?" Sherman asked.

"She didn't mention any. Duffy has gone to the hospital. I'm sure she'll have all sorts of news tomorrow."

Sherman said, "Yes, she might have actual news and will certainly have made-up news."

"That's the truth. How's the show prep going there?" Sherry asked.

"Everything is looking very nice. The opening is three days away, and we are ahead of schedule. Walls are painted. The stands and podiums are ready. We will start setting up the show this afternoon. Northburn should be here soon with the first load."

Sherry asked, "Only Northburn's work in the show?"

Sherman laughed, "Goodness yes. Only his work! He is the archetypical prima-donna artist. Only his ceramic sculptures and pots, and his drawings of his sculptures and pots will be allowed to grace this gallery during his show."

"Maybe he'll have drawings of him doing the drawings of his sculptures and pots. How long will the show be up?" Sherry remarked.

Sherman laughed, and responded, "Two weeks. I

hope the sales are good."

"Me, too. Northburn is a big-deal artist, isn't he? Should have a healthy turnout," Sherry suggested.

"Yes. Peter Northburn is one of the premier ceramicists in the country. He's the guy with the special glazes. The ceramic community is in awe of his glazes."

"And he lives here doesn't he?"

"Near here. He lives up in the mountains this side of Angel Fire, up Taos Canyon."

Sherry asked, "Isn't his studio at his home?"

"Yes. He's got a showroom, studio, home compound. We're supposed to visit it tomorrow. He wants to show the gallery staff his wood-fired kiln and general set-up so we can talk him up as we sell his art."

"That'll be a fun field-trip. With the clear weather now, it should be a beautiful drive over there."

"Should be. Cold but pretty. Snow covered mountain scenery. I'm looking forward to seeing his place. His ceramics are really very nice. And his glazes are incredible. But I'm told he's a princess to deal with. If we can get any traffic during his show, we'll sell art!" Sherman affirmed.

Sherry said, "Yeah, can only sell when there are buyers."

Sherman agreed, "Really!"

## CHAPTER 4

When Duffy reached Terry's room at the hospital, she found him asleep and no Gertie. It was as she'd hoped. She made a big show to the nurses that she'd brought the only flowers in the room. She told them she was going to sit with him for a while. They really didn't care if she stayed, and they told her so.

When the nurses were out of sight, she moved a chair close to Terry's bed. She held his hand as he slept. She caressed and kissed his hand, said his name, and then stood, leaned over him and kissed his lips. No response. She sat down again. She rested her head on the bed by his arm. Then she moved his arm to hold her head. She stayed like that for a few minutes. It was uncomfortable, so she stood, moved the chair slightly, and perched one of her sturdy buttocks on the edge of the bed. She was careful not to jostle his body. She sat like that, close to his torso, with her back to his legs up in traction. She moved his hand to her lap. She tightly snugged his hand to her crotch.

Suddenly, Terry woke. He twitched his hand away from her lap. His eyes were wide open and staring at her when he screamed. Duffy more or less fell off the high bed. She lost her balance, and tripping over the chair, she was stumbling towards the door when a nurse came running into the room.

"What? What's the matter?" the nurse asked intently.

Before Terry could say anything, Duffy said, "He must have had a bad dream. He just screamed. Scared me to death."

Terry corrected her, "No! I woke up to find you sitting on me with my hand in your..." To the nurse he said, "Get her out of here." All he could think about was the crippling realization that'd hit him in the parking lot while he was painfully pulling himself through the snow towards his truck. Duffy Dot was just like his mother! She talked to him like his mother had. She fussed about him like his mother had. Duffy even learned a few things about basketball and football so she could pretend conversation with him while they watched sports on TV at her apartment. His mother had done all the same things. Though, he had to admit, his mother had served him much better snacks. He had to get Duffy Dot out of his life. He knew couldn't have anything even resembling sexual anything with her ever again. Ever. It was all wrong. All wrong. Even to him.

The nurse turned to Duffy Dot and said, "Ma'am you'll have to leave now."

"No, I won't have to leave now! He's delirious. He doesn't mean that. I'm staying. I'm his...well, I'm staying. He needs me," Duffy announced. She looked at Terry for support.

He had closed his eyes, but he said very slowly and clearly, "Nurse, I'm okay. Just get her out of here."

"I'm not going to leave you, Terry."

"Nurse, get her out of here. Call security if you have to," Terry said firmly.

The nurse left the room. She returned almost immediately with a security guard. The nurse said to Duffy, "He will show you to the exit."

Duffy, not one to admit defeat, said, "I know you are tired. I'll let you sleep. I'll be back later."

"Don't come back," Terry said.

The security guard positioned himself between Duffy and Terry's bed. He motioned toward the door. "Ma'am. After you," he said.

Duffy dramatically retrieved her coat and huffed out of the room. The guard followed her. The nurse asked if Terry needed anything.

He said to her, "No. Just don't let her back in here."

"Okay. We'll try," the nurse replied.

When Gertie turned into the hospital parking lot, she saw Duffy hurrying from the building. The big woman was almost running. As Gertie pulled into a parking space, she said aloud to Duffy, who of course couldn't hear her, "Don't slip on the ice, hon. Might break something."

Gertie watched Duffy drive away before she went into the hospital. She stopped at the nurses' station to inquire about Terry's condition.

The nurse who'd summoned the security guard was there. She told Gertie about the incident. Gertie just laughed and said, "She's a bit of a looney tune."

The nurse said, "I'd hate to have her turn on me. She's a big ole girl."

"Glad you have a security person here," Gertie responded.

# CHAPTER 5

The snowstorm had moved to the northeast, toward Raton and on towards Kansas. The Sangre de Christo Mountains were rendered white and glistening in the bright sunlight. The morning air was crisp and clean. The high-altitude sun began evaporating and melting the snow everywhere the snow sat free from any shadows.

Peter Northburn, one of the most famous ceramic artists in America, had built his beautiful home, studio, and showroom in the Taos Canyon about ten miles from the town of Taos. US Highway 64 winds through the Taos Canyon tracking alongside the Rio Fernando de Taos. The river flows downhill towards Taos from above the Palo Flechado Pass. The pass marks the boundary between Taos and Colfax counties. The narrow two-lane winding road through the canyon is a fairly busy thoroughfare, as Highway 64 over the pass is the most direct route between Angel Fire and Taos.

The route Highway 64 takes from Taos to Angel Fire cuts through the Carson National Forest and a patchwork of private lands as it makes its way up and through the mountains. Sections of the southeastern side of the river fall in the shadow of the mountains most of the winter. The properties on the other side of the river and road are considered to be on the sunny side. But due to the serpentine lay of the river through the winding, climbing canyon, there are both sunny and shadowed sections of the canyon on both sides. About halfway between Taos and the Palo Flechado Pass, where Highway 64 nears the Valle Escondido turn off, the canyon opens up to gently spreading pastures on one side of the river, and steep forested terrain on the opposite side.

Just past Valle Escondido, Northburn's place is perched above the road on a narrow finger of land on the northwest side of the road. The dramatic incline of his driveway leads up from the highway to the buildings on top of the rise that is his property. Behind the high ground of the compound, there is a sharp drop-off into a steep canyon crevice. Only to the left side of his parking lot does the land lead quietly up into the mountains. His compound has magnificent views out the front, across the road and river, of wide meadows leading to the mountains beyond. On his side of the road, Carson National Forest is his only direct neighbor. The bottom of the deep ravine behind his property is a borderline of the Carson National Forest. The National Forest land rises high in the mountains above Northburn's property.

Northburn's claim to fame is not only his lovely ceramic work, both thrown and hand-built sculptural pieces, but also the notable surface effects he consistently achieves. For decades, other ceramicists have tried to duplicate the iridescent depth in his glazes without success. Peter Northburn's pieces are unique. His very large wood-fired kiln drives the extraordinary look of his work.

Wood firing is an ancient process. It goes back to the first clay firings humans ever attempted. Wood was the fuel of choice. It was the most readily available fuel for those earliest potters. In modern ceramic work, wood-firing is not as widespread as it once was. The less labor-intensive gas-fired and electric kilns have become the norm. It takes a dedicated artist to operate a wood-fired kiln. Peter is dedicated to his work and to maintaining his reputation. He has worked all of his life to become such an acclaimed artist.

Peter Northburn had instructed his helper, Oren, to be at the studio by nine. It was close to ten and the idiot wasn't there yet. Peter called the cell number of the phone that he provided to the young man who was supposed to be there by now. Where was the ungrateful moron? Peter provided Oren livelihood and a place to live. Peter thought of the boy as an indentured servant who'd probably never work himself free. Just the sort of helper Peter wanted.

Oren lived in the casita behind a large house down in the town of Taos. Peter'd bought the house in town and had lived there during the time he built his compound up in the Taos Canyon. After moving to his dream facility in the canyon, he consigned his former home in town to a property management company as a vacation rental. The annual stream of vacationers had maintained a healthy cash flow for him.

Oren was supposed to be some sort of a caretaker. However, he was stoned all of the time, which rendered him useless for most tasks. Oren had been smoking pot every day since he was about fifteen years old. Now, at twenty-one he presented a strong argument that marijuana was definitely not a gateway to intelligence and creativity. For Peter's purpose, Oren served him pretty well. Oren could help move heavy objects, drive the van to shows, not ask a lot of questions, and give Peter a blow job whenever he wanted one.

The call went to voice mail. Peter left a brief message: "Mr. Mackler get your ass over here. Now."

Sitting at his drafting table in his enormous studio building, Peter continued editing the list of the art pieces, and their prices, that he was sending to the gallery in Taos. He decided that he'd take the less phenomenal work to the gallery today. He wanted to deliver what he felt were the show-stopper pieces tomorrow. He heard Oren Mackler's motorcycle outside the studio. He could tell that the young man parked his bike exactly where Peter had told him not to park the bike.

Oren opened the oversized metal sliding door from the parking lot into the studio and said, "Morning boss!"

The thin, dark-haired, plain-looking young man stamped his snow-covered boots on the mat by the door as he slid the door closed. He jingled when he moved. As popular with the young men, Oren wore a long chain that looped down from his waist almost to his knees and back to his waist. Some young men attached their wallet to an optional shorter chain attached from their belt to their wallet carried in the back or front pocket. Oren never carried a wallet, but he did always wear a large key ring assembly attached to the long chain. He didn't wear a belt, so the chain with the ring of many keys was attached to a belt loop on his fashionably worn-out ragged jeans. The ring of keys attached to a carabiner that linked to the fashionably frayed belt loop via a leather snap closure at the end of the chain. The entire accessory drove Peter nuts. Oren jingled like a parade of circus animals. The effort of closing the sliding door created a loud jingling of keys and chain.

Without looking up from his desk, Peter sighed and said, "Move that motorcycle. You cannot leave it in front of the door! We are loading the van this morning. Get it ready."

Oren responded, "Uh. Okay. Be right back."

Oren went out the same sliding door he'd just come through. The jingling seemed louder. Peter shook his head and muttered, "What a complete moron!"

Peter heard the bike rev and drive just a short distance. The sound of the motorcycle stopped next to the studio building near the walkway to the wood-fired kiln building. Oren came in the door from the walkway.

"Oh wee, what a cold ride this morning!" Oren exclaimed.

Peter said, "You're late!"

"I couldn't find my helmet. I couldn't find my knit hat. It was so cold." Oren rubbed both hands very quickly back and forth over his short dark hair in his effort to warm his head.

"Stop that! Not only do you too closely resemble a monkey doing that, but you are throwing bits of...whatever... everywhere."

"Sorry. Okay. So we are loading the stuff for the gallery."

Peter stood and stretched his six-foot four frame to its full height. He turned to face Oren, and said, "*Stuff*??"

Oren smiled and replied, "Huh. Your art stuff? Art objects? Ceramic ware? Sculptures?"

"Let us think for a moment, Oren. Do you know the term 'perceived value?' Do you think my patrons pay the prices they do for my work and think of it as *stuff*? Do you think they would even want to see my work if it was *stuff*? I think not. What I create is fine art. My work is the culmination of my many years of experience with my chosen medium, and my honing of my genius, resulting in the highest interpretation of the universal concept of creativity itself. So, respect the results. Respect the fine art."

Oren said, "Okay, sure. Happy to. Want me to back the van up to the door?"

With a histrionic sigh, Peter Northburn said, "Yes. Back it up to the sliding door. Then bring the big cart from the kiln."

Oren went out the way he'd just come in, through the side door from the walkway to the kiln. The big wood-fired kiln stood in its own steel structure connected to the massive studio building, home, and gallery showroom building by a wide, covered walkway. There were three other kilns, gas-fired, inside the studio building. Northburn used those smaller kilns for bisque firing and the random special orders that did not require the special treatment of his wood-firing.

The large wood-fired kiln was his favorite. He achieved his famous special glaze treatments only in that kiln. No one had ever been able to duplicate his beautiful and extraordinary glazes. He'd built that kiln himself so many years ago. He'd poured the foundation, set every firebrick, and he'd welded the steel skeletal framework. He'd changed it over the years, altering the size of the firebox and the firing chamber, raising the chimney, redirecting the airflow, tailoring the dampers, all to perfect the kiln's performance. He now felt the big kiln was part of him. He could fire clay pieces six feet tall or six inches tall. He knew exactly how to handle the big kiln. He knew exactly what it would do for him.

Oren rolled a large four-wheeled metal cart into the studio from the kiln building. He pushed it carefully and slowly. His chain and keys still rattled and pinged against the metal cart. He moved cautiously. There was no way he was going to knock into any fine art. Not today. He parked the cart between Peter's drafting table area and the sliding door to the parking lot. He then went out the sliding door and positioned the van for loading. He was outside with the van long enough to suck down half a joint. When the van was in place, and Oren's high renewed, he went back in the studio building. Peter handed him the list of what to load and pointed toward the shelves by the door.

"You going to help me?" Oren asked.

"I will help you load the larger pieces. First, wrap the smaller ones in sufficient bubble wrap, and box them. Then put them in the van, to the front. After they are in, we'll deal with the larger pieces."

Oren looked at the art work on the shelves closest to the door, and asked, "Is that the stu...work?"

"That is some of it. I'll replenish the shelves as you

load up," Peter explained. "Same as always. You know the system. Do it."

Oren Mackler brought a huge roll of bubble wrap from the shipping room, some new cardboard boxes, and sheets of corrugated cardboard. He began wrapping. He packed the many small clay sculptures and vessels into cardboard boxes. When he had several boxes of objects packed, he put the boxes on the cart and headed for the van. When he slid the big steel door open, the van was right there. He opened the rear doors of the van and slid the boxes inside. He continued the process until most of the art from the shelves was in the van.

"The van's pretty full," Oren yelled at Peter who was in the rear of the studio behind more shelving and tables of art pieces.

"Come help me with this," Peter called back. "And close the door. It's cold!"

Oren helped Peter put a six-foot tall clay sculpture of a stylized figure of a woman onto a flat four-wheeled dolly. They rolled the standing sculpture to the front. There Peter wrapped her with layers of bubble wrap. He and Oren encased her in a double-walled cardboard box they fashioned from large sheets of heavy corrugated cardboard. Then they rolled the piece to the van. Peter rearranged the boxes in the van to make a bed of boxes onto which they lay the tall box. Peter brought out more small and medium sized pieces from the back of the studio. Oren wrapped and boxed until the van was full to its ceiling. It didn't take long to complete the entire project.

"Can we have lunch before we deliver?" Oren asked

Peter.

"We can. Plenty of time. Don't want to get to the gallery too early!"

"It might take us an hour to get into Taos. Slow going. The canyon road is cleared but still slick in the shady places," Oren said.

"They'll wait for us," Peter replied with a little laugh.

## CHAPTER 6

"When is he supposed to get here?" Sherman asked.

Marion Fleeo, the gallery owner, replied, "Oh, I really thought he'd be here by now."

"Want me to call him?"

"Oh, no. Don't call him. We can't appear anxious in any way. He needs to feel comfortable with us. We cannot be pushy or demanding. It took forever to schedule this show. He hasn't shown in Taos in over a decade."

Sherman asked, "A decade! Why not? He lives here."

Marion answered, "Oh, you never see him in Taos. He prefers to show in the important large art markets: Dallas, Chicago, New York. He just hasn't had time for Taos. He doesn't even show in Santa Fe."

"So what changed? Why is he showing here now?"

"Oh, well, maybe just the publicity. I really don't know. I have extended the invitation to him each year since I've owned this gallery. This year he said yes."

"Very persistent of you," Sherman said.

"Oh, yes. When I bought this gallery, he was the first artist I invited to show here."

"Do you know him?"

Marion Fleeo replied, "Oh, no. Well, I met him once years ago, at a party. He was charming, nice looking, very engaging conversationalist as I remember. That was some time ago. I've only spoken to him on the phone since then."

Motioning to the glass front door of the gallery, Sherman said, "This has to be him."

A very tall, handsome, blond-haired late middle-aged man swept in the front door. "Marion Fleeo! How wonderful to see you again!" he called out in a strong voice.

"Oh, Peter! You look terrific! Good to see you. Come in. Come in. Let me introduce my sales associate, Sherman Kroyton. We are such big fans of your work."

Peter Northburn hugged Marion, shook Sherman's hand, then twirled around to inspect the gallery space. "So sorry I couldn't get here sooner, to see the space, and you. Just always so busy. But this will do nicely. You've got a fresh clean space. We can adjust the lighting and make this work! My helper is outside in the van. Where should he park to unload? I want to unload as close to the gallery as possible, of course."

"Oh, ask him to just turn into the alley next to the gallery. He'll see our double doors, the receiving dock. Sherman, will you please unlock those doors and help get the art inside?" Marion said.

When Sherman had left to assist Oren, Peter Northburn said, "Marion, what kind of an opening event have you planned?"

The older woman smiled and said enthusiastically, "Oh, you're going to love it. I have invited everyone, your list and mine, including the governor! And she may be coming! I have media from Santa Fe and Albuquerque coming, both newspaper and TV. Also have the local art-blog folks coming, whatever that is...but all of the galleries invite them, so I made sure they were included! The caterer is top-notch. She caters for the local Hollywood and Washington celebrities."

"Good. Good. How many sales people will you have for the opening?"

She replied, "Me, of course, Sherman, and two others. Two women who have both worked for me in the past. Both are dedicated to selling fine art."

Peter said, "I will need to have a meeting, a sales-strategy meeting with you and all of your people before the opening. Can you arrange that for tomorrow afternoon or evening? We should hold the meeting at my studio."

"Oh, sure I can. What time is good for you?"

Before Peter could answer, they heard Oren and Sherman talking as they rolled a cart of boxes into the gallery's main showroom.

Sherman remarked to Marion, "There are a lot of boxes. We may need more display podiums."

Marion said, "Oh, we have plenty more. In the basement. I'll have Roger paint them tonight. They'll be fresh and ready by morning." To Peter, she said, "Roger is my maintenance man. Oh, and do you think you want more lights?"

Peter looked around at the track lighting in all three showrooms of the gallery, then he replied, "I don't think I want more lights, I know I want more lights."

Marion laughed and said, "Oh, Roger will take care of that tonight, too. Is there anything else we can do?"

"I'll let you know. I'd better see to the unloading.

Precious cargo and all," Peter said to Marion.

Peter, Oren, and Sherman moved all of the boxes into the gallery, and carefully unpacked the artwork. Sherman was suitably impressed with the pieces and he let Peter know it, as he placed the art on the floor around the periphery of the main showroom.

"Your glazes are stunning! So much depth and color!" Sherman remarked.

Peter said, "Yes, my glaze brings out the soul of each piece."

Sherman agreed, "I see what you mean. The iridescence almost breathes."

Peter smiled, "Sherman, you are a natural salesman! Use that line at the opening."

"I've been selling most of my life. That is many decades now!" Sherman replied, though he didn't explain to Peter that his sales career had been exclusively wholesale furniture and office furnishings, no art.

Oren had removed the cardboard and stood upright the tall bubble wrapped sculpture. As Oren began unwrapping the large figure, Peter Northburn, exclaimed, "Careful! You idiot. Don't just yank at the bubble wrap! Walk around the piece to unfurl the wrapping. Here. Let me show you."

Oren barked back, "I know! I can do it." His high was waning. He knew he should go outside and light up.

"Then demonstrate that you can! Be gentle with her," Peter retorted. He took control of removing the bubble wrap despite Oren's attempt to continue. Once the tall female figure was exposed, Peter exclaimed, "She looks stupendous!"

Oren said he'd go check the van for any more pieces. Really, he was going out to the van to get high again.

## CHAPTER 7

Terry pushed the button for the shift nurse. He closed his eyes and counted to ten. No nurse. He pushed the button again and again. At last, a beautiful young woman in a crisp white uniform appeared at the door to his hospital room.

"Everything alright Mr. Small?" she asked with a big smile.

"No. Everything's not alright. That's why I buzzed for you. I am hungry and uncomfortable. Bring me something to eat. Rearrange this harness. Do something," he said in a flat cold whiney voice.

"It is so late, Mr. Small. The kitchen is not serving right now. But I can try to adjust your legs a little bit."

"You can go to the kitchen and get something. A sandwich will do! Something."

"Mr. Small, I can't go to the kitchen and take food. But, I'll let my supervisor know you are hungry," the young woman said, as she carefully shifted his legs less than a millimeter in the traction harness. The effort was for show only.

"I don't remember you coming in here before. You new?" he asked watching her work on the harness.

"I've been in here several times. You are usually

asleep."

"Come closer. I can't see so well without my contacts," Terry said in a syrupy voice.

"Got to keep going. There are other patients, you know," she replied with a smile as she left the room.

Terry stared at the TV. It was on but muted. The news was on. Some plastic-haired dandy was talking. He hated newsmen. To him they all seemed either fake or gay. Or both. He retrieved the remote from the bedside table and found a sports channel, a basketball game. He left it muted. He closed his eyes.

The hospital at night made noises like a big machine. He heard whirring, and electrical motors cutting off and on. Air flow through the HVAC was loud. Terry heard carts rattling and elevators moving, opening, closing. Then he heard the door to his room open, but he didn't open his eyes. He felt someone touch his shoulder. He still didn't open his eyes. He was afraid it might be Duffy Dot. Then he heard his son's voice.

"Dad?"

Terry opened his eyes. He smiled and said, "Dude! How'd you get in here this late?" He tried to take hold of his son's arm, but his son quickly stepped back out of reach.

Bokshan replied, "I just walked in! Is it late? I flew in this afternoon. Took this long to get up here from Albuquerque. Shuttles don't run very often. How are you?"

"Both legs are broken in multiple places, dude. Pelvis is cracked. Ribs are bruised or broken or something. I hurt like hell. And the worst part is I am stuck here."

"How long will you be like this?" his son asked.

Terry replied, "Dude, the doc says I'll be learning to walk again in about eight weeks. I don't know when I'll be out of this contraption."

Bokshan asked, "Anything you need?"

Terry said, "Food. Good food. The portions here are tiny and tasteless. And some wine!! Bring me a bottle of wine!"

The door opened and the young nurse looked in. When she saw the attractive young man, she stepped in and said to him, "Who are you? Visiting hours are long past."

He said, nodding towards Terry, "I'm his son, Bokshan Small. Sorry, didn't know it was after-hours. Really I'm not sure what time it is. Just flew in from LA."

She said firmly, "You'll have to leave now."

Bokshan smiled at her and said, "Sure."

Terry said, "See you tomorrow, dude. Bring a bottle of wine!"

Bokshan left with the nurse, with only a wave to his father.

Once in the hall, he said to the nurse, "He's a bit of a jerk to deal with. Hope he hasn't been too bad."

She laughed and told him, "Well, he's not the first of his kind we've seen. Don't bring him a bottle of wine. He cannot have any alcohol with the medications he's taking."

"I'll bet. He's usually an ass, and way self-centered. He's a super control freak. That's his usual. And he can sure be a super dick to everyone around. He gives new emphasis to the 'dick' in addiction. A regular wino. Though, of course, he doesn't think so!"

"Your mother alerted us to the drinking issue. He's

in an imposed drying-out of sorts. He's on some potent pain meds, so no alcohol. We're monitoring the dosages carefully. Don't want to have a new addiction to deal with."

"He's a sneak, too. Just a heads-up. Watch out for his visitors bringing him wine," Bokshan added.

"Okay, thanks. So far, he hasn't had many visitors. You said you just got here? From LA? What do you do there?" the young woman asked.

Bokshan smiled and replied, "I'm trying to make a life in the film and TV industry. Currently I am a set builder for various TV shows. Not glamorous, but I do get paid!"

"How long have you been in LA?"

"Migrated out there right after college, a couple a years ago. Dad was 100% against it. Mom was 100% for it. Not that I needed their okay, but support is nice."

"Why was your father against it?"

Bokshan explained, "Like I said, he's a control freak. I was going to be far away in a world he'd never seen or knew anything about. He's seriously uncomfortable with anything he doesn't feel like he knows about. I think it scared him. He has a lot of personal crazy baggage."

"Goodness. Most parents are happy to see their kids pursue their own lives and careers."

"Not in his tiny world."

"How long are you going to be visiting?" she asked.

"Not long. I know I won't be able to take him for more than a day or two. He's always nice at first, and then he'll get ugly and pushy. He turns toxic. His paranoia and his prejudices manifest in unacceptably rude ways. That's when I leave."

"You have brothers or sisters?" the nurse asked as they walked.

"Yeah, I have a sister, Bricklan. She lives in St. Louis. I doubt you'll be meeting her. Brick doesn't like to come to Taos anymore."

"Why's that?"

"She doesn't want to deal with Dad."

"What does she do in St. Louis?"

Bokshan answered, "She manages a retail clothing store."

As they approached the elevator, the nurse said, "Didn't mean to pry. It's just quiet on the night shift. Enjoyed the conversation."

He said, "I enjoyed it, too. Guess it's a good sign when all is quiet at a hospital."

"That is true enough! Take care."

The elevator door opened, he stepped in and waved goodbye as the door closed. The young nurse continued down the hall.

## CHAPTER 8

Peter Northburn sat in his studio staring at the sizable rack of his ceramic pieces that he was sending to the gallery in the second load. The driveway sensor buzzed. Someone had driven up the steep entry from the highway. He walked through the studio into his showroom space to unlock the front door. Just as he got to the door, a young woman rang the bell.

"Good morning!" Peter said in his most welcoming voice. "Come in."

The forty-ish looking dark-haired woman smiled and stepped in. "I am so glad you are open. I saw your sign at the road, but I didn't see hours posted. Oh my god, you are Peter Northburn!"

Peter laughed and replied, "I am. And what is your name? Let me take your coat."

She laughed, too, as she handed him her coat. "Ooo, it's so cold out there. I'm from Texas, and I'm not at all used to this cold weather. Hi. I'm Karen. Karen Pilling. I love your work!"

Peter hung her coat by the door, and said, "Thank you, Karen. So you are familiar with my work? Of course you are."

"Yes! I teach art at a college in Texas. Houston, Texas.

I am a bit of a ceramicist myself. Nothing close to your level, of course. I teach your work in my classes. My students are as enamored with your work and your glazes, as I am! We're always trying to duplicate your surfaces. We've tried everything we could think of. We've not even come close!! I have always wanted to visit your studio here in Taos," Karen exclaimed enthusiastically.

Peter said, "To be accurate, this is not exactly in Taos. But you found me. I am preparing the final delivery of artwork to a gallery in Taos. The show opens soon, so I need to stay the course. But you are welcome to look around."

Karen replied, "I don't want to disturb you, but I would love to look around. Okay to take pictures?"

"No pictures, please. You can look around the showroom. Call out if you need help. I'll leave the door to the studio open."

She checked the pocket of her hoodie, and remarked, "Oh. My phone. Oh it's in my coat. But no pictures! So no matter! What gallery in Taos? Your show?" she asked as she stared up at his very handsome face.

"The Fleeo Gallery. It's on the plaza. You must come to the opening if you are still in town."

"Yes! I'll be here for a week. I'm on mid-winter break. Thanks for the invitation. How exciting! I'll be there!" she gushed.

"Bring whomever you are travelling with, too," Peter added.

"It'll be just me. I sort of snuck out of town. Left my boyfriend back in Houston. I didn't even tell him where I was going. We both needed time away from each other. Been together three years, too long to be so clingy. Oh, listen to me! You don't want to hear my story," Karen said blushing slightly.

"No problem. Where are you staying? I'll have an invitation sent to your hotel."

She laughed and said, "I haven't checked-in anywhere yet. Haven't decided. Silly, but I thought if I check-in somewhere, then I should call Leon and let him know, you know, where I am. I just wasn't ready to talk to him yet. Just been driving around thinking...then I saw your sign. Kismet!"

"Would you like to see my studio and my wood-fired kiln?" Peter Northburn unexpectedly asked, as he contemplated the surprising opportunity standing right in front of him. He was only slightly torn between acting on his impulse to take her, or to let her go. He really hadn't planned on a new one. Should he act this impulsively? His focus was the show. But, on the other hand, here she was travelling alone with no one expecting her anywhere anytime soon. Alone.

She replied, "Would I? Yes! Do you have time?"

"You can see the showroom afterwards. Follow me. Let's go into the studio. Let's go through there," he said motioning towards the door to his studio.

Karen almost squealed with delight, "Your studio! How great. You are so nice. I'd love to see your studio and kiln. Thanks!"

Peter smiled and led her through and out of the showroom space into the studio. Standing in his studio, looking around at the cavernous workshop, she said, "Mr.

Northburn, this is so much nicer and larger than the image of your studio that I've had in my head! This is phenomenal. So this is where you create?!"

"I create wherever I am. This is a good space in which to let my imagination spread its wings. Let's go out to the wood-kiln."

Karen followed him out the studio's side door to the large kiln area. It was cold in the covered, partially enclosed walkway between his main showroom and studio building and the metal building housing the large kiln. He slid open the metal barn door to the kiln space. Peter took Karen's hand in his. He stepped in to the building, and sliding the door closed behind them he said, "Come around here to the other side." He led her to the other side of the wood kiln. She was thrilled. She held his hand tightly.

"This is the largest wood-fired kiln I have ever seen," she remarked.

"It is a large kiln. The outside dimensions are eight feet long by three feet wide by seven feet high. It's called a train kiln. As you can see it resembles a train, with the firebox at this end, then the firing chamber, and then the chimney at that far end." Peter slid up and open the guillotine style steel firebox door. "This is where the beast comes to life. It takes five or six cords of wood for each firing. Feed the beast and it'll work magic."

Karen said, "This is so cool. How long is a firing?"

"It takes from forty-eight to fifty hours."

"That firebox can't hold all of those cords of wood at once. How often do you have to add wood?" Karen asked.

"It requires stoking about every three minutes. There

are heat sensors, thermocouples, inside the firing chamber, and of course I use cones in the chamber's spyholes. I have to watch the temperature closely throughout the firing."

"Every three minutes! You must live here at the kiln during the firings! I have read that you fire to cone twelve. That's hot!"

"The firings are both delicate and intensely fierce. It is a labor of love to load the kiln and run the firing process. Every time! And yes, it does fire hot. At the hottest during the firings, the temperature will reach at least twenty-four hundred degrees."

Peter closed the steel door to the firebox and said, "Let me show you the firing chamber." He led her back around to the other side, to the firing chamber's sliding door made of firebrick set in a steel skeletal frame. The door, with wheels attached top and bottom, and with a counterweight assist, rode smoothly on the steel tracks. Easily sliding the heavy door open, he said, "Look in here. The capacity is enormous. Has to be. I don't fire up my baby until I have a full load."

"Where do you keep all of the wood?" Karen Pilling asked, looking around the kiln.

"It's in large fenced bins, cages, at each of the two back corners of this structure, right outside the back door. I simply load the wood into a cart, roll it up to the firebox, and stoke. The wood is cut to size and sorted by species. I pick the hot fast-burning sticks or the slower-burning sticks as I need to keep the kiln temperature controlled as the firing progresses."

Karen walked around the kiln asking questions, and touching the firebricks, looking in the peep holes. She could only imagine what the now quiet kiln might look like, feel like when it was firing. She asked, "When are you firing again? I'd love to see this kiln working."

"Right now I'm planning to fire soon. If you are here, I'll show you exactly how it works," Peter said as they returned to the end of the kiln where the firebox door was closed and cold.

She said, "I can't pass up an invitation like that. I'll be here!"

"I'm counting on it." He smiled. He stepped in front of her and leaned in close, took her face in his hands. He kissed her mouth hard.

Karen said, "Uh. I wasn't expecting that."

"You probably weren't expecting this either," Peter said as he quickly took the steel stoking poker from a hook by the firebox. He swung the steel rod at her head. His backswing was too slow, and her reflexes were faster than he anticipated.

Shocked and panicked, she ducked and bolted for the closest door. She wasn't screaming: most of the others had screamed. She pushed the back door open and ran. She found herself outside in the snow behind the building. She looked to the right and left for a way back to her car which she'd left parked in the lot in front of the showroom building. Monumental stacks of firewood secured in tall fenced cages blocked both the front and rear routes from the side of the kiln building.

The wood was piled as high as the roof and many rows deep. The wood-filled cages went from the corners of the building right up to the edge of the drop off in front of her. Her only escape route was straight ahead into the steep and narrow ravine that ran behind the building. She ran forward awkwardly slipping in the snow. She hit the edge of the drop-off and slid down, hoping to go far enough into the ravine to be able to change course towards the highway. She couldn't stop the vertical slide on the frozen ground. She couldn't get any traction. She grabbed at trees and shrubs, but kept falling downward.

Peter laughed as he grabbed his compound bow and quiver of arrows from the rack on the wall by the back door. He knew she'd only have one direction she could go: down into the ravine behind the kiln building. She couldn't get to the front, to her car. Both sides around the complex from the rear were blocked by his carefully placed stacks of kiln wood. The wood was held in place by fifteen-foot high fence corrals that went from the building to the precipice of the deep ravine.

He stepped outside. He heard her thrashing through the frozen underbrush as she slid and fell down into the snowy crevice. She hit the bottom hard enough to break through the ice into the partially frozen little creek. He waited patiently to position his shot until she scrambled out of the cold water and began her climb up the other side. He watched her frantically grab at the bushes, slipping and pulling herself up the steep snowy incline. The sound of the snapping sticks and branches echoed through the cold air across the narrow ravine.

When she reached an open area, she turned to look back at him. She saw him lift what looked to her like a compound bow. Before she could take another step, the arrow sliced into her neck. Surprised and confused, she coughed and dropped into the snow. The last thing she saw was the thick white snow absorbing her blood, like syrup on a snow cone.

Peter Northburn went back into the kiln building and returned his bow and quiver to the hooks by the back door. He heard Oren calling his name from the studio building. As Peter opened the door from the walkway into the studio, he said, "Why are you yelling?"

Oren replied, "I was looking for you. I have the van ready for the next load."

"No need to yell like that."

"Sorry. Didn't want you to think I was late again. That's all."

"I hope you remembered to get gas while in town this morning."

"Yep. All gassed up. Ready. Whose white Camry is that in the parking lot?"

Peter replied casually, "I don't know. Had some tourists here a while ago. Maybe they left a car here…for some reason."

"It has Texas plates. Looks new."

"I really don't care," Peter said. "We need to get this art packaged up and loaded."

"All of this? Everything on this cart?"

"Yes. Start with these pieces, and then load the framed drawings. I have two large pieces in the back. We'll put those in last," Peter instructed as he headed for the door to the showroom space.

Oren asked, "Where are you going? Not going to help me?"

Peter turned around and said to Oren, "You are here to help me. Don't forget that."

"Yes, sir!!" Oren replied with attitude. He wanted to go outside and smoke a joint. Should have done that before coming inside, he thought, but he was too rattled to think straight. He hadn't had a smoke since the gas station in town.

Peter continued in to the showroom area closing the door to the studio behind him. He went straight to Karen's coat hanging by the entry door. He checked the pockets as he took it from the coat rack. He confiscated her cell phone, and car keys. He folded the coat and tossed it in the cabinet behind the central display and reception counter. Then Peter returned to the studio.

"You want me to put the boxes in the van as I fill them?" Oren asked.

"Yes. I want to be sure there is ample room for the large pieces," Peter replied as he went to the back room to begin wrapping the two tall pieces. Each piece was five feet tall. One was a stylized male figure and the other was a stylized bear reared up on his back legs. The position suggested the bear was pawing at some unseen prey, or initiating a fight.

Oren stepped into the back area, looked at the bear and said, "I love the bear. Very cool. That'll sell right away!"

"Good to know," Peter remarked facetiously. "Help me get the bubble wrap around these two."

## CHAPTER 9

Terry Small was lying very still in his hospital bed staring at the ceiling feeling very sorry for himself. He heard voices outside his door. His wife Gertie came in with his son Bokshan.

"Hey dude! Hey Gertie," Terry said.

"Hi Dad. How're you feeling this morning?" Bokshan asked.

"Feeling hardly anything, dude. I can't move much at all. Just my arms. Can't even sit up. Did you bring me any real food?" Terry complained.

"No food, Dad. I was told you are on a strict regimen and some serious drugs," Bokshan replied.

Gertie said, "The hospital will take good care of you. Don't burden Bok with your complaints. He has to get back to LA. Has to get back to work. I'm taking him down to Albuquerque to the airport. He came by to say goodbye."

To his son, Terry whined, "You're leaving? Already? Dude, you just got here!"

"Yeah. Just wanted to check on you. I need to get back to work. We're working on a new sitcom set. I have to be there."

"What crap. TV! Can't believe it. Fag job! My son is working in Hollywood. Christ! When are you going to get a real job in some respectable industry?" Terry Small suddenly snapped.

Bokshan looked at his mother and rolled his eyes. Gertie said, "We gotta go."

Terry whined, "Dude, stay another day. One more day."

"No can do, Dad. Take care. I'll call you."

"I'm nearly killed, and you can't stay and be with me for another day?"

"Glad you weren't killed, Dad. Take care. I'll call you," Bokshan repeated.

Gertie and Bokshan left. As the door clicked shut behind them, Terry really felt sorry for himself. He closed his eyes. After an indeterminate length of time, he heard the door open again. Then he heard Duffy's voice.

"Hi darling!" she said in her sing-song voice. "I brought you some chocolates."

He opened his eyes. Duffy Dot was standing by his bed holding a small box of candy. "What are you doing here? How'd you get in here?" he asked.

"Oh darling! Of course I'd come visit. I'll be here as often as possible!" she said gleefully as she put her coat on the chair by his bed. "How are you feeling?"

"I feel horrible. I am trapped in this bed."

"Are you in pain, darling?"

"Stop calling me darling. I'm not your darling. I'm not your anything, except maybe your employer for the time-being."

"I understand...you are on a lot of medication. You really don't mean that. I love you. I know you love me."

"I don't love you. I am through with you."

Duffy giggled and said, "You *are* drugged up, aren't you? You want a quickie? I'll bet your 'little self' could use some attention."

She moved close to the bed and slipped her hand under the sheet to his crotch. She took hold of his flaccid penis and trilled her fingertips across his balls. He couldn't shift away from her, but he did slap at her arm.

"Get away from me," he cried. "Don't touch me."

Duffy let go and stepped back. She said, "Okay. We'll catch up when you feel more like yourself. I'd be happy to help you, and your 'little self,' relax whenever you want. You just say the word. You want some chocolate?"

"Just leave the chocolate and go," Terry said without looking at her.

She stepped up to his bedside again, and before he could react she leaned in and kissed his mouth. "There, now. I'll be back later," she said as she picked up her coat.

Terry suddenly asked, "How's everything at the office?"

Duffy replied, "Everything is fine. Erlene filled-in for you at the courthouse as expert witness. She said it went fine. Sherry is covering your appointments."

"Okay. Tell them to call me if they have any questions," he said.

Duffy laughed as she picked up her coat, and said, "Yeah. I'll do that. They're fine. Don't worry about the office."

"I can call my clients from here. Just bring me my calendar, bring my laptop. Bring my blackberry! I think

Gertie has it."

"No you cannot call or email anyone, young man!" Duffy admonished. "The only job you have is to get well!"

Terry closed his eyes. He was sure she was channeling his mother. He said, "Get out of here."

"See you later, darling."

## CHAPTER 10

Once all of the art was in the van, Peter instructed Oren to drive it down to Taos to the Fleeo Gallery. He told him he'd follow shortly. Peter said, "Be careful! Drive carefully."

"Why don't you ride down with me?" Oren asked, but hoping he wouldn't. Oren really wanted to get high.

"I have a call to make. I'll be there within the hour. Go ahead and unload and unpack."

Peter watched Oren slowly maneuver the van down the steep driveway to the highway. It occurred to him that Oren might just make it to Fleeo without losing any of the pieces. Maybe. But the first order of business was to retrieve Karen's body from the snowy far side of the ravine.

Peter gathered the usual equipment: rope, tarp, block and tackle. He bundled up and went to get his prize. At the top of the ravine he attached the block and tackle to a tall fence post at the backmost corner of the backmost woodpile corral. He'd set the posts in deep concrete footings, strong enough to handle the weight of the wood piled behind it, as well as any weight pulling from the ravine. He wove the rope through the pulleys of the block and tackle and loosely rappelled down the steep slope. At the bottom he knew where to cross the icy water without getting wet. Carrying the rope and tarp, he easily climbed up the other slope towards the body. Peter knew every foot of his ravine.

When he reached the body, he turned around to enjoy the view back to the kiln building. He wanted to see what she last saw. He smiled. He ripped his arrow/bolt from her neck, wiped it in the snow, and stuck it through his belt, arrow head pointed down, of course. He lay out the tarp on the hill and rolled her into it. He wrapped the body-filled tarp bundle with rope like a big smudge stick. He affixed the bundle to the rope from the block and tackle. He dragged the wrapped body down to the bottom, to the creek, slid it across a patch of ice, and then he climbed back up towards the building. At the top he used the block and tackle to easily haul the sizable bundle to the top. Once he had the package at the top and untied from the pulley system, he picked up the bundle and carried it inside the kiln building. He carried it through that building and through the studio building, and then out the back door of his studio. She wasn't as heavy as he'd thought she'd be. To him, she'd looked bottom-heavy, but overall she was easy to maneuver.

In a separate shed behind the studio, was his special twenty-two cubic foot chest freezer. He thought of it as a bank of sorts. He deposited Karen in the bank. He locked the freezer and the shed. He returned to the kiln and went back out to collect his block and tackle. He stood at the top of the ravine looking across to the kill site. He knew that the animals would take care of the blood in the snow in no time. "Santé!" he called out to the forest. He felt invigorated.

The bigger problem, in his mind, was the car she'd left in his parking lot.

For the moment, though, he needed to get to Fleeo Gallery. So, changed into wool-lined chinos, a flannel shirt, clean boots, and leather jacket, he hopped into his Mercedes and drove to Taos. By the time he got there, Oren and Sherman were breaking down empty boxes and rolling up the bubble wrap. All of the art pieces were lined up along the walls of the gallery's three showrooms. The three large sculptures: the bear, the male figure, and the female figure, were standing in the center of the first showroom.

"Those look good right there," Peter said of the placement of three big pieces. "Just need a little positioning and lighting."

"Do you have a scheme in mind for the arrangement of the art?" Sherman asked Peter.

"I do! Put the lower profile vessels and platters in this front room with the large sculptures. And hang the drawings in this room that correspond to the work in the room. Then put the smaller sculptures and their drawings in the middle room. And put the remaining pots and drawings in the back room. I'll adjust the lighting after the spacing is right."

Sherman said, "Okay. Got it. Can do."

"Excellent. Where is Marion today?" Peter asked.

"She's out triple checking the catering menu, flowers, and such. She'll be here later," Sherman explained. "Roger will be here shortly. We should have this show together in no time!"

"I like your attitude, Sherman," Peter announced. "Oren and I need to get back to the studio for a little while. But we'll return. We were going to have the sales planning meeting there this evening, but I think we should have it here in the morning. Can you call Marion's other two salespeople? Let them know."

"Sure. We thought that might happen. Time flies when getting a show put together. I'll call Marion. She can set it up. What time?" Sherman replied.

"You are right about time. Never enough! Let's say ten in the morning," Peter said. "Right now we have to get going. Come on Oren. Any problem with me leaving my van in your alley?"

"No problem at all. See you later," Sherman said to Peter and Oren.

As they got in the Mercedes, Oren asked, "Why are we leaving the van here? Where are we going? I thought we were going to set up the show."

Peter explained, "Those tourists that were at the studio this morning, the ones who left that Camry in the parking lot, called after you left. They seemed to have some kind of an emergency or something. I really didn't ask a lot of questions."

"That doesn't sound like you," Oren interrupted.

Peter ignored the comment and continued, "Well, they requested that we take the car to Mora and leave it at a gas station. They've continued on their trip and will be able to pick it up there."

"You said you'd do that? Now that's really not like you," Oren said laughing. "They must have spent some serious money with you."

"You don't seem to know me very well. Hey, no smoking in the car!" Peter said to Oren just as he was about to fire up a joint.

"Sure. But I need a smoke before going to Mora!" Oren declared.

"I'll be sure to factor your pot time into the schedule. You're going to drive the Camry. I'll follow and bring you back."

"You think we can get this done and back to Taos for the sales meeting?" Oren questioned.

"The meeting is in the morning," Peter said.

"Oh, where was I?" Oren mused.

"Stoned."

Once back at the studio, Peter told Oren the key to the Camry was supposed to be in the car. He knew it was because he'd put it there before he'd left for the gallery in town. He'd carefully gone through the car. He removed the flyer he found on the seat, advertising his studio and showroom. He put her suitcase and backpack in the trunk. He didn't find a purse. He thought that was odd. He'd never known a woman not to have a purse. Maybe it was in the suitcase or the backpack. He didn't open either. He wanted those contents left undisturbed. Oren said he needed to smoke a joint and grab a sandwich before he could drive. Peter gave in. He'd rather have Oren in his usual state of stoned.

After Oren was newly high and fed, he was ready to drive the new Camry to Mora. "This is a nice ride," Oren remarked to Peter as they stood in the parking lot next to the car.

"You have a car kind of like this, don't you?" Peter asked him.

"My Camry is ancient and barely runs. That's why I ride the bike," Oren said laughing. "This is new! Nice! Let's go."

"You head out and I'll follow," Peter said. "You know how to get to Mora?"

"I know how to get to Mora. Going through Angel Fire, right?"

"Yes. Stop at the first gas station as you get in to Mora. The big station. Park along the side. Just leave the keys in the car under the front seat, and lock it. I'll be right behind you."

## CHAPTER 11

The drive to Mora on Highway 434 out of Angel Fire was as beautiful as ever, Peter thought. The roads were clear and the sky was bright winter blue. He noticed Oren seemed to be smoking in the Camry. Peter saw smoke coming from the driver's window every so often. No problem. Maybe good. Maybe they'd think Karen was high when she disappeared. Peter was thinking about the show more than about the silly woman's car.

Peter lagged back a few miles. He wanted Oren to reach Mora well before he did. They should not get there at the same time.

Oren pulled into the gas station and parked on the side of the convenience store building as Peter had instructed. He finished a last deep hit of some very potent weed. He smiled as he saw Peter wasn't right behind him. He had time to grab a snack from the convenience store. He got out of the car. As he stepped out and turned, his big key ring and chain assembly caught on the inside door handle. He gave the chain a tug. The result was an unexpected splash of keys on the pavement by the car. Oren looked down and saw the torn belt loop from his jeans still attached to the old leather snap connector still attached to the chain still attached to the big key ring which had opened and spilled his inordinate number of keys onto the pavement. "Oh fuck," he said as he knelt down to pick up the keys, ring, and chain. He had to slide under the Camry to retrieve a few of the keys that had bounced under there. When he had all the keys collected, he threaded them back on the big ring and snapped it closed. He reattached the whole thing to another belt loop, closed the car door and headed for the front of the store. He needed a snack.

Oren still didn't see Peter anywhere, but he did see a biker he recognized. He hadn't seen the guy in a long time. The man was leaning on a motorcycle parked in front of the store.

"Hey bro! No see long time!" Oren said as the two men attempted an awkward multi-motion hand shake fist-bump, man-hug.

"What's going on?" the guy asked.

Oren couldn't remember the guy's name. He couldn't remember where he'd met him or last saw him. "Nothing. What are you doing?"

The guy answered, "We're on a road trip. Florida to California."

Oren then noticed there were five other motorcycles parked alongside his friend's. "Cool. That's definitely a road trip, bro."

"You live here?" the guy asked, looking around for a motorcycle or car.

"No. Live in Taos. Just dropping off a car. It's in the back. My ride is supposed to be here…right behind me."

Peter turned into the gas station and stopped along the side of the lot by the dog walk area. He waved at Oren.

"Here he is. Gotta go. Have a good ride," Oren said as he sort of ran towards Peter's car.

"Who's your friend?" Peter asked when Oren got in the car.

"Can't tell you. Don't remember his name. But I met him somewhere at some bike thing. I don't know."

"Okay. You left the key in the car and locked it?" Peter asked.

"Oh shit! No. I'll do that right now," Oren said, touching his giant key ring. He hopped out of the car.

Peter watched Oren walk around to the side of the building. Peter took Karen's cell phone out of his pocket, turned it on and waited for it to boot up. After it was on and ready, he called the last number called. He hung up after one ring. He turned off the cell phone. Oren returned to the Mercedes and Peter headed north on Highway 518 towards Taos.

Oren said, "That Camry is brand new. Only a couple thousand miles on it. Sweet drive. So, we're going to Taos? Not back to your place?"

"You have somewhere you need to go?" Peter asked.

"No no, I'm along for the ride. I left the van at Fleeo, remember? My bike's up at your place."

"We're taking a scenic drive. Not stopping at the gallery. You sure you have enough weed with you to last through to morning if we go back to the studio?"

Oren replied, "Always."

## CHAPTER 12

Gertie sat in the restaurant of the Taos Country Club with a handsome middle-aged silver-haired man, her friend, Nevel. She asked him, "You okay?"

"Fine. Just sorry the impromptu assassination was only attempted! I should have backed over him, too. I thought of it, but then decided it was too much. Sorry."

"No matter. He's suffering and out of action, so almost like I'd hoped for."

Nevel said, "Bokshan came to see him? That was nice of him. Is Bricklan coming?"

"Yeah, Bok is always nice. Just took him back to the airport early this morning. Terry was his usual weird and rude self to him. I don't think Brick is going to be coming any time soon. She can't deal with Terry at all anymore," Gertie replied.

Nevel asked, "Terry realizes Brick is gay, doesn't he?"

"Nope. He still harps at her to find the right man. And he makes no secret that he doesn't like her 'roommate' Julie. He thinks Julie is gay, so he's extremely rude to her. He can't understand why his daughter is living with a lesbian. Terry is such a severe homophobe. He really and truly gets angry when he is dealing with anyone he even suspects might be gay. And that suspicion is based entirely on Terry's imaginary world criteria for gays. It's insane."

"Doesn't Terry see that he has alienated his kids?" Nevel posed. "Both of his children are gay. And he hates gays! That's totally nuts."

"Terry is so self-centered. He doesn't think he's alienated the kids. He doesn't notice. Even if he could get it that his kids are gay, he wouldn't know what to do. He'll never be able to just love them. He'll be the judgmental asshole till he dies. I think the staff at the hospital is beginning to catch on to his crazy-assed…" Gertie began.

A loud-talking woman standing in front of the waitperson's station startled the whole dining room. The big woman was pointing at them. The woman yelled, "There she is!"

Gertie sighed and said, "Oh Christ, it's the Duff."

Nevel said, "Oh my. I've never met her. Please introduce me."

Duffy pushed past the waitperson and marched to the table where Gertie and Nevel were having their late lunch.

Duffy pulled out a chair and sat down. She glared at Nevel, and then to Gertie she said, "I've been looking everywhere for you! Don't you ever answer your cell phone?"

Gertie replied calmly, "What's the matter with you?"

Duffy looked from Nevel to Gertie and back to Nevel, then asked him, "Who are you?"

"Who are you?" he responded.

"I am Duffy Dot. I am Terry's office manager."

"Well, hon, I'm Nevel Montana. I am the other golf pro here."

Gertie interrupted their banter, "What do you want?"

Duffy said, "Golf pros! What does that...? Anyway, we need some checks signed at the office. I took them to the hospital. Terry still has use of his hands. He can sign a check. But the hospital won't let me see him! They said I am not on the visitors list! That's outrageous. I'm his office manager!"

"I'll sign them. Did you bring them?" Gertie stated, ignoring the rest of Duffy's tirade.

"No, I didn't bring them. They are at the office. I've been driving all over town looking for you. Might have known you'd be lunching with your golf pro friend at the Country Club, while Terry's in his hospital bed. Alone," Duffy said snidely.

Nevel said, "Simmer down. Don't be ugly. Why don't you go get the checks. We've just started our lunch. You have time to go get them. We'll wait for you."

Duffy was startled that this stranger was telling her what to do. She didn't like it one bit, but she couldn't think of anything to say. She stood up and said, "I'll be back." She literally stomped off.

"You handled that very nicely," Gertie said to Nevel.

"I think I took her by surprise. She's not what I'd envisioned at all."

"How so?"

Nevel explained, "I didn't picture her that large.

She's taller and bigger than I thought. What does Terry see in her?"

"She's not that tall."

"She's at least five nine, five ten," Nevel said.

"Maybe. But admittedly the rest of her sure makes her seem pretty damn big," Gertie said. "I hate to say it, but she's not unlike Terry's mother in stature."

Nevel said, "No! Really?! And he's a psychologist! His mother?!"

They both laughed. Lunch was served. They ate and chatted. Then, as promised, Duffy returned. The waitperson just stepped aside when she saw her marching in. Duffy again sat down, again uninvited, at Nevel and Gertie's table. She slapped a file folder in front of Gertie.

Gertie calmly opened the folder, then asked, "Do you have a pen?"

Duffy's expression changed from haughty to confused. "Uh, no. I'll get one." She stood and headed back to the waitperson's station. The waitperson turned and walked away. Duffy went after her.

Nevel handed Gertie a pen. Gertie read through the checks, signed them and closed the folder.

Duffy returned to the table out of breath but with pen in hand. "Here."

Gertie just slid the folder towards Duffy. "All done. Bye."

Duffy slapped the pen on the table, looked in the folder, saw the checks were signed, stood up and without a word stomped away.

"Nutball," Nevel remarked.

"Yes she is," Gertie agreed.

"Why'd she really come here?"

"She wants to know what I know about her affair with Terry. All she knows right now is that I don't like her. That's all Terry knows either."

Nevel asked, "You've never confronted Terry?"

Gertie laughed, "Not about that fool. But money, now that's different."

"Yes I know. He really is an asshole. Taking nearly two hundred thousand of your inheritance from your father, without asking you, and buying that little office of his shows the extent of his assumed entitlement," Nevel said shaking his head.

"That's right. And on top of everything, he never had anything nice to say about or to my father. Ever! In fact he was always downright nasty to my father. Terry is so fucked-up," Gertie said.

"What is the next phase? What are we going to do about him?" Nevel asked. "I know you don't want a divorce. He cannot have half. You've worked too hard to give away half to that psycho!"

"Are you sure you want to continue? You've been wonderful. But you could get in some serious trouble," Gertie said.

Nevel replied, "You're my best friend. Well, until I find the love of my life. But for now, I'm with you! We can do this. You certainly have the upper hand. Why don't you just go to the police?"

"I'm not sure. I've waited so long. There might be unwanted repercussions for me."

"Let's think of ways to get him investigated. There are so many choices."

Gertie said, "Yeah. I'd like to have him investigated and indicted. He's practicing without a license. He is lying about his whole life. He never graduated from college. And he certainly never played any pro football. He's a fake on every level. His entire life story is bullshit."

"Doesn't he fear you might turn him in?" Nevel asked.

"Not in the least. He believes his own fabricated life story. I don't think it has ever occurred to him that I know the truth. He really believes he has everyone fooled. He's been living his lie for a very long time."

"But you've known him since high school! You know the truth. Is he that crazy?"

"He is. He probably doesn't remember that he confessed the worst to me years ago."

Nevel said, "He probably doesn't. We could remind him."

Gertie laughed. "We could indeed! Hey, to change the subject, you want to go with me to an art opening tomorrow night?"

"Sure. Where?"

"Fleeo Gallery. Peter Northburn show. Sherman Kroyton works at the gallery. He's married to Sherry, one of the actual licensed psychologists in Terry's office. He extended the invitation to Terry and me."

"That'll be fun. I'll pick you up," Nevel replied. "The love of my life could await me there!"

"I'll keep an eye out for him. He'll have to pass muster

with me though, you understand. I'll not have you going off with just any smart, good-looking, successful man!" Gertie replied laughing.

"Understood. Nor you either."

# CHAPTER 13

At ten sharp Peter Northburn arrived at the gallery for the sales meeting. Oren rode in to town with him. Oren told Peter, "You don't need me for the sales meeting, do you? I'd like to take the van and go to my place and clean up, get clothes, you know."

"You go ahead. But come back here in about an hour. This won't take long. We may need to run back to the studio for something. This is the dress rehearsal."

Marion Fleeo was front and center ready for the meeting. She'd brought in pastries and coffee. Her two additional salespeople were there, and of course, Sherman was ready for the meeting. Roger, Marion's handyman lurked in the background in case Peter wanted any lighting or other changes made.

Marion said, "Oh. Peter we are all set. What do you think? Let me introduce my sales staff. This is Margie and this is Irene."

Peter said hello to the two saleswomen. He knew he'd never be able to tell them apart. They were both wearing similar flowing clothing and scarves that late middle-aged women favored. They had the same bobbed haircut and orange hair color. They looked like twins to him. They appeared lively and personable. That's all that mattered to him.

Peter walked through the three rooms of the gallery. He approved of the way they had arranged his art. He instructed that the refreshments be placed in the back area of the gallery so the guests would be forced to walk through the entire show in order to get their bite to eat and a drink.

Peter gave the group a little pep talk. "My work will sell itself, but needs you to negotiate the sale. Stick to the marked prices. It is important that the pricing stays consistent worldwide. As you know, if a piece is discounted in one market that diminishes the value elsewhere. You can offer to ship at some discounted price to make the buyer feel good. Any questions?"

Margie asked, "Do you give tours of your studio? I know that's a question we'll hear since you live here."

Peter replied, "I have given one-on-one tours of my studio. By appointment only. No groups. And never children."

Sherman asked, "If anyone wants a piece that is sold, are there like-pieces available at your studio?"

Peter laughed, "Every piece is one-of-a-kind. I do make multiple platters, for example, but no two are alike. Never have been, never will be."

Marion asked, "Oh. Is the lighting good for you, Peter?"

"It is fine. Do you have the banner for the front of the gallery?" Peter inquired.

"Oh. It will be ready this afternoon. You'll love it," Marion said. "It has your name in letters two feet high!"

Oren appeared at the front door and quietly joined the meeting. Peter wrapped it up and told Marion and her staff how much he was looking forward to the opening. "I'll see you people tomorrow evening. Thank you," Peter said in a smooth sales-voice.

Peter and Oren drove back to the studio. Oren drove the van, following the Mercedes. When they got to the studio, Oren asked what was on the agenda.

"I'd like to get ready for another firing. Load the firebox, and fill the wood cart. Be sure the firebox grate has been brushed clean before you load it with the starter wood."

"Glad I put on clean clothes!" Oren complained.

## CHAPTER 14

Marion Fleeo was a nervous wreck. This was the second biggest artist she'd ever hosted. The most important artist she'd ever had a show for was the painter from New York who'd done the famous portrait of Jackie Kennedy, the one of her before she married Jack. It was one of the painter's last shows before he died. That show was the very first exhibit Marion Fleeo hosted after buying the gallery. That was in the final healthy moments of art sales as they had been: the good old days of retail art in America. After that, the art market slowed to a crawl. Now finally it was beginning to percolate just a little. It was beginning to run as it used to. Payoffs here and there, kickbacks to ensure certain artists had the media accolades necessary for high-dollar sales. Money was speaking loudly once again in the art world. There really is no such thing as a better artist or a best artist. All artists are artists are artists. The factors that lift one or another artist to fame and fortune are mostly media marketing and word of mouth among art patrons. If one person buys an artist's work, then they are going to talk up that artist to their friends. Their friends will buy it to be just as smart or cool, which in turn validates the purchase for all. It is fashionable. Everyone wants to fit in with their friends. Everyone wants to belong, to be alike. That sells art.

That sells a lot of things.

Marion Fleeo prayed the money she was spending with the media and decorators was going to come back tenfold or better. She wasn't that into clay art, but the Dallas and Chicago markets had been good to Northburn for a while. Long enough for her to believe that he had some amount of staying power in the fickle art world. This was going to be her last hurrah. She planned to close the gallery and retire after this show. Not right after it. She did want the commissions from any subsequent Northburn sales.

The gallery looked beautiful. The lighting was spectacular. Roger worked wonders. He knew just how to light art. He'd ignored Peter's prattling about the lighting. Thanks goodness, she thought. And the caterer had laid out a lovely display of delicious food and drink. The flowers were spectacular. In the dead of winter in the mountains it was invigorating to have this array of colorful flowers in such abundance. Marion began to calm as she surveyed her gallery. All was ready.

Peter Northburn arrived dressed to kill. He looked spectacularly handsome in a tuxedo. His ego would propel his salesmanship. Shortly after Peter, the invited media, and celebrities showed up. The gallery filled with wealth. Marion circulated and mingled. She sold the tall bear piece right away. A woman from Oklahoma wearing her weight in turquoise jewelry bought it. She told Marion she'd pick it up in the morning. No need to ship it. It'd easily fit in her Suburban. Marion wondered if it had been priced too low.

Peter himself sold the tall male figure piece to a young decorator from Denver. Sherman, Margie, and Irene were selling the smaller figures and vessels non-stop. Marion could not stop smiling. An older man wearing a plain white dress shirt, with a narrow black tie, black ski jacket, and jeans with old cowboy boots, made an offer on the tall female figure. Marion told him the price marked was firm. But she took his contact information just in case.

Gertie and Nevel wandered through the gallery, said hello to Sherman and Sherry, had a bite to eat, then left. They walked around the plaza, window shopping. Most of the holiday lights were still up, for the skiers, even though it was mid-January. The plaza was sparkly. The sky was clear and moonlit. The snow on the ground and clinging to the adobe walls and buildings glowed blue in the moonlight. As the show wound down at the Fleeo Gallery, other guests walked the plaza, too. Soon the plaza was busy with people and voices.

Nevel asked Gertie, "Did you meet Peter Northburn in there?"

"Nope, but I saw him. Nice looking man! Did you talk to him?" Gertie replied.

"I did indeed. He puts out a strange vibe," Nevel said.

"What do you mean?"

"He's self-assured and outwardly charming, but I felt an underlying weirdness about him," Nevel said. "He was alluring and repulsive at the same time."

"Maybe he's like Terry, a psycho homophobic bigot," Gertie suggested.

"Could be. Whatever it is, he works hard to hide the bad juju side," Nevel insisted.

## CHAPTER 15

Marion was worried that the tall female figure hadn't sold. Nearly all of the guests had left. She spotted a middle-aged woman looking carefully at the sculpture. The woman was dressed in a full cowgirl ensemble. Marion approached her casually. "Oh. Lovely piece, isn't it?"

The woman replied, "Captivating."

"Oh, hello. I'm Marion Fleeo. Can I help you make a decision regarding this piece?"

"Maybe so. My decorator tells me that Peter Northburn is the very best in the country with this sort of stuff."

Marion replied, "Oh, he is. Would you like to meet him?"

"Sure."

Marion motioned to Peter to join them. She introduced Peter to the cowgirl. "Peter, this is..."

The woman stepped up to Peter extending her hand, "Hi. I'm Lisa Mordant."

Peter said, "I hope you are enjoying the show. Where do you live?"

The woman replied, "Phoenix. Yeah, this is nice stuff you have here. The sheen on this stuff is pretty nice. I've never seen anything exactly like this look you have going on here."

Peter smiled and said, "Yes. I am focused on making the most extraordinary glazes that I can. The glaze brings the soul to the surface of each piece."

"Well okay. Whatever. But they are pretty nice. I like this tall girl here. I think she'd look great by my pool. Can she be outside? Will she be able to take the weather, the heat in Phoenix?"

"Yes indeed. She came to life in my wood-fired kiln at about twenty four hundred degrees. She is ready for Phoenix!"

"Then I'll take her. I'll pick her up tomorrow. She can ride in the horse trailer. Wrap her up good. She's pretty," the woman said as she handed her platinum American Express card to Peter.

He thanked her. Handed the card to Marion. He told the woman he'd wrap the figure himself. Of course, he never planned to fulfill that promise. As he walked away from the cowgirl, he muttered, "*Stuff!?*"

So after all transactions were completed, Marion headed for the food table. There were a few hors d'oeuvres left. She took a little plate and a small bottle of Perrier and finally sat down. Success. Sherman joined her.

"Good sales tonight!" he said.

"Oh, yes. It was a wonderful opening," Marion replied.

"I didn't see the governor. Did she turn up?" Sherman asked.

"Oh, no. I never saw her. But we sure had the moneyed people in here."

"Yeah. I'm always surprised at who has the disposable income to buy art at these prices."

Marion corrected him, "Oh, it isn't disposable income. It's just wealth. Money. Assets. Most of these people are not earning money. They have money."

Sherman remarked, "Now some of them have less money. Yeah!"

Marion smiled and patted Sherman on the shoulder. She pointed towards the front door. Sherman looked up in time to see the end of a roundhouse punch hit Peter Northburn square and hard on his left ear.

Peter fell back nearly crashing into the trio of standing ceramic sculptures in the center of the room. If the cowgirl hadn't caught him, tens of thousands of dollars in clay would have crashed to the ancient highly polished wooden floor. Sherman jumped up to quell the melee. Marion didn't stand up. She remained seated with her snack in her lap, staring open-mouthed at the fracas.

She saw the man who'd punched Peter go towards him again. The cowgirl, Lisa, stepped between the two men and hollered for them to grow up. The man assaulting the artist was the man who'd made a low-ball offer on the tall female figure piece. He didn't look quite as old to Marion in this moment as he had when he made the offer. In fact, he looked fit and now oddly vaguely familiar. She was sure she knew him from somewhere. She could hear bits of the exchange of incivilities between the two men. How ridiculous, she thought: time to put a stop to this. Marion put her plate on the chair Sherman had vacated, stood up and assumed her authoritative self.

"Oh, Peter, what is the problem?" she called out as she walked calmly towards the scene.

Peter Northburn didn't reply. He looked dazed and angry. His face contorted and red. Still no words were offered to Marion.

She looked at the assailant. "Oh. What happened?" she asked the man.

The assailant was ready to talk. "This putz said he never does consignment work. Said he doesn't want to dirty his artistic consciousness with the pathetic visions of ordinary people like me. He also said I was one of the ugly reasons that he had to make the world beautiful."

Marion, feeling like a kindergarten teacher, looked at Peter. "Oh. Did you say that to this man?"

Peter had caught his breath and could now speak. "Yes. I replied to the little turdwad's request exactly as I meant to. Of all the nerve! He wanted me to make another female figure, but with his dead wife's likeness in the face. I don't *do requests*. I'm not a fucking disc-jockey!"

"Oh, Peter!" Marion said exasperated. She flapped her arms at her sides like she wanted to fly away.

The man said to Peter, "Rot in hell, you pretentious asshole." The assailant coolly exited out the front glass door, yanking the banner from the front of the gallery. He tossed the banner into the street as he walked away.

Peter turned and smiled at the few remaining guests in the gallery. He ran his hand through his thick blond hair and said, "Well, we can't expect everyone to..."

Oren interrupted him, "To be as sophisticated as you?"

Peter turned around to find the very drunk and stoned Oren standing, swaying unsteadily right behind him. Oren was laughing heartily. Peter was about to do something physical to Oren when all of the people in the gallery started laughing with Oren, at Peter.

Peter looking very grim managed with a salesman's enthusiasm to say, "Let's all have some wine."

Sherman whispered to Marion, "Who was that guy?"

Marion replied quietly, "Oh, I don't know, but I do have his name and number in my pocket...along with about ten other shoppers. I talked to him earlier this evening."

Sherman said, "I'm sure I've seen him somewhere before."

Marion said, "Oh, me too. But I can't place him right now."

Sherman remarked: "I hope this doesn't hit the papers...or the internet."

Marion Fleeo said, "Oh, thank goodness the media people left long ago!"

Out in plaza, the buzz about the fight in the gallery spread through the remaining crowd like news of free hamburgers. Gertie and Nevel were amused.

Nevel said, "Damn, we left too soon. Told you Northburn was somehow simmering something dark beneath that polished exterior. Crack in the old glaze!"

## CHAPTER 16

After the opening, on the drive back to Peter Northburn's compound of home, studio, showroom, and kiln, Oren said nothing because he'd passed out. Peter said to the unconscious young man, "You're lucky I don't fire you!" Peter burst into hilarious laughter, and hummed happily for the rest of the long drive back up Taos Canyon. Oren didn't stir.

Once home, Peter dragged Oren by his collar out of the Mercedes which roused him. Oren sputtered, saying, "Hey! Where the hell am I?"

Peter said, "Back at the studio. You can sleep off this, whatever you've done to yourself, in the showroom, on the couch. Don't say anything else. Just go in there and crash."

Oren did as instructed. He passed out once again as soon as he was horizontal on the couch. Peter went upstairs, above the showroom area, to his home. His home consisted of two rooms, well three, if counting the large bathroom. He also had an outdoor balcony patio off the kitchen. His kitchen/living room and his bedroom were surprisingly small for the size of Peter's ego.

Only the bathroom was spacious and grandly appointed. Peter loved to soak in his oversized jetted tub.

He also loved the huge walk-in shower space. The many showerheads and jets could calm him down like nothing else, or they could rev him up like nothing else. He thought of it as a magic shower. He took a long magic shower. As usual, he wacked off and sprayed the shower wall, then watched the results disappear down the drain. He never tired of seeing his perfect penis perform.

Tonight he was very hungry. He decided a grilled tenderloin steak and a salad would hit the spot. He often grilled on his balcony right outside the kitchen space. The second-story covered balcony looked out over the ravine behind his property and up into the Carson National Forest bordering beyond. Stepping out on the balcony, looking off to the side he could just see over and past the woodpiles, the area where his sure-shot had taken down his most recent prize. It was late and even though the starry and moonlit night reflected off the snow, he couldn't see into the woods. But, he could still picture her body and the blood. He said aloud, "Another perfect shot!" He stepped back in the kitchen after he started the gas grill. It'd heat nicely while he finished putting together the salad. He poured a large glass of red wine, humming while he prepared his dinner. Tomorrow was going to be a busy day.

## CHAPTER 17

The next morning was a stunningly gorgeous mountain winter morning. The clear cold air was invigorating. Peter was up early, took another long magic shower whacking off with gusto, and then dressed in his work clothes of chinos, cotton flannel shirt, and steel-toed boots. After his coffee, eggs, and toast, he descended to the showroom. He found Oren just where he'd left him, unconscious on the couch. Peter kicked the couch. Oren sat up.

"Uh, hi boss," the bleary eyed young man said.

"How're you feeling this morning, you idiot?" Peter asked.

"Felt better. Felt worse. I need a smoke. Going outside."

Peter said, "Good plan. Go outside, smoke your weed, get on your bike and go back to town. Don't come back today."

"Can do." Oren stood up and made his way to the door. He left.

Peter went to the studio. He sat at his drawing table to tally the sales from the opening. He'd taken notice of most of the sales. Almost everything in the show must have sold, he thought. Marion should be emailing him a report before the end of the day. The vases and bowls are always the last to sell. People like the platters more than the other pieces. "Next firing, lots of platters," he announced to himself. He finally heard the stupid little motorcycle start and drive away. Now it was time to check the bank.

He went out the back door of the studio to the locked shed. Once inside the shed, he unlocked the chest freezer. The tarp-wrapped bundle felt mostly if not completely frozen through. He lifted it out. He carried it back into the studio where he laid it on a table in the rear part of the building by the smaller gas kilns. Peter Northburn cut off the rope and removed the tarp from the body. The outer clothes came off rather easily. He removed the hoodie, jeans, and tall lace-up boots. Then he had to cut the frozen clothes that he couldn't readily pull off the stiff cold body. She had on more clothes than he'd imagined. He had to work a little harder than usual to remove the thick tall socks, thick knit over-shirt, turtleneck undershirt, and her ridiculous gold colored lace bra and panties. He then rewrapped the naked body in the tarp. He tied the bundle with thinner rope than the rope used to haul it out of the ravine. He redeposited her in his chest freezer bank.

Now it was time to eliminate the clothes. Since it was such a nice morning, Peter thought it would be fun to have a little bonfire outside instead of the usual disposal up in the woods. He carefully folded the now thawing clothes, retrieved Karen's coat from the cabinet in the showroom then went outside. He opened the big front sliding door to the kiln building. He dragged a sheet of four by four steel roofing out of the building. There in front of the kiln building, he built a small bonfire on the sheet metal. He piled scraps of bark and pieces of wood discarded during the last firing. The small bits of wood would've spiked the temperature and burned off too fast. But that is exactly what he wanted this morning: a fast little bonfire. He placed the clothing on the wood and then covered it with additional wood. He doused it with lighter fluid and sparked it. What a nice fire. The still thawing clothing sizzled. He added more hot-burning wood to the fire to counteract the cooling from the cold wet clothes. The woolen coat stunk when it burned. He pulled a chair from the kiln building. He sat contentedly watching the fire, feeding the fire as needed. He relaxed. Peter loved the view looking down from his compound across the highway and river to the meadows and mountains beyond. Eventually it looked like the flames had consumed nearly everything. He knew when to stop feeding the fire. He put the chair back in the kiln building, closed the sliding door and returned to his studio. He left the steel sheet with the ashes outside to cool. He knew in the cold air, it would cool quickly enough.

At his drawing table, he began a list of items to produce for future firings. He hadn't planned on a firing just yet, but with the prize in his bank, he wanted to get things moving. He had a lot of work ahead of him. He liked it that way. He made lists and some preliminary sketches of new pieces. Then it was time to clean up the bonfire residue. He grabbed his coat and gloves.

Except for the snaps, metal buttons, zippers, and various other metal pieces that didn't burn or melt completely, the clothes and boots were ash. He shoveled the ashes onto a screen covering a five gallon metal can. The ashes fell through into the can and the unburned bits and pieces were captured by the screen. Once the ashes were all in the can, he picked the larger mostly burned leather bits of the boots off the screen and tossed them in with the ashes. He emptied the small items from the screen into a small cardboard box. He shook out the screen and steel sheet before putting them back in the building.

Then he walked to the far end of the parking lot in front of his main building. From inside a small shed he rolled out an ATV. He drove it over to the front of the kiln building and picked up the ash can and the cardboard box. He drove his ATV down his steep driveway to the highway. He turned left. After about a hundred yards, he turned right onto a dirt track that lots of hunters and campers used to access a National Forest campground. He continued on the frozen dirt track for a mile. It took him higher and higher into the National Forest. He didn't stop at the first or second campsite, but went further, to the third one. No one was around on this January morning. But people had been there recently enough that the campfire pit had dry ashes in it that had not been snowed on. Peter added his can of ashes to the pit and stirred all the ashes together. He got back on his four-wheeler and continued up the mountain on the dirt track. Further up, the terrain leveled out to a meadow. He drove across the snowy meadow, staying on the trail.

On the far side of the meadow there was a stream that was nearly frozen solid. Peter took the cardboard box and left his ATV. He walked alongside the stream until he reached the point where the stream began to fall downhill.

Some water was moving slowly under the ice. He poked a hole into the ice with his gloved hand and deposited the unburned items from the cardboard box into the icy stream. He knew that as the winter eventually subsided and snowmelt accelerated the water flow, those items would be scattered downstream, not ever to be noticed or found again. He went back to his ATV and headed home. A beautiful morning.

## CHAPTER 18

Enough days had passed since Terry Small had wound up in traction in a room at the county hospital, for him to come to the horrible realization that this was not going to be over soon. He hurt all over. He had sweats and headaches like he'd never experienced. His intestines actually stung. He was suffering from alcohol withdrawal, despite the fact that he maintained he wasn't addicted to anything, least of all alcohol. He only had an occasional drink. The bottle of wine every night was good for him. That wasn't drinking. It wasn't an addiction. It was wine.

A doctor who had a thick Indian accent tried to counsel him regarding alcohol withdrawal, but received only a sneer and insults from Terry. Terry said he was not going to listen to nonsense regarding alcoholism. Terry told the doctor to leave. The doctor gladly obliged.

The nurses were tolerating Terry because, as trained nurses, that is what they do. The orthopedic surgeon who told him that surgery on his knees was mandatory if he wanted to walk again was dismissed by Terry in a deluge of insults. Terry didn't see the logic in waiting on his broken femurs to heal before performing the procedures to rebuild his knees.

"Just do it all. I'm stuck here for fuck's sake. Just do

everything, get it over with so I can go home."

"We cannot do your knees just yet. It would only delay or impede your complete recovery."

"But if you wait to re-do my knees, I will just be delayed in getting out of this fucking harness. You don't know what the fuck you are doing, do you? I want a new doctor."

"Great. Fine by me. Your insurance agent can give you a list to choose from."

Gertie made the bad-timing decision to visit Terry just as the orthopedic surgeon was leaving. She encountered him in the hall. He spelled out what had happened with her husband. "Terry is a complete ass. Sorry you had to deal with him," she said sympathetically to the doctor.

"Not a problem for me. Happy to be rid of him. Life's too short. Good luck to the next doc!" the surgeon said with a sigh.

Gertie opened the door to Terry's room to find him leaning as far as he could off the side of the bed. "Lose something?" she asked.

"The remote. It slipped off the bed. Get it. It's right there," Terry barked pointing at the floor by the bed.

"Can you say please?" Gertie asked.

"Please. Flippin' please," he replied.

Gertie picked up the remote and handed it to him. "What does flippin' mean? Are you cursing at me, or not?"

Terry said, "It's a frigging polite way to say fucking!"

"So if you use flipping or now, as you have pointed out, frigging, then are you not cursing?" she inquired.

"I am not cursing if I don't say fucking," he said in a stern tone.

"Really. So are you using the polite, as you say, vernacular for the word fucking to not curse at me? But if frigging and flipping mean fucking, then you are cursing at me."

"Flipping really?"

She countered, "See there, what you mean is fucking really?"

"But I didn't say fucking. I said flipping."

"Are you a better person if you substitute those one-meaning-synonyms for curse words? Why use any of those words if you don't mean to curse? Just omit the modifier altogether."

"It is for emphasis," Terry said lamely.

"Really? You can't think of any other word in the entire language to modify your spoken thoughts...flipping, frigging, that's it? What about fudge? I've heard you use that word when you mean fuck. And fricking? That's a fucking substitute, too."

"You're being fucking hard on me. I'm strung up here like a dead deer, and you are beating me up about my language."

"I'm just trying to get a handle on when you are cursing at me and when you are not."

"Does it matter?" Terry asked.

"Do you curse at the Duff? Does she understand that when you say flipping or frigging or fricking or flip or frig or frick or fudge that you are actually cursing? Hypothetical question. Duff really doesn't understand very much, does she?"

Terry insisted, "She's a bright woman. Don't talk about her like that."

"Really. Fucking really?" Gertie responded.

"What's got you so worked up?" Terry asked defensively.

"I signed some checks for you. The Duff brought them to me to sign because the hospital won't let her in here to see you. I saw a check to Willow Park Apartments for over a thousand dollars. I signed it. Then I did some checking and it turns out that is where Duffy Dot lives. I visited the leasing office, and do you know what I found out?" Gertie asked.

Terry's face went pale. "What?"

"The sweet young woman in that office told me all about that lucky Duffy. Duffy is a chatty person, you know. She told the sweet leasing office woman all about you and how much you and Duffy love each other. Duffy is so lucky to have such an attentive and generous boyfriend. Seems you have been paying not only for her apartment, but also for her car, her car insurance, health insurance, everything since she went to work for you. You also pay her a wage beyond the going rate for her position. The young woman described you fucking perfectly."

"There must be some mistake..." Terry said in a small voice.

"I don't think so. I think you have been spending my money not just on that little condo office space you bought, but on the Duff. The office I can resell, recoup my money. But the Duff? That's money down the toilet, don't you think?" Gertie said. "How stupid are you?"

"Wait a minute...your money? I work for living. I make money. I spend my money," Terry said.

"Oh really? You are not actually licensed to practice as a psychologist in New Mexico. You once were licensed in Colorado, but you haven't kept that license current. So, you aren't licensed at all anywhere. Your office generates income thanks to the work that Sherry and Erlene do. You don't do anything. You are living off of them and me."

"I will be licensed in New Mexico," Terry whined.

"No you won't. You've been saying that for years. You know you can't meet the requirements. You could study until your legs heal, and you couldn't pass the tests."

"I did. I was licensed in Colorado," he said.

"That was long ago and far away. Way before you got Duff dumb."

"I support my family. I have always supported my family," Terry responded.

"That's absurd. You know very well that I have always supported our family. You have added some to the income, but my work at one of the most exclusive, aka richest, golf clubs in Colorado is what set our lifestyle, and I've maintained it all of these years."

"I admit that your being a golf pro has paid off for us. I never thought it would, but it has," Terry admitted.

"Your psychologist's office in Snowmass was no money maker. You spent most of your time skiing, fishing, doping, drinking, and playing. I hope you have a bit saved away," Gertie said.

"Why do you say that?" Terry whined.

"I'm not giving you anything. This whole Duffy Dot escapade has slammed the door, and nailed the coffin shut, as they say. And, you are going to have to repay me for the money you spent on your office. That was from my inheritance from my father, whom you hated by the way."

"What are you saying?" Terry asked quietly.

"I'm saying that I have had it with you. We are going to divorce, go our separate ways, split up."

"What about the kids?" Terry asked.

"What about them? They are grown people. They have their own lives. Lives, by the way, that you cannot participate in because you are such a fucked up homophobe bigot."

"I am not against gays. I just don't believe my children are gay. It's a phase they are going through. I'm not going to encourage it."

"You dumb shit! It isn't a phase, Bok and Brick have always been gay. I've known since they were little. Hell, I knew before they knew."

"That's ridiculous. They were never gay. Bok played football. He should have played harder and kept with it. Could have been a pro."

"Oh like you?? Listen to your stupid self! Good god! So, a gay man can't play football?"

"Gays aren't into sports. Bok was a great sportsman. Now he's building sets for TV shows in Hollywood! How embarrassing!" Terry declared.

Gertie shook her head in dismay and said, "I am not even going to have this conversation with you. You are such a fool."

Terry said, "We'll see who the fool is. You have a lot of money, why is it so important to you that I pay you back for the cost of my office? I don't get it. You are a very rich woman! That office was a great deal. I bought it from the bank! A foreclosure."

"You were always so mean to my father. You never had anything good to say about him. You made fun of him. Really you have always been an asshole to my entire family. I don't want you to benefit even a tiny bit from my father's life. That's the issue. And I know I don't want to give you anything from my life either. I have spent over thirty years married to you. I can't believe it! But I have. Maybe I should see a psychologist! A real one!"

"You can't do this to me. I won't let you. I'll fight you for half of everything," Terry snapped.

"Really?? Two words: James Phinn," Gertie said, as she opened the hospital room door. She left.

Terry Small was too shocked to even blink. He stared at the ceiling. It hit him that his broken legs were not his biggest problem.

## CHAPTER 19

"Well what's that ass doing up here?" the older man asked his horse, Pokey. He'd heard the noise of the all-terrain vehicle as he was riding his horse down from the ridge high above the creek that traversed the side of the mountain. He'd descended towards the noise in time to see Peter Northburn leave the four-wheeler and walk alongside the creek.

Quinton Quigley sat on his horse watching Peter from deep in the trees above the creek. He saw Peter stop at the point where the creek changes course and heads almost directly downhill. "What is he doing?" Quinton asked Pokey. The horse shook his head. "We'll just wait and see," Quinton said.

Once Peter was again on his ATV and barreling back towards the highway, Quinton rode down to the creek. He went to the spot where Peter had been kneeling by the frozen water. As Quinton dismounted, he said to his horse, "Well look at that. The neighborhood artist has put something in the ice. Let's see what it is."

Quinton retrieved the small pile of scorched metal notions from the shallow hole in the ice. He looked carefully at the odd collection. He said to his horse, "He sure went to a lot of trouble to dispose of pieces of, looks like a zipper, and maybe snaps. Metal buttons, rivets. How interesting. Let's hang on to these." He put the scorched items in an old saddle bag, got on his horse, and resumed his ride, with his ultimate destination of his home which was not far down and just across the highway from Peter Northburn's compound.

Quinton Quigley had lived on his mountain ranch for forty years. His property of a thousand acres swept from the highway back thru a pass into a valley that was bordered on three sides by Carson National Forest. He'd bought the ranch those many years ago with the Oklahoma oil and gas money he'd inherited from his parents.

His family never lived in Oklahoma, but that's where the money came from. Quinton grew up in Texas. He always thought it ironic that his money was from Oklahoma, but his life was from Texas. Not a bit of Texas oil money. He never knew, growing up, that his parents were so wealthy. They lived a regular life in Dallas, nothing special or ostentatious about their home or lifestyle.

When he was twenty-nine years old, his parents were killed in a car crash on a wide-open empty flat stretch of north Texas highway. They had been driving from Dallas to their lake house on Lake Texoma. A dumbass teenager was just driving around drinking. Quinton was suddenly and unexpectedly an orphan and a very rich man.

He'd just finished law school at Southern Methodist University in Dallas when his parents were killed. He was engaged to a beautiful brilliant woman who'd passed the bar a year ahead of him. They planned to open a law firm together as soon as he was licensed. Life looked like it was on track, a plan was being actualized. They married and bought a small thirties era home in central Dallas. Then the woman he loved, the woman he worshiped, died in a car crash in Dallas. Another drunk driver had killed another part of his life.

He packed up the few things he had and headed for the mountains of northern New Mexico. He knew he wanted land. He wanted to be away from people.

He met an eighty year old woman at the newspaper office in Taos when he went in to inquire about land listings. Her name was Frank Armire. She happened to be in the newspaper office to list her ranch for sale in the classifieds. She said she was selling it herself because she didn't want to deal with realtors and lookers. She liked Quinton right away. He liked her, too. Over a cup of coffee, she explained to Quinton that she and her husband, also named Frank Armire, had worked the ranch all of their lives. He'd died the previous year of exhaustion at eighty-eight years of age. His widow didn't want to stay there without him. Frank sold the big ranch with all of the livestock, equipment, everything to Quinton at a fair price. He helped her move to Amarillo to her sister's house.

Quinton loved the ranch from the first night he spent there sleeping on the covered porch, which stretched the full length of the front of the house. He still sleeps outside on the wide front porch when weather permits. He learned how to be a rancher. And he brought Frank to spend a month with him at her old ranch during each of the four summers until her death. Both Frank and Frank are buried on the ranch. Quinton takes good care of their graves and their ranch.

Today, when he and Pokey, his favorite riding horse, got back to the ranch, Quinton cleaned Pokey and turned him out to the sunny pasture by the house. Then he took the saddle bag onto the porch. He wanted to take a closer look at the bits and pieces of whatever that asshole artist had secreted in the frozen stream.

He found two metal zippers. One was longer and smaller-toothed than the other. He counted eight metal buttons; one was larger than the others. There were four small rivets, twelve small hook and eyes, and six metal snaps. "What an odd collection. I think I'd like Emma and Harry to see this. Maybe they'd like to come to dinner," Quinton said aloud to himself. He usually spoke to himself if the thought was important enough. He took the cell phone from his jeans' pocket and walked out to the barn. The only spot on the ranch with dependable cell connection was right in front of the big metal barn. Since the barn was such a large steel structure, he was convinced that the mass of metal assisted in the wondrous life of the cell phone's invisible information gathering and dispersing.

Emma Spruce picked up, "Hello Quinton!"

Quinton explained what had happened, what he had sitting on the long table on his porch. "I think something's not right over at the asshole artist's place. He never and I mean never visits the National Forest on this side of the highway. I've seen him in the forest above his property, but not over here. Why don't you and Harry come for dinner soon? I'll grill some elk."

Emma compared her schedule with Harry's and

replied, "I'm on duty through tomorrow midnight. But we can come the next afternoon. That good for you? We'd like to see you, and what you found."

"Good deal. See you at four PM. Senior early-bird special grilled elk! Bring me some coffee if you would please. I'm about out," Quinton said.

"Out of coffee?? How'd that happen? With your storehouse of supplies, I can't believe that!" Emma laughed.

"Well, not being a real survivalist, more of a non-shopper, I do run low, then all of a sudden I run out of this or that. Thank goodness for UPS and FedEx! If they and Amazon weren't there...I'd be calling you for shopping favors all the time!" Quinton said laughing.

"Not a problem. We'll see you day after tomorrow at four PM, coffee in-hand! I'll bring a salad, too. Look forward to it," Emma said.

Quinton thanked her. He set about on his usual chores.

## CHAPTER 20

Peter was excited to begin some new pieces. After disposing of the ashes and metal pieces from Karen's clothes, he returned to his compound. He parked his ATV in the shed without the customary obsessive cleaning, and went straight to his studio. His nervous energy was high. He sat down at his throwing wheel and began a platter with a thrown round shape. Then as it hit just the right diameter, he let it swing wide into an oval shape. He stopped the wheel before the piece reached the point it would tear apart. He lifted it from the wheel and finished it by hand into one of his signature platter shapes. He could throw faster and more effectively than anyone. In no time he'd used up all of the prepared clay, and he had an impressive shelf of plates and platters. He covered the raw clay platters with plastic so they could begin the controlled drying process. In a few days, he'd bisque fire them in the gas kilns and then they'd be ready for the wood-firing. But that seemed too long to wait. He paced around the studio. His adrenaline was pumping. He made a decision. He wasn't going to wait until the new platters were ready. He wanted to fire up his wood kiln now. He looked further in his shelves of ready clay work. He didn't care if the work was new. If he could find enough to fill the chamber, he'd lite her up.

He found enough.

He had some other vessels ready and waiting, as well as a four-foot tall hand-built sculpture of a tree. The tree was basically a trunk with a couple of bare stick shapes coming out of it. Not too unusual, he thought, but when his glaze brought it to life, it would be phenomenal.

Peter mixed a fresh batch of glaze to coat the pieces. He used the ashes and crushed particles harvested from the kiln's ash box and the floor of the firing chamber from prior firings mixed with feldspar, kaolin, spodumene, nepheline syenite, soda ash, and ball clay to create his special glaze mix. Although the base ingredients were common for a wood-fired potter's glaze, it was his tailored combination of the components that made his glaze work with his special ingredient. Peter had developed his highly guarded recipe over the years to a perfect mix of chemistry that reacted exactly as he wanted with his individual orchestration of the firing. He coated the clay vessels, platters, cups, and the tree sculpture with his glaze mix.

The wood-fired kiln takes on a life of its own when it is fired up. Stoking surges the fire that consumes oxygen pulled in through the front air intake ports urging the fire and heat into the firing chamber. This reduction of oxygen, consumed by the fire, acts on the clay and glaze chemistry in its own ways. When the fire burns down prior to the next stoking cycle, the air in the chamber is re-oxygenated, and that reacts in a different way on the clay and surfaces. This alternating oxygen, less oxygen, oxygen, less oxygen is the breathing that Peter controls. He controls the kiln's breathing to guide the chemical reactions in the chamber to create his special glaze colors and surface effects. He also has his special ingredient for firings that excites him more than anything does. The special ingredient makes him the extraordinary artist he knows he is.

He was excited to begin the firing process. With his focus heightened, he began. He first went to his bank in the shed behind his studio. He brought the nearly frozen corpse to his studio. He put it on his stainless steel worktable and removed the tarp. The naked body was glistening with the frozen moisture crystals coating the skin. He began cutting the extremities from the trunk with a sawzall. Cutting it frozen kept the body fluids contained in the corpse. He finally beheaded the body. He bisected the trunk just below the rib cage, above the hipbones. The sawzall chomped easily through the spinal cord. He looked at the bounty. He had legs with feet, arms with hands, two pieces of the trunk, and the head. The extremities were frozen through, but the trunk was thick enough that the chest freezer had only frozen the outer few inches. The organs were not completely frozen. They would vaporize quickly enough. Perfect.

He tossed the tarp that the body had been wrapped in over the body pieces on the stainless steel worktable. He rolled the big cart of clay pieces out of the studio over to the wood-kiln building. He parked the cart by the loading door of the firing chamber. Even though Oren was supposed to have swept out the kiln, Peter always had to sweep it again before each firing. He swept out the firing chamber carefully picking out the larger unburned pieces of debris from the prior firing. Any unburned pieces of the previous corpse would be crushed and incorporated into his next batch of glaze. No waste. No evidence.

He went back to the studio, loaded the body segments on a cart and rolled it to the kiln. When he had the kiln shelves, stilts to hold the shelves, the clay artwork, and the dismembered corpse arranged by the chamber door, he began loading the firing chamber. He carefully arranged the work to maintain the needed airflow through the kiln, forcing the flames around the objects within. He put all of the body parts, except the head, at the spots within the chamber that he'd learned from trial and error over the years would produce the desired effect throughout the population within the chamber. He placed sets of pyrometric cones in front of the two spy holes he knew were his prime temperature indicator spots in the chamber. He made sure the thermocouples were correctly placed and working. He went outside to visually check the chimney. After closing up the firing chamber door by stacking firebricks to block the opening completely, he went to the other side of the kiln to inspect the firebox. Oren was supposed to have cleaned it, but Peter knew from experience that his always-stoned assistant was a flake when it came to cleaning his beloved kiln. Peter got after it. He cleaned the firebox and the ash box under the fire grate of remaining ash debris, putting all of the cold ashes into an ashcan. He then stoked the firebox with the first load of wood for this firing. Always a precious moment for him, it had to be just right. It's important to bring the heat up properly. He ignited the kindling. It had begun! He returned to the kiln, double checked everything. Arranged the damper. Secured the chamber door. All systems go!

He went back to the firebox and began in earnest to get the fire up and going. Peter Northburn's heart was racing. His adrenaline was climaxing. He watched the fire slowly grow hotter and hotter. He stoked it until ashes were falling into the ash box below the fire. Then he began his ritual cycle of stoke and rest. He gave the kiln life. It was breathing.

Peter checked the spyholes and thermocouple readings every thirty minutes. He stoked the fire approximately every three minutes. After each round of wood stoking, he checked the chimney. When the smoke cleared, he would stoke again. This created the rhythm he wanted for the firing. At the beginning of the firing, a gentle wisp of smoke rose from the chimney. As the firing progressed, the amount of smoke increased until a dark blackish-grey plume bellowed from the kiln's chimney sending the thick pungent smoke into the surrounding landscape.

Whenever he had a moment to spare, he watched the chamber through a large spy-hole. He slid open the door on that spy hole and saw the chamber was barely beginning to glow red. It was early yet. Soon the wood ashes would ride the tongues of the fire and heat from the firebox through the chamber creating wonderful effects, color, and blushing on the clay. The ash melts into the glaze at such high temperatures. Peter modified his assortment of wood species to burn, not only to guide the heat production, but also in order to control and optimize the ash effects on the surfaces. As the human body parts burned, vaporized then swirled in the heat, they also added a very special touch to the surfaces of the clay. That vaporizing and the chemical changes of all the elements swirling and racing through the chamber provoked the transformation of the clay pieces into his phenomenal art.

The wood-fired kiln reaches its hottest towards the end of the firing. Peter's kiln dependably fires to twenty-four hundred degrees. At that point the pieces in the kiln appear liquid; almost translucent they are so hot. That is when Peter tossed the head into the firebox. He really loved watching the partially frozen head explode as it hit the heat in the firebox. The ash flying into the chamber on the shoulders of the incredible heat will be loaded with the chemical elements of the head: hair, bone, teeth, and brain. This last elemental licking of the molten clay is the final touch in his special firing technique.

After stoking the firebox with the head, he continued to fire for approximately four hours. He held the temperature at a constant, stoking the kiln heavily with more wood. With each stoke he opened the firebox door peering in at the disintegrating head. This was such an exciting part of the firing for Peter. The visual of the incredibly fierce strength of the fire consuming the flesh, hair, and brain provided Peter with an indescribable rush.

He'd spent forty-eight hours straight tending to his kiln. He'd expected Oren to return sometime after the first day of the firing. But the pot-head never showed. Oren was never allowed to assist with the loading process, for obvious reasons. Peter had trained Oren to help him with the firings, but only after the work was loaded and the fire going, Oren was a tolerable stoker. Peter always sent Oren away at the end of the firings when it was time to toss the heads into the firebox. This time Peter had done it all. He was exhausted, truly exhausted, but so exhilarated. He left the kiln. It would cool down slowly, as would he. He went to bed. Smiling.

## CHAPTER 21

Quinton Quigley rolled his sizable smoker out of the barn and set it by the water trough next to the horse corral just to the side of the barn. He loaded it with charcoal and wood. He lit the fire and waited for it to burn to coals. It didn't take long. He then put thick slabs of elk backstrap on the grill. A sweet sizzle preceded the sweet smell of elk cooking. He closed the lid and set the timer on his cell phone. He planned to smoke the elk for the shortest time. Don't overcook elk!

Just before four, Harry and Emma Spruce arrived. Quinton had left the gate open for them. The gate was near the highway, about a half mile from his house. When he saw their truck coming up his long drive, he took out his cell phone and tapped in a command to close the gate. Smart gate.

Emma and Harry hugged him. They'd brought their four dogs with them. Quinton's two dogs were absolutely delighted to see their pals. The six dogs ran in figure eight patterns around Emma, Harry and Quinton. After a few rounds, they shot off to the barn and corral. Too much fun to be had.

Harry put the salad on the long table on the porch. "We have about thirty minutes more of sunlight," he called from the porch. "We eating inside?"

Quinton said, "Go on inside. I'll get the meat." Quinton retrieved the elk from the warming drawer on his fancy smoker and joined them inside.

The temperature drops quickly in the mountains once the sun sets. It was warm and cozy in Quinton's house. It still looked a lot like it did when Frank and Frank lived there so many decades ago. Quinton liked Frank's taste in décor, so he left it just like she'd had it. He had laid a healthy fire in the big stone hearth. Emma and Harry set the table and served salad. Quinton served the elk. They sat down to eat.

Emma told Quinton, "I put your coffee delivery in the kitchen along with some grocery surprises."

"Thank you! I love grocery surprises," Quinton replied.

"You have bread in the oven?" Harry asked Quinton.

"God! Yes. I forgot."

"I'll get it," Harry said. He was already at the oven. "Looks fine."

"I rarely make bread. I just forgot all about it," Quinton said laughing at himself.

"Smells great," Emma said.

Harry set the bread on the table, along with a small plate with a stick of butter on it. He asked, "Speaking of smell, what is that I smelled on the highway...just before we got to your road?"

Quinton said, "What'd it smell like?"

Emma said to Harry, "I smelled it, too." Then to

Quinton, she said, "Smelled to me like a house burned with a victim inside."

Quinton laughed, "Only you would! D'you have any interesting deaths in the last couple of days?"

Emma Spruce is a field deputy for the New Mexico Office of the Medical Investigator. She'd just finished a forty-eight hour duty shift. "I did! A young man killed himself working on his car."

"What? How'd he do that? Where?" Quinton asked.

"Out near Tres Piedras. He had his car's front end lifted up with the wheels off. He'd put old rotten tree stumps, each about eighteen inches high under the car to hold it up. I found him under the fallen hood. Apparently he had the hood up, engine running. He climbed up on the fender, was leaning over the running engine when one of the rotten stumps crumbled. The hood slammed down on him and his head was violently pushed into the running engine. His long hair was grabbed mercilessly by various moving belts. His face was a mess, scalp was ripped up. He probably didn't die quickly. His girlfriend was so high, she couldn't tell us anything. It was a very sad scene."

"Good Lord! What's in the water out there?" Quinton exclaimed.

Harry asked, "What do they put in their veins out there?"

Emma said, "Unfortunate. Young man was probably as high as his girlfriend."

"Okay. Back to the smell in the canyon. There was a fair amount of dark smoke hanging in the air, too. Was there a fire today?" Harry asked.

"Probably the neighborhood artist's kiln. He stinks up the canyon for a couple of days whenever he's firing," Quinton explained.

"What does he burn? It smelled like wood and something else. Not just wood," Harry said.

"Smelled like he might be cremating something. Had that particular odor of the old crematoriums. The way they smelled before the EPA made them clean up the emissions. But more recently I encountered that smell in Red River when a man killed his wife, then torched their vacation cabin with her body in it," Emma said. "The aftermath smelled a lot like what we just drove through."

Quinton said, "No fires today. It wasn't my smoker. So that leaves asshole's kiln. Emma, you live such an interesting life!"

Emma laughed, "Guess I do. I sure see a lot of stupidity, or rather the results of stupidity."

Harry said, "Is that Peter Northburn's kiln we're talking about?"

"Yes. His studio is up in the foothills across the road, about a quarter mile back from my road. He has a sign at the highway," Quinton said.

"Really, how long has he been there? I've driven this highway millions of times. Never noticed," Harry said. "In fact I'm going hunting not far from here on that side of the highway next week. Private land elk hunt on Charles McMarlin's ranch."

"Northburn's been there about twenty years I guess. He built the compound to house his home, studio, and kiln. It's a big-ass wood-fired kiln. It has its own building. The chimney is high. The fire marshal designed a spark screen for the top of the chimney. Seems safe enough, just kind of stinks sometimes," Quinton explained.

Emma suggested, "Does he keep animals? Cows? Sheep? Goats? Pigs? Chickens?"

Quinton replied, "I don't know if he does. I've never been up there and don't plan to go up there."

"Well anyway, this elk is great. Good job on the smoker!" Harry said.

They enjoyed a wonderful dinner. Then Quinton brought out a shoebox-sized cardboard box with the pieces he wanted to show them.

Emma examined the pieces carefully, then said to Quinton, "Tell me again where you got these."

"Just west of here in the National Forest, there is a creek that comes from way up high and swings across a meadow, then it turns downhill and runs into the river at the bottom of the canyon. Pokey and I were coming down from the top of the ridge two days ago when I saw Northburn on a four-wheeler coming up towards the meadow. I never see him over there. I don't ever see him on this side of the highway. So I watched him park his noisy little off-road toy and walk along the creek. He goes all the way to the point where it turns downhill. I saw him kneel down and stick these things in the ice. He made a little pit in the ice and put them in it. Weird. I waited until he left, then retrieved them. I was just too curious."

Harry was picking through the collection. He asked Emma, "These are bra hooks, aren't they?"

Emma said, "They sure look like it. This melted

plastic zipper looks like the kind on a pullover turtleneck, the kind that zips up the back, you know, at the top. These rivets and zipper are from some kind of a hoodie or sweater, maybe a jacket. And this other zipper is from pants, I bet. The pull has a Land's End logo on it. And this is a Land's End metal button."

"All women's clothes, you think?" Harry asked her.

"Can't tell. But the bra hooks most probably," she said laughing.

Quinton said, "So what the hell was he doing hiding them in a frozen creek? What else has he hidden over there?"

"Good question. OMI does not have its own lab. They consign a lab. They only deal with lab work for specific cases."

"You think the sheriff would be interested?" Quinton asked.

"Seems like suspicious behavior, but the sheriff and the state police both would ask a lot of questions and need some event to get involved. I don't think either of them would want this at this point," Emma replied. "But I think I might know who would be interested enough to run these curiosities through a lab."

Harry asked, "Who?"

Emma said, "Jackson Avery."

"Who's that?" Quinton asked.

"FBI. Jackson always tells me not to hesitate to let him know if I have anything for him. I'll call him tomorrow."

Quinton told Emma to take the box of curious items with her. The dogs were on the front porch. All six were worn out. They'd fulfilled the goal to sniff everything around the house, around the barn, in the barn, in the corral, and in the pasture nearest the house. Harry let them in and fed them. Emma and Quinton stayed by the hearth speculating about Northburn's motives.

"How about some dessert?" Harry asked.

"Great idea," Quinton said. "There's some ice cream in the freezer."

When Harry brought the ice cream over to the hearth, his herd of dogs followed him. He sat down and asked, "So why did the artist cross the road?"

Emma and Quinton laughed. Emma suggested, "Maybe it was a ritual thing. You know, some kind of religious thing."

Quinton said, "Doubt that. He's a complete ass. I went to his opening at Fleeo Gallery. There was a sculpture I liked. But it'd sold. It was a figure of a woman. Kind of modernistic, not realistic. Tall sculpture. I asked him if he could make one for me, and maybe put some aspect of my deceased wife's facial features on it. He went ballistic. Said he never does commissions. Acted like I'd insulted him. But he insulted me. So I hit him. I smacked him on his ear."

"What'd he do after you hit him?" Harry asked.

"Nothing really. I left. Northburn is just a self-centered pompous ass. But I guarantee he is up to something. He's doing something he shouldn't be doing."

Emma said, "I'll talk to the state police. See if anyone else has reported anything regarding Northburn. Just curious."

"Let me know. Better put my animals up for the

night. Take the rest of the elk and bread with you. Leave the ice cream!"

Emma and Harry thanked Quinton, rounded up their dogs and headed home.

Quinton used the gate operation app on his cell phone to open the gate for them as he walked over to the corral whistling for his horses. Quinton tapped another app on his phone to activate the outside spotlights on the barn. His barn, corral and pasture were suddenly fully illuminated. His horses compliantly came from the far side of the pasture to meet him. They were ready for their dinner.

## CHAPTER 22

As usual, Duffy Dot arrived early to the office. She went straight to Terry's office. She was going through his desk, when she heard Sherry open the front door. She jumped up and strolled awkwardly back to her reception station. She said in a choked voice to Sherry, "Good morning."

Sherry looked at Duffy only because the tone of voice was out of the ordinary. Sherry replied, "Good morning." Sherry went to her office.

Erlene arrived a few minutes later. She went straight to Sherry's office. She told Sherry, "Jane at the courthouse told me that the word is Terry is going to be out of commission for at least six months. Could that be right?"

Sherry replied, "Let's call Gertie and ask her."

Erlene asked, "Why not call Terry?"

Sherry just stared at Erlene, then said, "Because Terry won't know what the hell. Gertie will."

They called Gertie who verified that six months was a fairly accurate guess. "Terry is scheduled to be transferred to a rehab center in Albuquerque next week. Then when his legs are determined to be healed enough, he's going to have his knees rebuilt. Then he'll be in the rehab facility until he's able to walk again. Could be a few months."

"Should we keep the practice…going? Like we have?"

Sherry asked.

Gertie replied, "Please. If you and Erlene can, do keep working. You are welcome to fire the Duff anytime…"

"Should we check with Terry? About anything? We really haven't been in touch with him. I went to the hospital, but he was asleep," Erlene added.

"He's on serious medication, for pain and whatever. Really, you both are the practice. He's useless. Just keep doing what you're doing. If you need anything, anything at all, let me know," Gertie instructed.

Sherry asked, "Don't we need a reason to fire Duffy? Can we just let her go?"

Gertie said, "Tell her Terry won't be back for six months, and since she was his assistant, that she's not needed anymore."

Sherry said, "We can do that. She really doesn't do much here anyway."

Erlene concurred, "Hardly anything at all."

"It'll save some money. You can consider whatever money comes in from prior billings, and whatever you generate as your earnings. Nothing needs to go to Terry," Gertie said.

"What about this office? Isn't there rent?" Erlene asked.

"I own the office now. You pay the utilities, and your other expenses. I'll pay the office insurance, condo fees, property tax, and such. Don't worry about the office. Just keep the lights on," Gertie said with a chuckle.

"That's generous of you. Thanks," Sherry said.

"And get the Duff out of there," Gertie reiterated.

"You bet," Sherry said.

After the call, Sherry asked Erlene, "So who gets the honor of booting the Duff?"

"Let's do it together. We're psychologists! We should do it now!"

"Right now?"

"Great idea!"

They opened the door from Sherry's office and saw Duffy sitting at the reception desk playing a game on her computer. "Makes it easy," Sherry said.

Sherry and Erlene positioned themselves behind Duffy. Duffy didn't stop playing the game of matching rows of confections.

Sherry said, "Duffy, Terry is going to be out for at least six months. You're his assistant, so you aren't needed any longer. Nothing to assist."

Duffy still didn't stop playing or even look at them. She said, "What?"

Erlene said, "You are fired."

Duffy laughed and said, "You can't fire me."

Sherry and Erlene laughed and said, "Yes we can. And we are."

Duffy spun around in her chair, looked at them and said, "No, no you cannot fire me. I work for Terry."

Sherry said, "Gertie has taken over for Terry since he is no longer capable of running an office, at least for the next six months, and she gave us the authority to let you go. So, get your things and go."

Duffy suddenly stood up. She said, "You'll be sorry. I'm going to go see Terry. We'll see who has the authority to do what around here!"

"You do that," Erlene said.

Duffy got her coat and giant tote bag. Huffing loudly, she headed for the door.

Sherry said, "Your key."

Duffy turned around and with great effort removed the office key from her keyring. She threw it at the reception desk's counter. She turned and left.

"That went well," Sherry remarked.

"And quickly!" Erlene said laughing.

Duffy Dot drove straight to the county hospital. She marched in to see Terry. She was about to walk around the nurses' station and go to Terry's room, when one of the nurses stepped from behind the desk and blocked her way.

"Ma'am. You can't go in. You are not on the visitors list."

"What do you mean? You don't even know who I am."

"I do. You are Ms. Dot. I have instructions from Mr. Small himself. You are not to visit him."

"You can't tell me what to do. I am going to see Terry. Out of my way."

The nurse stepped aside. Duffy continued to Terry's room. She pushed open the door to his room with such force that it slammed against the wall. Terry was startled awake by the loud noise.

"Oh Terry! Those women said I am fired!" Duffy said through sobs and copious tears.

Terry was in a morphine-haze. He could only muster, "What? What are you...?

"Your office! Sherry and Erlene said I am fired. They said your wife told them they could fire me," Duffy sobbed.

"Good. It's over," Terry said as he closed his eyes and drifted back to sleep.

Duffy was shaking him, trying to wake him, when the security guard showed up. "Ma'am. Ma'am. Let go of him."

Terry opened his eyes wide. He screamed.

The security guard threw his arms around Duffy Dot. He pinned her arms to her sides. He backed her out of the room. In the hall, she began screaming, "Let go of me! Let go of me!"

The guard released her but stood in front of the door to Terry's room. He said in a calm voice, "You'd better go now."

Duffy said, "I'll be back. You'll be sorry."

She left.

Once out in her car, she called Gertie Small's cell phone. Gertie picked up.

Duffy said, "I cannot be fired by you or those women. I work for Terry. He is my employer."

Gertie said simply, "Oh Duffy. You are fired. Get over it." Gertie hung up.

Duffy sat in her car for an hour or more. She was very cold by the time she went back into the hospital. It was easy enough for her to get to Terry's room from the other end of the corridor. That's what she did. This time she opened the door to his room slowly and quietly. He was awake and watching TV. She approached him slowly.

"Hello Terry. Sorry about the fuss before. I was just so upset."

"Duffy, you shouldn't be in here," Terry said. He didn't take his eyes off of the TV.

"I don't know what to do. Sherry and Erlene told me I was fired. Can they do that? I work for you."

Terry still looking at the TV said, "I won't be back at work for months. I am being moved to some rehab place in Albuquerque next week. I have no say in anything. I can't do anything. Do you understand? I am a prisoner. It's worse than being a prisoner. I can ask for a ham on rye and a glass of wine until I'm hoarse, but they bring me whatever they choose to bring me. I have no say in anything. I can't move. I can't do fucking anything. Do you get it?"

"But, Terry. You can't fire me! What'll I do?"

"I didn't fire you. I can't help you. Your big mouth got you fired."

"What? What do you mean?"

"Gertie talked to some person at your apartment complex, in the office there. Apparently you'd told the woman there all about what I'd been paying for you and that I regularly visit you at your place. Told Gertie all kinds of things. Gertie blew a gasket of course."

"But what does that have to do with the office? We've been…involved…but I work for you. I have a job with you."

"Not any more it seems."

"But it's your office! How can Gertie step in like this and take control?"

"Because she can. It's her money. It's her decision. Nothing I can do."

"But..."

"Goodbye Duffy."

Duffy stared at him. He still wouldn't look at her. She heard voices out in the hall and decided it was best to walk out calmly. She left.

# CHAPTER 23

Peter Northburn woke early. He went straight out to the kiln building. He wanted to unload the kiln. It'd only been a few days since completing the firing. It might still be too hot to unload. But he'd left the building's big front sliding door slightly open. And it was cold out! He checked the kiln. It was still hot. He was anxious to unload, so he rolled the big cart up next to the firing chamber. He removed the firebricks used to close off the chamber door. He was hit in the face with a wave of hot air. He heard a couple of pinging sounds from the fired clay that indicated he should wait a little longer before taking any of the pieces out. A glance in the hot kiln verified for him that the work looked beautiful. The firing had been successful. As always.

He knew he'd be able to get some new work to the Fleeo Gallery as soon as Oren reappeared.

## CHAPTER 24

Leon Ranler, Karen Pilling's boyfriend, decided he'd been patient enough. Time to talk to her. He called her cell phone. No answer, straight to voice mail. She'd been gone just over a week with no word. Leon worked at the University of Houston, as did Karen. He taught in the computer science department, and she in the art department. Leon also worked for the Texas Department of Public Safety. He served as an IT consultant for the Texas Rangers Division.

His father, Tommy Ranler was a retired Texas Ranger. With his father's help, Leon began tracking Karen's movements as best he could. He started with her cell phone. The cell phone call records are only available with a court subpoena. He couldn't get that at this point, but he could trace her route by the towers that picked up her cell phone's number as she passed through their sectors.

Using his connections with the Department of Public Safety, Leon easily tracked her cell phone's route from Houston, to Marble Falls, to Lubbock, to Amarillo, to Santa Fe, to Taos. Karen had the locator feature on, so the towers kept track of the cell phone as long as the phone was on. The last ping was seven days earlier from a relay tower between Taos and Las Vegas, New Mexico. That tower picked up from several transmitters scattered throughout the few small mountain towns nearby.

Leon checked her credit cards. He had access to those statements online. She stayed at a Comfort Inn in Amarillo. She'd bought gas at Santa Rosa, New Mexico along the route to Santa Fe. She last bought gas with a credit card in Espanola between Santa Fe and Taos. He asked the Rangers to check with New Mexico State Police. Had Karen's car been in an accident?

Leon called Karen's sister in Austin. He told her how worried he was. He asked her if Karen had given any indication of plans for her trip. Her sister said she hadn't heard from Karen in at least a week. She didn't know where she was staying, or where she was going. She told Leon not to worry. Karen just needed some time away. Maybe she'd gone north into Colorado. Cell phone service was spotty in the mountains.

"When you heard from her a week ago, where was she?" Leon asked.

"She said she was near Santa Fe. She was heading north. She said she was on an art tour."

"She's with a tour?"

"I don't think she meant that. She was visiting art galleries and studios. She said she was stopping at the Shidoni Foundry and the Tesuque Glassworks just outside of Santa Fe. She's making her own art tour. She sounded fine. Don't worry."

But Leon was already worried. He called his father, Tommy Ranler, to report what he found regarding the cell phone and Karen's sister. Tommy said he'd get in touch with an FBI agent he knew in Houston, Special Agent-in-Charge

George Baden.

"Tommy! You old kitty cat! How are you?" George said when he heard Tommy Ranler on the other end of the phone.

"George! You still playing G-man?" Tommy asked laughing.

"I sure am! Hope you're calling to invite me to go hunting."

"Sorry, not today. But soon! I'm calling on behalf of my son, Leon. His girlfriend, a serious girlfriend, is missing. Well, we think she's missing. We hope she knows exactly where she is."

George asked, "How long she been missing? From where? Tell me the story."

Tommy told George everything he knew about the matter. George said he'd put it out to FBI in Dallas and Albuquerque and Denver.

"Something will turn up. Tell Leon I'll let him know as soon as I know anything," George Baden assured Tommy.

## CHAPTER 25

A couple of days after the visit to Quinton's ranch, Emma called FBI Special Agent Jackson Avery at the FBI offices in the Shanklin Building in Dallas, Texas. Emma knew Jackson from previous investigations that had brought the FBI and Jackson's team to northern New Mexico. As a field deputy for the Office of the Medical Investigator, Emma had worked hand-in-hand with the FBI to resolve those cases. Since Emma had been the critical element in stopping one of the FBI's Most Wanted killers, Robert Woodson, a few years ago, Jackson Avery and his partner, Charlie Black, encouraged her to call if there was anything she needed assistance with.

"Hi, Jackson. How are you? How's Charlie? Sam? Carlos?" Emma asked.

"I'm fine, just a little older. Same for Charlie. We're both here in Texas for the moment. Sam and Carlos are up in Wyoming on a claim jumping matter."

"What? Claim jumping?" Emma said with a laugh. "They tumble into a time warp?"

Jackson laughed and explained, "Just tumbled into a complex mess of titles to mineral rights. A Canadian family says the minerals are theirs. They did have ancestors who lived in Wyoming and owned real estate with mineral rights. In fact they owned huge areas. They were ranchers. The documents the Canadians have seem to verify the land was sold but without the mineral rights. Now the current land owners and also nearby Native American people are claiming the mineral rights. I think Sam is about to resign the Bureau. It is a thankless investigation. No paperwork seems to trump another at this point."

"Oh jeez. Guess someone found some minerals to fight over."

Jackson laughed and replied, "Yes. Prospecting has been fruitful. Oil and gas both. What's happening there?"

Emma explained to him what Quinton found and the circumstances of the find, then said, "Adding to Quinton's story, and the scorched items, there was smoke and the smell reminiscent of human cremation coming from Peter Northburn's ceramic kiln. He has a wood-fire kiln, a big one, and he was firing the day Harry and I drove up to Quinton's place. We drove right through billowing stinky smoke. Something wasn't right."

Jackson asked, "What do you hope I can do?"

"I'd like to send to you the items that Quinton recovered. Perhaps the FBI lab can get some DNA or something from them. They are not burned thoroughly. There is some scorched fabric still attached to the zippers. And there's a button that looks like it was on the waistband of some pants. It's a two piece metal post button. Could have some DNA stuck in it."

"Sure. Send the package FedEx overnight. Send it to me here at the Shanklin Building. I'll get it to Quantico. It'll be a good test case for some newbie lab tech."

"Thanks so much. I'll get it over to FedEx right now. I wasn't sure if you'd be interested in this. I mean, it seems like a long shot to think it is related to some crime."

"Well, there is a reason I am interested. The Bureau has received a report from the Texas Rangers of a missing teacher from Houston. She was headed to Taos last anyone knew. She's not officially a missing person just yet. But no one knows where she is."

"I hope the items Peter Northburn hid in the stream have nothing to do with that teacher," Emma said.

"Me, too. Anything else going on in northern New Mexico?"

"Not anything that I know about...yet," Emma replied.

## CHAPTER 26

Charlie Black and I were taking our time. We'd been at the breakfast table for over an hour. The east Texas late January morning was grey and cold. It looked and felt like it was going to rain soon.

"I wish you could go with me," Charlie said for tenth time.

"I wish I could," I replied for the tenth time.

"Come just for a few days. You love it out there," Charlie insisted.

"I know I do. But I have to stay here. I'm into my tax season already," I responded.

"Okay. You're a CPA. You have to do what you do according to schedules beyond our control. I know. I don't know how long this case will keep me in New Mexico, or wherever it leads. I'll miss you. I'll miss Henry," he said.

"I know. We'll miss you, too," I said. "When do you have to leave?"

"In the morning, Jackson and I are flying to Taos. I have to drive to Dallas tonight," Charlie explained. "So let's have a fabulous day today, and a good dinner this afternoon."

"I'm on for that!" I said.

"I'll fire up the deck heater. We can spend the day

huddled out there on the covered deck. Enjoy the east Texas winter cold dampness!"

"Uh, I'd rather spend the day in front of the fireplace in the living room!"

Tyler, Texas is only about an hour east of Dallas, but the climate is different from Dallas' climate. Tyler is in the pine forest of east Texas. Dallas is on the north Texas plains. Tyler is generally wetter than Dallas. East Texas winter can be bone-chilling damp cold or crisp clear sunny winter cool. Today was cold and overcast with low ceiling grey dampness. The scent of the pines permeated the air. This kind of winter day had a charm all its own. This kind of winter day could seem cozy. It could, if you could stay warm and dry and just look at it. Not a day to linger outside unless necessary.

Our wonderful big dog, Henry, wanted out. I got up to go out back with him. I said to Charlie as I donned my coat, "You better work on a menu for our afternoon feast. I'll run to the grocery for anything we need."

Charlie said, "You feel like beef?"

I smiled and replied, "You mean lean grass-fed Angus tenderloin, I presume. The answer is yes."

He laughed and said, "Indeed, yes, of course. I'll have a list in a flash."

"Come on, Henry. Let's let the FBI Special Agent work on our dinner menu!" I said.

Henry and I went outside. He headed for the farthest edge of the back yard. I sat on the deck. Our back yard is a large grassed area edged by thick pine forest. Henry liked to run the periphery of the lawn right along the tree line. He was on his usual route, when he stopped abruptly giving his full attention to the pine trees at the back of the yard. He barked into the forest, but stayed on the grass.

"What is it?" I called to him. Then I saw what it was.

The very familiar vertical slit of cobalt blue light shown from deep in the pine trees. The light pulsed as it floated among the tree trunks. The damp air shimmered with the cobalt glow as it glided through the trees. It was beautiful. Finally, it made its way out of the forest into the yard. The blue light intensified and seemed to open up. Burkie stepped out.

The tall dark-haired handsome smiling man hugged an exuberant Henry. I called out hello. Burkie waved and called back, "Hi! We'll be right there." He and Henry headed towards me on the deck. As they approached, the deck heater came on. The area under the covered deck immediately began to warm.

Burkie had been visiting me since I was very young. He began by appearing in the large closet in the room I shared with my brother Ed. Ed and I were still sleeping in high-sided baby beds. We were very young. At night we climbed out of our beds and retreated to the closet to look at the many books we'd stocked there. Problem was we couldn't reach the pull chain for the ceiling light. Sometimes we remembered to put a flashlight with the books. But not every night did we have a working flashlight. One night a cobalt blue vertical light appeared. It widened then opened like a narrow door, in midair, right there in the closet. A tall handsome man with thick dark hair combed straight back, wearing a black suit, tie, white shirt, and shiny black dress shoes stepped out of the blue light.

He was accompanied by the most extraordinary and wonderfully serene aroma. He wasn't scary to us. He smiled at us, then gave the pull chain a tug and turned on the light. We thanked him. He always waited until we were through with our nighttime book session. He just stood there smiling at us. If we asked him something, he answered, but he didn't say a lot. When we were ready to return to our beds, he turned off the light in the closet for us. Then he told us goodnight and stepped back through the blue light. The blue glow faded and that was it. It happened reliably for years. He saw us through our childhood.

Eventually we asked him who he was. He told us his name was Burkie. We didn't know what he was or where he came from or went to. We just knew he existed. It was always good to see him.

Throughout these many decades of our lives, Burkie has visited both Ed and me. It took some time, but now Charlie can see and talk to Burkie, too. Though Ed and I have aged in the expected way through our lives, Burkie has never aged or changed a bit in all of these years.

This morning I was warming by the newly ignited deck heater when Henry bounded up on the deck. Burkie stepped up on the deck and gave me his usual magnificently comforting hug. He smelled so good, and the kindness emanating from him engulfed me. It always brought tears to my eyes.

"Warm enough?" he asked me.

"Fine now that the heater's going. How'd you do that?" I asked.

"Do what?"

"Turn on the heater from way out there in the yard?"

"Just an energy thing. Not magic!" he replied laughing.

We sat down at the table under the covered part of the deck. Charlie came out the back door carrying a pad of paper and a pen.

"Whoa! We have company! Hello Burkie!!" he said happily.

"Hello Charlie," Burkie said as he stood and hugged Charlie.

We all sat at the table and chatted about the dinner menu, then Charlie said to Burkie, "My keen investigator's mind has deduced that your appearance this morning has something to do with Jackson's call. My new assignment to go to Taos, New Mexico."

Burkie laughed and replied, "Indeed. What a good investigator you are! Yes, I'm here because there are some sad energies, tragic energies in the area of northern New Mexico. Energies that you are most likely going to encounter."

"You have always told us that you don't get information regarding any future prognostications, but that you do receive data of various kinds. So what energies do you mean? People? Dead people?" I asked.

Burkie chuckled and said, "You are right, I'm no soothsayer, but I have picked up on the sadness and confusion that some energies are experiencing in that area. They are energies that were human."

Charlie asked, "They? How many? From when? Are

you talking about one event that killed these people?"

Burkie explained, "My understanding is limited to the emotional language, if you will, of the energies. There are quite a few of these voices, so to speak."

"What are they saying?" I asked.

"They don't actually speak of course. They emote. They react," Burkie replied.

Charlie asked, "What are they reacting to? How?"

"They are reacting to something evil which is still doing whatever it has been doing. And whatever it has been doing has agitated these energies, and the universes feel that agitation. These energies are focusing their attention on the source of the evil. They will help you find it. I cannot tell you what the evil is. I don't know. I know about the energies' reactions. As I've explained to you in the past, when there is good done, it is felt throughout the universes. And when there is evil done, it, too, is felt throughout the universes. Since these energies want to stop this evil...whatever it is, and it is located where you are going, Charlie, I am here to tell you that they, the energies, are going to be there. You need to stop whatever needs to be stopped," Burkie said. "These spirits will try to assist you if they possibly can."

Charlie said, "Thanks for the heads up. I appreciate your help. Always."

Burkie remarked, "Since you affect her," motioning at me, "I was included in the loop, as you call it. It was my responsibility, because of that connection, to pass the information to you. I realize this information might seem vague to you, but I believe you will see it is helpful in some way once you get out to New Mexico."

I said, "Thanks."

Charlie said, "I'd love to be able to tap into your 'loop' sometime. It has to be fascinating."

Burkie laughed, "You will someday, Charlie. You'll be right there in the 'loop.'"

Charlie laughed and added, "You want to stay for dinner?"

Burkie ruffled the fur on Henry's head and replied, "Nice of you to ask, but I'll be going. Be careful in New Mexico."

I said, "I'm not going with him. It's tax time for me."

Burkie said, "I know." To Charlie he said, "I'll keep an eye on her, as always."

Charlie and I hugged Burkie goodbye. We watched him return to the blue glow at the edge of the pine trees. Henry followed Burkie out to the trees. Burkie leaned over to hug Henry just before he stepped back in to the cobalt blue light and then vanished.

When Henry returned to the deck, we all went back into the house. Charlie said, "Burkie only comes with info for me when I'm about to fall into some strange or very interesting case. Wonder what is going on out in New Mexico."

## CHAPTER 27

Terry Small was sweating bullets as he lay in the hospital bed. He knew he was going to be moved to a rehab facility. He didn't want to go to a rehab facility. He wanted to go home. He wanted to have a heart-to-heart talk with Gertie. She wasn't visiting him anymore. She wouldn't talk to him on the phone. She'd cut him off completely. He was very worried about himself. Where was he going to end up?

The door to his room opened slowly. A middle-aged dark-haired man stuck his head in.

"Ah, you're awake."

Terry said, "Yes. Who are you?"

"I'm Marvin. Marvin Persler. I represent your wife, Gertie Small."

"What do you mean, you represent her?"

"I'm her attorney."

Terry gulped audibly and said, "What do you want? What the hell are you doing here?"

Marvin Persler replied, "I'm here, as a courtesy from Gertie, to give you a copy of the divorce papers filed today at the courthouse."

"What?"

"Today, your wife has filed for divorce. Since you

are...um...stuck here in the hospital, Gertie asked me to bring you a copy of the divorce papers. My suggestion is that you share this information with your attorney as soon as possible."

"I don't have an attorney."

Marvin said, "It is always a good idea to have an attorney! I have to be going now. Nice to meet you Mr. Small."

Marvin laid the large manila envelope on Terry's bedside table and left.

Terry lay quietly in his bed for a while before he began chanting, "Fuck, fuck, fuck."

He buzzed for the nurse. A young man in white responded.

"Who are you?" Terry demanded.

"Hi. I'm John. I'm your nurse this afternoon."

"Hell you are! Get out of here. Send in a real nurse. A woman!"

John said, "Mr. Small, I am a real nurse. And I am here to check on your condition, and your medications if needed. How are you today?"

Terry Small replied, "I don't want any man-nurse. I want a regular nurse."

"Sir, I can relay that request to my supervisor, but right now there are only two nurses on duty for this section."

"So send in the other one!"

"You sure?"

"Yes! Get out of here."

John left and almost immediately another young

man wearing white entered Terry Small's room.

"Hello, Mr. Small," the young man said.

"You're a new doctor. Haven't seen you in here before. What kind of doctor are you?" Terry asked.

"I'm not a doctor. I'm an RN," the young man said.

"RN? You mean a nurse?? Holy crap. What's going on? Why am I getting the men nurses? Is this some kind of joke?"

"Sir?"

"I don't want any men touching me."

"I don't intend to touch you. I am here to check the traction harness and your drips, your meds. Don't worry," the nurse said laughing.

"What's so funny?"

"What are you afraid of, Mr. Small?"

"No man is going to touch me!"

"Are all of your doctors women?" the nurse asked.

"Don't be a smart-ass. Of course not. Doctors are men and nurses are women."

"Really?! Mr. Small, that's not true. At all."

"It's going to be true in this room!" Terry said. "Get out."

The young man left without another word.

Terry closed his eyes. He drifted off to sleep without opening the manila envelope left by Mr. Persler.

Sometime later he woke. He wondered if he'd dreamed about the men nurses or if they really had been in his room. He looked at the bedside table and saw the manila envelope. He opened it and read it. He picked up the antiquated looking phone by his bed and called his office.

"Small Psychology and Counselling," Duffy's voice intoned.

He started talking, "Duffy, this is Terry. I need you to..."

Then the voice continued, "If you want to speak with Terry Small, please press star two, if you want to talk to Sherry Kroyton, please press star three..."

He said, "Shit!" He hung up.

He called Duffy's cell phone.

Duffy answered immediately, "Hello."

"Duffy, it's Terry. I need you to..."

"Terry! I knew you'd call! Darling, how are you?"

Terry said, "I need you to call Ellis Grantpin. Tell him I need his services. Ask him to come see me at the hospital. ASAP!"

"Grantpin is a lawyer. You need a lawyer? What for? What's happened?" Duffy squealed.

"Gertie's filed for divorce."

"What? Well, divorce might..."

"Don't go there, Duffy. Just call Ellis. His cell number is in my phone and Gertie has my phone. You'll have to find Ellis' number somehow. He only has a cell number, no land line. Go to his office. It's over by the plaza, you know. Find him. Tell him to come see me ASAP."

Duffy replied, "I'll go to his office right now. Be strong, darling. I'm here for you."

## CHAPTER 28

Gertie and Nevel waited in the restaurant at the country club for Marvin Persler long enough to eat an order of French fries. "What time did he say he'd be here?" Nevel asked. "Let's order lunch. We can't just munch fries all afternoon!"

"He'll be here soon. He runs late. Yeah, let's go ahead and order lunch," Gertie agreed.

They were into their salads when Marvin arrived. He ordered salad, too. Then he pulled a folder from his briefcase, opened it on the table, and said, "Got the counter from Ellis Grantpin, Terry's attorney. In a nutshell, Terry wants half of the equity of everything."

Gertie laughed and said, "In a nutshell, hell no!"

Nevel said, "Grantpin is an accomplished golfer. He's a probate and real estate attorney, not a divorce attorney."

Marvin replied, "He is. But he's Terry's attorney for this divorce. Gertie, it is a community property state, and you have built, acquired, the estate in the marriage."

Gertie replied, "But the assets are ninety percent mine. I built it. He did so little. Since the beginning, he has done so little."

Nevel said, "Well, his name is 'Small.'"

Gertie and Marvin both gave a hearty laugh at that

remark. Marvin said, "What is our argument for the court, for the ninety/ten split."

Nevel asked Gertie, "Other than he is a mean, biased, paranoid, lying jackass, ummm what else?"

Gertie took a bite of her salad and said, "He told me he killed a man."

Marvin stopped eating and looked at Gertie. "What?? Are you serious?"

Gertie replied, "I am. Long ago when we were first married, he told me that. He was stinking drunk and high when he told me the story. So, I don't know if he remembers telling me. He's never mentioned it again. Ever. And I've never asked him about it since then."

"What story?" Marvin Persler asked.

Gertie glanced questioningly at Nevel. He said, "Tell him. Now's the time."

"Okay. Here's the story that Terry told me," Gertie began. "When we were first married we lived in Colorado, in Aspen. I had a job as golf pro at the Aspen Country Club. It was a very well-paying job. Terry was just starting out as a psychologist. He was licensed in Colorado at that time. That's another story.

"Anyway, he opened an office. He had a couple of clients, but for the most part he didn't try to grow his business. He just played. He skied, he fished, and he drank and got high. He has always been kind of immature. At first I found that endearing and fun. But he's never changed. In fact he's become crazier over the years.

"He is not a licensed psychologist any more, in Colorado or in New Mexico. Hasn't been for years. He never graduated from college. He quit in his senior year to drink and get high. He likes to think he is fooling everyone. His ego has grown and blossomed under this adolescent misguided belief that everyone buys his crap."

"Who'd he kill?" Marvin asked.

"Well one night in Snowmass after he'd had a long day of skiing, I met him at a bar. We were sitting on a deck next to one of those outdoor heater towers. He was already drunk when I got there. He smoked some weed, drank some more, then started crying. Nobody else was on the deck with us. The waiter came and went, but nobody else was out there. I asked him repeatedly what was wrong before he finally explained himself.

"He said that when he was a freshman in college, he and a high school friend, his best friend, went skiing at Steamboat. He'd known the guy since first grade. Anyway, he said that when they were up on the mountain, at a spot where they always stopped to change trails and catch their breath. They'd been skiing together there for years. Well, the guy told Terry that he had feelings for him. He told Terry that he'd been in love with him for several years. The guy put his hand up to Terry's cheek. This was way before helmets. The young man leaned in to kiss Terry. Terry said he pushed guy away and cursed at him.

"The guy lost his balance. They were both on their skis. His friend fell on his butt. He sat there crying and telling Terry it was alright. He still loved him. Terry side-stepped in his skis around the guy, picked up a rock by the side of the trail and hit him square on top of his head. The guy was still sitting on his skis, feet locked in, knees up, when Terry hit him. The guy fell over sideways and didn't move. Terry dropped the rock by the guy's head, left him there and skied down the mountain.

"Terry said the guy's head was spewing blood when he skied off. He skied to the base. He waited. He didn't go for help. Then he got on the lift and returned to the site. When he got there, a crowd of skiers had gathered and the ski patrol medics were loading his unconscious friend on the sled to take him down the mountain. He skied up to the crowd and asked what had happened. Someone said it looked like a guy fell and hit his head on a rock.

"That's when Terry began the lie. He told me he pretended to be horrified that his buddy was injured. He gave the ski patrol medics his friend's name. His story to the ski patrol was that he'd skied ahead and had been waiting for his buddy the bottom. He followed the ski patrol and the sled carrying his friend down the mountain. By the time they reached the bottom the young man on the sled was dead.

"The authorities in Steamboat never questioned Terry's account of the day's events. No one witnessed the incident. It was called an accident. The young man was sent home to his family in Grand Junction for burial."

Marvin asked, "What the hell? Why'd he hit the guy with a rock?"

"That night on the deck at that bar, I asked the slobbering asshole that same question. He said he couldn't have anyone think he was gay. He said that friend of his must have thought he was gay, or he wouldn't have approached him like that. That's the thing, if a man thinks it is okay to tell him that he is interested in him, then that man must think he's gay. Terry cannot have anyone think he's gay."

Marvin said, "Why didn't he just say no thank you?"

"The whole thing runs much deeper with Terry. He said he'd had some kind of feelings for a coach when he was in junior high. He didn't elaborate, but I gathered he was talking about sexual feelings. His parents and their church drummed into him that being gay was the worst thing in the world. He felt so guilty about his feelings for the coach, he quit high school football. He is phobic about anyone thinking he's gay. It's absurd. Apparently he thought being gay was bad, but murder was okay."

"Holy shit! Did he tell you the young man's name? The fellow he hit with the rock?" Marvin asked.

"James Phinn," Gertie said.

"Is she in any trouble for not telling anyone sooner?" Nevel asked.

"Did you believe him when he told you the story?" Marvin asked Gertie.

"No. He was so drunk and high. I thought it was a story he'd made up. He was always making up stories about himself. Though, usually his tales were to enhance his self-perceived status in some way or another. This one was so different. I didn't know what to think really," Gertie explained.

"Do you believe it now?" Marvin asked.

"I do. He is severely homophobic. Almost exaggeratedly so. He is living so many lies. The lies have grown over the years. I don't think he can tell the difference between fact and fiction anymore."

Marvin asked, "May I ask, aren't your children gay?"

Nevel laughed, "Let me answer, Gertie. Yes, they are. Brick and Bok are happy and living far away from their father."

Gertie added, "That's right. I am so proud of my children. They have grown into fine adults. Neither seems to have been tarnished by their father's psychotic personality. They see him for what he is, misguided at best."

Marvin Persler said, "What a tangled web Terry has created for himself."

"And all by himself," Nevel added.

"So you said you've never mention the story about the killing to Terry, since that night he told you?" Marvin asked.

"Well I did simply say James Phinn's name to him as I left the hospital when I told him I was going to divorce him. When he said he'd take half of everything, I just said the name and left."

"His attorney has counselled him to demand half. So we have to either have him voluntarily take that request off the table, or challenge him," Marvin said.

Nevel asked, "Is there any way to open an investigation into James Phinn's death?"

Marvin said, "Yes, no statute of limitation on murder. It would be a matter of enticing a Colorado prosecutor into wanting to pursue the matter."

"How?"

"Well if Terry really did hit the boy over the head, square on top of his head while the boy was sitting, then that top of the head blow would not appear to have been an accidental head injury. In an accident, the skier probably would have fallen to the side and had a side of the head or face impact. Wonder why the coroner didn't question that."

Gertie said, "Maybe they did question it. I only know the version Terry told me."

Marvin said, "I'll check into it. I have an old friend in the state prosecutor's office in Denver. Let's see if we can get justice for James Phinn. What year did he die?"

Gertie gave Marvin the few details she remembered Terry mentioning regarding the year of death, and James Phinn's family. They finished lunch and Marvin said he'd respond to the divorce counter-demands with a simple delay.

## CHAPTER 29

OMI Field Deputy Emma Spruce was on her way to an unattended death near Red River, New Mexico. Her cell phone rang through to the Bluetooth in her Subaru Forester. "Emma Spruce," she said.

"Hey Emma, it's Jackson. You have a minute?"

"Sure. On my way to a death scene. Let me pull over so I can talk. My client isn't going anywhere. He's dead."

"So the lab did recover useable human DNA from the bits and pieces you sent. The stuff your friend Quinton found. The DNA didn't match anything in the CODIS database. But it's in the database now. I can tell you it's from a female. There was also horse DNA found."

"Quinton did carry the find in his saddlebag, on his horse, an old saddlebag. Have you compared the human DNA to the teacher from Houston that you mentioned? Is she still missing?"

"We're going to get something from her boyfriend. Hair from her hairbrush or something. We'll find out if there is a match. More interesting right now is that when we looked though the database for missing people thought to have been to northern New Mexico prior to disappearing, we found too many. We compared the DNA to those people of course. Nothing. But why would there be so many people travelling to that area and then vanishing."

"When did that happen? I don't recall seeing missing persons reports. Especially not in any volume," Emma said.

"The people were reported missing over the past decade. No pattern to timing or ethnicity. The common element is that the people went missing after they strayed off on their own to do something or another. They either were on a solo trip, or left their family or group to go somewhere alone. They just never came back."

"That's scary. Who's been looking for them?"

"We have, the FBI. But there has never been a successful result. We haven't found the people or their remains. Nothing. People do sometimes go missing deliberately. They simply leave their lives."

"Charlie and I are coming out there. My goal is to find the missing teacher and determine if there is anything nefarious going on with regard to the items you sent to us," Jackson explained.

"It'll be nice to see you both. Remember it is much colder here than in Dallas. Dress appropriately!" Emma said with a laugh.

## CHAPTER 30

"Oh, Peter, this is Marion Fleeo," the voice on the phone said.

"Hello Marion. How is everything at the gallery?" Peter responded.

"Oh, everything is great. I'm calling because we need more of your work. Do you have pieces you can send? People want platters, and the larger pots."

"I have a few platters I could send. I have just unloaded the kiln. I'll send some pieces that you'll love."

"Oh, wonderful! Please send what you can. I'll be excited to see what emerged from your firing!" Marion said.

"I'll send Oren with some pieces. I'm preparing to fire again as soon as I can. There'll be more work available."

"Oh, great. Thanks."

After talking to Peter, Marion Fleeo told Sherman that more Northburn work was forthcoming. Sherman said, "I've been pleasantly surprised at how steady the sales of his work have been."

"Oh, I know what you mean. I'd hoped the sales would meet the hype. And, oh, it has!" Marion replied.

The front door of the gallery opened and a large medium-tall woman with a dyed yellow-blond helmet-style haircut entered. She looked sort of dazed. Sherman told Marion he'd deal with her.

"Hi. Welcome to the Fleeo Gallery. Have you been in before?" Sherman said.

Duffy Dot replied, "Uh. No. I'm looking for work. Do you need any help?"

Sherman asked, "You have experience with art? Sales?"

"I'm not a salesperson. Looking for office or reception work," she muttered.

"Well I'll let you talk to Marion Fleeo, the gallery owner." Sherman went to the back of the gallery to get Marion.

Marion approached Duffy Dot. "Oh, you're looking for work?"

Duffy said, "Yes. But I'm not an art person. I do like this pottery though. The colors are pretty."

Marion explained that the artist, Peter Northburn, lives near Taos. Marion ran through the sales pitch. Duffy took a flyer with the map to Northburn's studio and showroom, thanked Marion and left. After she'd gone, Sherman asked, "So did she buy anything?"

"Oh, no. I think she's kind of a lost soul. Maybe depressed, or medicated, or something. Poor old thing."

Duffy Dot drove around Taos, stopping in here and there to ask random businesses if they needed any help. She really had no plan. Then she looked again at the flyer from Fleeo Gallery. She headed towards Taos Canyon, towards Northburn's studio.

## CHAPTER 31

Harry met up with his hunting buddies at the intersection of Highway 64 and Highway 585. That's where Taos' south bypass meets the road to Angel Fire. The four hunters were in three pickups. They caravanned up 64 towards Angel Fire. They followed 64 along the Rio de Fernando to the turnoff of Baca Canyon Road. They turned left and climbed up the road that would take them up to the high mountain meadowlands where they were going to elk hunt. It was a private land hunt. The ranch belonged to Michael McMarlin's uncle. Harry had known Michael since grade school. They both grew up in Taos. He and Michael had hunted at Uncle Charles' ranch many times over the years. The other two men were from Albuquerque and had hunted with Michael and Harry before. It was always a treat to spend time on the beautiful property. The high mountain meadows were in full sun all winter. The elk hung along the edges of the fields in the aspen and pines. Always good hunting.

The ranch bordered Pueblo land on the north and mostly National Forest on all other sides, though there were strips of some private lands that touched the ranch here and there.

There really wasn't much ranch work anymore,

other than maintenance, for his eighty-year old uncle to do. He lived there because he always had. His wife had died ten years earlier, and he didn't want to go anywhere. Mostly he patrolled for trespassers and poachers. There was no on-going business of the ranch. It was simply a beautiful place for wild game to call home. Charles also found it a beautiful place to call home. Michael and his uncle were all that were left of the family.

Michael's parents were killed in an airplane crash when he was in high school. After the crash Michael moved in with Uncle Charles and his wife at the ranch. Michael's father had only the one brother, Charles. Michael had been an only child, and Charles and his wife didn't have children. Michael'd always felt blessed that Charles and his wife had embraced him as their own son.

The men looked forward to stopping in at the ranch house to say hello to Michael's uncle, Charles McMarlin. After a bumpy ride climbing uphill through the forest, the hunters pulled into the circle entryway at the ranch house. They parked the pickups as Charles hurried out to greet them.

"Hey, you made it!" he exclaimed.

They hugged and went inside the big old house. For the most part, the interior hadn't changed over the years. Uncle Charles had always treated Harry like family. Harry felt at home in the familiar environment. He and Michael were stunned to see that Uncle Charles had installed a gigantic TV over the fireplace.

"Oh my God, Uncle Charles! You have a TV! A new TV!" Michael exclaimed.

Charles laughed and said, "I thought it time to step up. That old TV was unable to receive the satellite signal."

"You have satellite service now???"

"Yes, I do. I have cell service, a cell phone, and all sorts of TV stuff, you know channels. Can't imagine how I'll ever have time to watch it all. Now I'm just like the rest of the world!" Charles added laughing.

The men ate an early dinner at the ranch house before heading out to scout the hunting sites. Charles had the ATVs ready and waiting for them. Michael and Harry went one direction and other two men went the opposite direction. The property was so large that they could easily hunt different areas without infringing on each other's game territory.

Michael and Harry, on separate ATVs, followed a path they knew well. They wound through the beautiful tall pines eventually emerging into a high mountain meadow. The meadow was at least ten acres of tall winter grass surrounded by pine and aspen trees. The meadow was golden in the sunlight and blue in shadows where the snow lay quiet and smooth. They parked the off-road vehicles, got their rifles, and Michael's compound bow, and each climbed to their respective tree blinds to wait and watch. Harry was hunting with his rifle, a Ruger 308 M77 Mark II. Michael was sure he could take an elk with his bow, but he did have his rifle with him, too. Just in case.

The evening began closing in on the meadow. The temperature dropped dramatically as the shadows of the trees blanketed the wide meadow. They saw a small herd of elk move along the tree line. They were looking for the perfect place to bed down for the night. Harry and Michael watched silently. There were two bull elk and eight cow elk. The elk ate a last bite of grasses then slipped into the trees for the night. They disappeared.

Michael and Harry waited until it was almost completely dark to climb down from their blinds. As they were about to start up the ATVs, Michael said, "Those are such beautiful animals!"

Harry agreed, "If they weren't such good eating..."

The four men rendezvoused back at the ranch house. They sat in the big living room staring at the crackling fire in the stone fireplace, and the giant TV over the fireplace. Michael and Harry described the group of elk they'd seen. And their friends described the huge herd of elk that they'd seen. They made plans for the early morning hunt.

Uncle Charles provided snacks and beers for them. He sat with them while everyone engaged in the usual and mandatory hunting chatter. Harry brought up Peter Northburn's excursion into the National Forest land on the other side of the canyon, and what Quinton Quigley retrieved from the stream.

Uncle Charles said, "Northburn is not very well liked up here. His kiln smells horrible when he is firing whatever...art! He litters the woods when he wanders up behind his property."

Michael exclaimed, "Litters!? What? Is he dumping his trash? That's illegal. We can get him on that."

"No not his trash. Well, it might be some of it, but I'm talking about the clothes he leaves in the forest," Uncle Charles explained.

"What? Clothes? His clothes? What do you mean?" Harry asked.

"I don't think they are his clothes. I've seen him drop off men's clothes, women's clothes..." Charles said. "But interesting also are the lights I've seen in his dumping place."

"What do you mean he drops off clothes? Lights??" Michael asked.

"He hangs the clothes in the trees. A set of shirt, pants, shoes one day, different set of shirt, pants, shoes, etcetera another day, just random. He takes his four-wheeler up into the Carson National Forest land behind and above his place, then he rides over onto my land. I don't imagine he knows whose land he's on. He hangs the clothing on various trees in a small clearing, a very remote clearing. You know, he hangs them to look like a person is wearing them. I thought they were scarecrows or something. He seems to favor certain trees."

"Scarecrows? In the forest?" one of the other hunters said.

"The clothes were hung in the trees like you'd hang them to make an image of a person standing there. Hat at the top, if there was a hat, then the shirt and coat below the hat, then pants below the shirt, then shoes on the ground at the bottom. He even puts the underwear under the clothes. Made it look like a scarecrow, only hung on a tree instead of a post, and not stuffed," Uncle Charles explained. "Kind of weird."

Michael added, "Kind of? Yes, very weird!"

"How many scarecrows did you find?" one of the

other hunters asked.

"The first time I saw the clothes was the evening I first saw him, well, heard him on his ATV, then saw him. After he left is when I looked carefully around the clearing. That time I found remnants of older clothes. Lots of them. Pieces scattered all around the area. He'd been making the scarecrows for a long time. Or someone had. Looked like animals and weather had worked on them."

Michael asked, "You say, the first time, so you've seen the clothes again?"

Uncle Charles responded, "Oh yes. I check the area pretty regularly now. I remove whatever he's hung up there. But he's still hanging the clothes on the trees. He's a strange one."

Harry asked, "What about lights?"

Uncle Charles explained, "In the clearing where he puts the clothes, I've seen balls of floating lights. They pulse and move around the trees. Like a movie special effect."

"You seem kind of calm about it."

"What am I supposed to do? They're just lights. They show up at dusk and after dark. When I move in to see them closer they shoot off into the treetops and vanish."

Michael interrupted, "Has Northburn ever seen you up there?"

Charles answered, "No, don't think he's ever noticed me. I've always been on horseback and then on foot. And other than that first time, he's rarely been there when I was. But I have seen him a few times. He's the only one doing it. I'm pretty sure of that."

Harry asked, "What were you doing up there in that

remote area when you saw him?"

Charles said, "Well, I like to follow the animal paths. Sometimes I hunt small game, you know, to eat. I look for signs of poachers. Mostly I just ride around. The horses need to be ridden. When I heard a gas engine coming fast through the woods that evening, I hid. That's when I first saw him. He was on his ATV."

Michael said, "Uncle Charles! Somebody's liable to shoot you by mistake!"

Charles said, "I always wear my blaze orange hat. And that Northburn character is the only one who tears through the woods like that. He has no respect for anything."

"You said he hangs the clothes on some favorite trees? Do you leave the clothes there?"

"No. After the jerk leaves them hanging, I take the clothes down. Don't need that trash and all that human scent up there."

"What do you do with the clothes?" Harry asked.

"I put them in a box in the barn."

"You still have the box of clothes?" Michael asked.

"Sure. Been meaning to take the clothes that are still good down to one of the churches in Taos. Maybe they could find folks who could use them. For the most part, they are not old clothes at all. Look like the stuff from Cabelas and such, catalogs."

Harry said, "Okay if I tell Emma about this?"

Uncle Charles said, "Sure. You think something is screwy with Northburn?"

"Yes, I do. Hold on to that box," Harry said.

## CHAPTER 32

Emma and Harry met the FBI jet at the Taos Airport. Special Agents Jackson Avery and Charlie Black emerged from the plane. Jackson called out, "Emma! Harry! How good to see you!"

"And you two, too!" Emma called back.

Charlie said, "What a beautiful mountain winter morning! Perfect. Clear Cold. No wind!"

"Where are you staying?" Harry asked as they all climbed into his big Silverado extended cab pickup.

"Same old same old...we got the same vacation rental we had last time we were here," Charlie replied.

"That's a nice place. Central location. Big house," Harry noted.

"Yes, we like it," Charlie said laughing. "Just so you know, we have asked for a Suburban, of course, to be sent up from Albuquerque. Should be here tonight. So we're not going to ask you to chauffeur us indefinitely!"

"No problem, FBI asks, FBI gets. Happy to help you!" Harry said.

"So what was it that made you decide to come to Taos?" Emma asked.

Jackson replied, "Couple of things. The missing teacher's car's been found. It was in a field over near the town of Mora. No Karen Pilling found yet. Her suitcase and backpack were in the trunk of the car. No cell phone found, but her phone did ping a tower in that area on January seventeenth."

Emma asked, "Who found the car? What kind of car?"

"The land-owner found the car, a Camry. Whoever was driving it, plowed through his fence then drove out into his field until the snow was too high to go any further. The perp left the car, and from the state police report, the footprints in the snow went right back to the highway. They went out just where they'd come in. There were two sets of prints."

"They left the belongings in the trunk?" Harry asked.

"They didn't have a key. Well they didn't have the right key. There was a key jammed into the ignition, but it didn't work. They went to a lot of trouble to take the car. They removed almost the entire dash and steering assembly to hot wire it. Suppose they didn't have any interest in breaking into the trunk too. Might have been simply a couple of locals out for adventure. Left the license plate, but maybe they took cell phone, purse, and other stuff, if anything was in the car," Charlie explained.

Emma said, "Kids. So state police pulled it out of the field and impounded it?"

"Yes. It's somewhere in Taos or Albuquerque by now. We'll take possession of it. Kidnapping, crossing state lines, etcetera. It's our case."

"I heard that Karen Pilling's boyfriend works with

the Texas Rangers as an IT specialist," Emma said.

"You read that on the internet?" Charlie asked with a laugh.

Emma laughed and replied, "State police told me. They said the boyfriend really got everyone moving to find Karen. Guess you'll be able to get Karen's DNA from her car."

"That's true. Our lab will have something shortly. Her boyfriend's name is Leon Ranler. He sent samples of Karen's hair to the Texas Rangers' lab for DNA profiling. But, they haven't reported any results yet. We're going to get whatever they have and whatever we can from her belongings left in the car. The boyfriend is a part-time IT guy for the Rangers. He tracked Karen's cell phone and gave the Rangers and the bureau some excellent intel. Her boyfriend's father, Tommy Ranler, is a retired Texas Ranger. He's been a big help, too."

"Do you know where the car was last seen, you know, before the field?" Harry asked.

"A gas station in Mora, according to the state police. We're going over there in the morning," Jackson said.

Charlie asked Harry, "So, you been hunting this winter?"

Harry replied, "I just went last weekend. Elk hunting. Got a big cow elk. The freezer is loaded up."

Charlie remarked, "Hope we get a chance to try a little fresh elk."

"You bet. We'll have you over. Oh, and I have a story about Peter Northburn that you're going to love," Harry said.

Harry told them about Michael's Uncle Charles' retrieval of the clothes Northburn had been hanging in the trees.

Jackson asked, "How long has this been going on?"

"Charles said he first saw Northburn up in the woods a couple of years ago, or so. He wasn't sure. Charles was so horrified by the jerk's behavior that after the first time, he made a point to check the area for clothes periodically. He found clothes frequently, and then every so often he actually witnessed Northburn hanging clothes and leaving them there."

Emma said, "Tell them about the lights, the balls of lights."

"Charles said he's seen balls of lights floating in the air around the trees where Northburn hangs the clothes. He's even approached the lights for a closer look. They shoot up to the treetops and disappear."

Charlie Black asked, "How big are these balls of light? What color?"

"Baseball size and bigger. He said the colors change, pulsate."

"I want to meet Uncle Charles," Jackson said.

"I'll arrange it," Harry assured him.

## CHAPTER 33

Oren sat for over an hour in the lobby of the Taos Inn listening to local musicians play. He drank two beers in the hour. Finally his buddy showed up.

"Hey man, sorry I'm late. My car gave out on me! I walked from the blinking light! Man, walking is tiring! I need a beer!"

"Okay. Let's get beers somewhere else. This music is not exactly, um, my kind," Oren said. "Let's go up Bent Street. There's a little restaurant bar place up there."

His buddy, TJ, said, "I don't know if I can walk any further, man!"

"It's just a half a block! We can smoke one on the way."

"Okay."

The two young men smoked a joint as they walked up the alley behind Bent Street. When they got to the restaurant, there was a line out the door.

Oren said, "No way am I waiting in line. Let's go to my place."

TJ agreed. They walked back to the Taos Inn where they hopped on Oren's bike and headed the short distance to the casita behind Peter Northburn's vacation rental. Peter's rental house and the casita were right in-town, just behind the plaza. Once in the little building, they immediately focused on more weed and beer. Wasn't long before they were hungry.

"Let's go get a pizza. I'll call it in, then we can pick it up," Oren said.

"Hell. Have it delivered, man," TJ countered.

"Naw. I'll go get it. Delivery means a tip. I don't have that kind of money."

"Just don't tip."

"I wouldn't do that to somebody," Oren said. "I'll pick it up."

The two guys decided on a meat pizza, called it in and sucked down more weed while waiting to go get it. TJ asked Oren if he could borrow his Camry until he could afford to get his car fixed.

Oren said, "Sure. I don't use it hardly at all."

"It won't be for long. I should have money next week," TJ said.

"I know, let's see if the old Camry will start. We can take it to pick up the pizza. I'll put some gas in it for you," Oren said.

"Thanks, bro."

The two very high young men stumbled out to the car. Oren took the Camry key from his overpopulated keyring. He pushed the button on the key fob. No click, no nothing. "Guess the damn key battery is dead," Oren muttered. He couldn't get it in the car's door lock. Key didn't fit.

"What's wrong?" TJ asked.

"Don't know. Key won't work."

"Let me try," TJ suggested.

TJ tried to insert the key into the lock. He studied the key closer and laughed, "This is not the key to this car, bro."

"What??"

"Wrong key, bro. This is a new Toyota key."

Oren stopped breathing for a second. He suddenly wanted to vomit. "Oh fuck! Oh fuck! How did this happen??"

"How did what happen?" TJ asked.

"How'd I mix up the keys?" Oren said in a squeaky scared voice.

"What are you talking about, bro?"

Oren replied, "Uh, nothing man. Let's take the bike. You can hold the pizza."

They got the pizza and went back to Oren's place. They ate, drank, and smoked while they watched TV. Oren didn't say much. Finally TJ asked, "You have another key to your car?"

"Uh, yeah I do, somewhere," Oren replied. "Lemme take a look."

After a few minutes of rooting around in the bedroom, the only other room besides the bathroom, Oren found another key to his old Camry. He returned to the couch and tossed it over to TJ.

"Thanks, bro," TJ said. "Think it'll start?"

"Go find out," Oren said. He was lost in thought and not at all interested in whether his old car would start. His problems were far greater than that.

The car started right up. TJ left it running while he went in to tell Oren he was leaving. "Thanks again, bro. I'll have this back to you next week."

"Yeah, okay," Oren said absently. He was close to a full blown panic attack. He couldn't move. He heard TJ drive off in his Camry. He looked at the key in his hand. He knew it was the key to the Camry he'd parked at the gas station in Mora. He knew there was something crazy about the whole scheme of leaving that new car at the gas station...in Mora. Fuck, what was he going to do now?

Then it hit him, he'd just go back to Mora, unlock the new Camry and switch out the keys. It was a long motorcycle ride to Mora. It was getting late. It'd be completely dark soon. He decided he'd better wait until morning. He passed out from anxiety, weed, and beer.

## CHAPTER 34

Very early the next morning, before any direct sunlight shot over the mountains, Oren was on his motorcycle on his way to Mora. The morning air was well below twenty degrees. He was bundled up, He'd even put the plastic face shield on his helmet. The wind chill was outrageous. He thought that the ride might kill him. He could certainly freeze.

When the sun's rays did break over the mountains, Oren felt he had a chance to survive the ride. By the time he rolled into Mora, the temperature was in the upper twenties. It felt almost warm to him as he parked his bike in front of the big gas station. He walked around to the side of the building to switch keys. He stopped cold when he saw the car was gone. "Oh fuck!" he murmured to himself.

He went inside the gas station's convenience store. A loud buzzer sounded when he stepped on the inside mat. He asked the man behind the counter, "Uh, my buddy left his uh car here, parked around the side over there. It's gone. Did you see him get it?"

The man replied, "What kind of car?"

Oren explained, "A Camry. A new Camry. White."

The man laughed and said, "Sorry...have to laugh... that car has been quite the news around here. It got stolen.

The state police were here about it."

"Stolen? When? Did they find it?"

"It was stolen last weekend. Yeah, the police found it in a field over near the raspberry farm. Way out in a field. It went about as far as the front wheel drive would take it through the snow!"

"Oh shit. Was it stripped?"

"Not really. It was messed up. Whoever took it, hot wired it somehow. Not easy to do on the newer cars. But the dash and steering column was trashed. State police took it."

Oren bought a cup of coffee and a box of small chocolate covered cake donuts. He sat at one of the plastic table bench units and ate the entire package of donuts before he went back out to his bike. He couldn't decide whether he should tell Peter about the car. As he put on his gear to ride back to Taos, he decided. He wasn't going to say anything to Peter about the key mix-up or about the Camry being stolen. Nope, not a word to Peter. Oren headed back to Taos.

Within thirty minutes of Oren's departure, a new black Suburban pulled into the gas station. The man behind the counter watched as two tall, handsome, white-haired men emerged from the big SUV with dark-tinted windows. They were wearing suits with no ties, but both were wearing winter boots and had tucked their suit trousers into the boots. The man behind the counter smiled as the two men entered the store. The buzzer sounded loudly as the men stepped on the inside mat.

"You boys ought to have coats on today. Gonna get colder they say," the man behind the counter said jovially.

Jackson stepped up to the counter, showed the man his ID and badge. "I'll bet it is going to get colder. There are clouds moving this way. Probably snow tonight. I'm FBI Special Agent Jackson Avery and this is Special Agent Charlie Black."

"Nice to meet you. I'm Rusty."

"You look okay to me," Charlie said with a chuckle as he showed Rusty his badge and ID.

"Good one!" the man replied. "So what can I do for you?"

Jackson explained they were there regarding the Camry that the state police had recovered from the field. They'd been told by the police that it was stolen from this gas station. "State police said you have the car on a surveillance recording. It shows it being driven out of the station last weekend. Can we see that recording?"

"You sure can," Rusty said. "Follow me back to the office."

Charlie asked, "You want me to watch the store for you?"

Rusty laughed, "I got it covered. Cameras. Thanks."

The three men sat in the close quarters of the office and watched a computer screen mounted on the wall above a bookshelf. Rusty played the segment that he had tagged for the state police. The recording showed the white Camry driving quickly from around the side of the station through the pump area and out onto the highway. The car was in view of the camera only a few seconds.

Jackson asked, "No camera on the side of the building?"

"No. But now I'm thinking about putting one there," Rusty said.

"Do you know when the car was left here, parked on the side?" Charlie asked.

"My wife said she thinks she first saw it there about two weeks ago."

"Did you call the state police about it?"

"No. People leave cars here sometimes. We don't mind as long as they don't leave them where it interferes with our customers."

"Okay. Were the state police looking for the car?"

Rusty shrugged and said, "I don't know. I guess they picked it up because the guy who owns the field where it was left musta called them."

"Okay. Thanks. If you think of anything else, just let us know. Number and email are on my card," Jackson said as he handed Rusty his card.

"Well, just before you came in, a guy was in here asking about the car..." Rusty offered.

"Really. What did he want to know about it?" Charlie asked.

"He said his buddy left it here. Wanted to know if I saw it get picked up," Rusty said.

"You know this man?"

"No, but he's on camera. Let's go look," Rusty said.

They went back into the little office and watched Oren come in, talk to Rusty, eat donuts, and leave. The outside camera got a clear picture of his arrival and departure on his motorcycle.

"Would you please send those clips to my email?"

Jackson asked Rusty.

"Yup. Can do," Rusty replied while reading the card. "You think he's involved in the car thing?"

"He seemed to you to know about the car?" Charlie inquired.

"Oh yeah. He knew the make and color. And he seemed upset that it was gone," Rusty explained.

"Okay, thanks Rusty. Call me if anything else comes up about this car," Jackson said as he and Charlie left.

Once back in the Suburban, Jackson said to Charlie, "This is kind of interesting. Let's run the plate on the motorcycle. And let's go see the state police. Now I'd like to see Karen's car."

Jackson heard back almost immediately that the motorcycle is registered to Oren Mackler, address in Taos. "Interesting. Let's go look at the Camry, then find Mr. Mackler," Jackson said.

"Where is the Camry?" Charlie asked.

"I don't know. Call the state police office in Taos. Ask them."

Charlie called, talked to Criminal Investigations Officer Mike Pelis, whom he knew from previous investigations in Taos. "Mike! Hi, it's FBI Special Agent Charlie Black. How are you? Yes Jackson and I are in Taos. We're investigating a developing case. There was a car, a new Camry, retrieved from a field in Mora."

Mike Pelis said, "Yes it's still here at the Taos station. We're about to send it to Albuquerque for eventual processing. You want it, you can have it. It's just a stolen car to us."

Charlie asked Mike to hold the car. Told him that he and Jackson were on their way.

Jackson Avery and Charlie Black pulled into the parking lot of the little state police office in Taos just as Mike Pelis was getting into his car.

"Hey, Mike!" Jackson called out.

Mike stopped and greeted the FBI agents. "The Camry is right there," Mike Pelis said pointing to a dirty white Camry parked next to the building.

"Do you know a man named Oren Mackler?" Charlie asked Mike.

"Sounds familiar. Let me go in and run the name."

Jackson said he'd look through the Camry and then join them inside. Jackson found the suitcase and backpack still in the now open trunk. There wasn't anything much in the car itself. He saw mud on the floor on the driver's and the passenger side, some empty beer cans and snack food wrappers. Since those items were on top of the mud, Jackson surmised they were discarded by the car thieves rather than Karen. He took some pictures with his phone. Then he called the FBI office in Albuquerque and asked them to pick up the car. He headed into the office to join Charlie and Mike.

Charlie Black and Mike Pelis were sitting at a computer in Mike's tiny office looking at the image of Oren Mackler's driver's license. Charlie said to Jackson, "Oren Mackler is a local stoner. He's been picked up for DUI, marijuana. But the interesting thing is he lives in a house owned by Peter Northburn."

Jackson said, "Small town."

Mike Pelis said, "I think Mackler works for Northburn, but I'm not positive. Now that I see his picture, I know I've seen him up in Taos Canyon. I think I've even talked to him. If it was him, it was at a campground up there. He and a friend were camping as I remember. Well, mostly they were getting high. I'm pretty sure it was him. That was summer before last. He's been around here for at least a few years."

"Were you headed out?" Jackson asked Mike.

"Yeah, I'm expected at a hearing in Santa Fe in about two hours. I'll be back up here in Taos tomorrow."

Charlie told Jackson, "I've got Mackler's address. Let's go see if he's home."

"Yes, good idea. Mike, we'll see you tomorrow maybe. Thanks for the help," Jackson said.

## CHAPTER 35

Lisa Mordant and six of her friends from the Mesa Country Club sat in the fading evening light on Lisa's luxurious patio just outside of Phoenix, Arizona. They had been drinking margaritas and eating nachos since mid-afternoon. The pool lights and the lights in the trees and flowerbeds lit up all at once.

"Ohhh, so pretty!" one of the women exclaimed.

"I love to sit out here and watch the night sky take over," Lisa said.

"I agree! This is the best time of year. Cool days, cold nights."

The women decided to get their jackets and stay out on the patio a little longer. Lisa suggested they stay for dinner. Most of them were too drunk to drive anyway.

As they tottered from the pool area to the sliding glass doors, somebody bumped into Lisa's new big ceramic sculpture. The tall stylized female figure statue tumbled into the pool with a big splash.

"Oh nooo!" Lisa cried as she jumped into the pool. She was wearing her usual full cowgirl gear of boots, jeans, big turquoise belt, and leather vest over a long-sleeved western shirt. She made a bigger splash than the sculpture.

Lisa Mordant pushed down in the water to execute

a rescue of the sculpture. She held the figure from behind, across the chest, and swam it back to the shallow end of her pool. Her friends waded down the steps to help Lisa get the piece out of the pool. It took three drunk women to get the big stylized female figure sculpture out of the water and onto the deck.

In the light on the patio, Lisa saw that something was wrong with the left side of the piece. The sculpture didn't have defined legs, but rather a single shapely podium with legs subtly represented on it. It resembled a floor-length dress just tight enough to give a hint of the legs beneath. The injury was where the left thigh would be if there were legs. The abstract rendering of the legs portion was cracked and a section of it opened up on the left side. The cracked piece hadn't fallen out but was going to if the piece was moved much more.

"Let's leave it here," Lisa directed. She snapped a few pictures of the damage with her cell phone. She emailed them to the Fleeo Gallery with a request for the artist to repair it.

Lisa and her friends enjoyed the rest of their evening together. The next morning Lisa took a closer look at her damaged art by the pool. She saw something in the precarious crack which ran vertically about eight inches down the left side of the lower part of the figure. There was something smooth and light colored inside the leg.

Her housekeeper looked at the statue and said, "Looks like a big chicken bone to me."

Lisa illuminated the whitish thing in the sculpture with a high powered flashlight. "I've never seen inside a big clay sculpture before. Maybe that's the, what do they call it, armature! But it does look kind of like a bone. Looks like the bones I see out in the desert when I go riding."

"Why would they use a bone in an art thing?" her housekeeper asked.

"I don't know. Don't know if it is a bone. How can we find out?" Lisa said.

Her housekeeper suggested they call Lisa's friend from the art museum. Lisa agreed that was a good idea and called him.

"Mathew, this is Lisa Mordant. I have a peculiar request..."

Mathew found her story intriguing. He said he'd come to her house during his lunch time if she'd provide a bite to eat. Lisa happily agreed.

"So this is the art piece. Peter Northburn! Very exciting," Mathew said as he looked over the injured sculpture on Lisa's patio.

Lisa said, "She fell in the pool last night."

"Yes. She sustained a rather serious gash on her leg here," he said as he began examining the crack.

"What is that in there? Inside the crack?" Lisa asked.

Mathew asked for a flashlight and an ice pick. He scratched at the smooth white object in the sculpture and examined the resulting marks. He said, "It could be a bone. It scratches like an old bone. I think maybe I'll call the natural history museum. Mick'll come check this out."

Mathew called his friend at the Arizona Museum of Natural History in Mesa. Mick was also intrigued and said he'd love to come take look. Mathew and Lisa ate lunch on her patio. They mostly stared at the sculpture. But Mathew was also interested in hearing about the Northburn exhibit where Lisa had purchased the piece.

"You met Peter Northburn?" Mathew gushed.

"Yes. Nice looking man. Very tall. He's older than I'd imagined, but seemed fit. Not a personable sort, I will say," Lisa said.

Mathew asked about the other work in the exhibit. Lisa really couldn't say much else about the show, because Mick arrived.

"That was fast! Thanks for coming," Mathew said.

"The museum is not far!" Mick said shaking Mathew's hand.

Mathew introduced Lisa and the sculpture. They all looked at the crack and the mysterious cylindrical white surface peeking out from the crack.

"That's a bone. It looks old and/or weathered. What's it doing inside a clay sculpture?" Mick said without hesitation.

"Can you tell what bone it is? What animal?" Mathew asked.

"It's a femur. I think it's human."

Lisa gasped and said, "Human! How do know?"

Mick explained, "This looks like the midsection of the bone's length. See that bumpy lateral ridge as a feature running down the part of the bone that's visible? That's the linea aspera. That's an attachment assist for the muscles. In animals, that feature is usually double or more plateau-like. This definitely looks more human. Should we notify police or someone?"

"Oh my god!" Lisa exclaimed. She looked from Mathew to Mick. "What do we do?"

Mathew said, "Call the FBI. Don't call local police. They wouldn't know what to do. They'd just bust up this sculpture looking for whatever."

Lisa agreed. She began googling FBI on her cell phone.

"I do think the FBI could probably handle this appropriately. But realize the piece will probably be destroyed in the effort to get to the truth," Mick said.

"What'll they do to it?" Mathew asked him.

"If it was brought to my lab, I'd X-ray it first. Then if any other bones were found, I'd have to remove them. Just to get to this bone, the whole bottom section will probably have to be excavated."

Lisa spoke with someone at the FBI. When she hung up, she said, "The Phoenix FBI office is going to send an agent to look at this. They said someone would be here late this afternoon. Mick, can I have the agent call you if necessary?"

"Sure. I'll come over when they get here. Just call me." He handed her his card.

Mathew thanked Mick. As the men were leaving, Mathew said to Lisa, "What a fascinating lunch break! Talk to you soon."

## CHAPTER 36

The morning had been horrible. Breakfast was soft greasy toast and cool scrambled eggs, with a small plastic cup of old-looking chopped pineapple. A male nurse had dealt with his bedpan and bathed him. He'd gotten through it by keeping his eyes fixed on the TV. He had tuned in ESPN, a football game played loudly. He had to admit the nurse was professional about everything, but still...it was a male nurse. It didn't help that his penis decided to bone up when the nurse cleaned it and changed the catheter. Terry was mortified.

After the male nurse left, the door opened and two uniformed New Mexico State Police Officers entered. "Mr. Small?"

Terry Small was startled and dry-mouthed, but he managed to respond, "Yes."

The two officers introduced themselves and gave Terry their cards. Then they began an informal interview, as they called it.

"What's happened? Why are you here? Is my family okay?" Terry asked as his mind cleared enough to say what he thought was appropriate.

"We're here to ask you about a couple of things. We're going to record this interview. Okay? First of all, you are a licensed psychologist, aren't you? Office here in Taos?"

Terry's mouth went dry again. He reached for the glass of water by his bed. One of the officers handed it to him. "Thanks," Terry said after a long drink. "Interview? Why? What about? Record? Uh, I do have an office here in Taos. Why?"

"Sir, are you a licensed psychologist?" the officer pressed.

"Well my license was originally in Colorado. I've been meaning to file for a reciprocal license with New Mexico. Just been so busy. You know. Why are you asking?"

"So your license is in good standing in Colorado?"

"Uh, it may have expired."

"How long ago do you think it might have expired, Mr. Small?"

"Several years ago...maybe," Terry said weakly. His mind was racing. Had some disgruntled patient filed some kind of suit against him? Why were they asking these questions?

"Sir, do you realize that practicing as a licensed psychologist without a valid license is fraud?" an officer said.

"Uh, officer, I don't know that I fully understand what is going on here. I am on lots of pain medication. I have broken legs, pelvis, ribs. Have you found who ran over me?"

The officer said, "There was no evidence at the scene of your accident that could corroborate your account of the incident. The woman who called in your accident, didn't leave her name. There was no surveillance video. The official report states you had a bad fall."

Terry exclaimed, "What? A bad fall?? Can't you trace the call, the woman who called?"

The officer said, "She called from a blocked cell phone, a burner."

The other officer asked, "You went to school in Colorado? What college did you go to?"

Terry was thrown a little off kilter by the change of subject. He said, "Yes Colorado. Uh, Colorado State University."

"Where is that school?" one of the officers asked.

"Uh, Steamboat…no, uh, Fort Collins. In Fort Collins," Terry stammered.

"When did you graduate?"

Terry was reeling in confusion from the line of questioning. Why did these guys come in here and why were they asking about his license and his schooling? What was going on? "Wait a minute. Why are you here?" he asked the officers.

"We need to verify some information we received."

"What information? Just get to the point," Terry demanded, trying to take some control of the situation.

"Okay, sir, fair enough. Do you know, or did you ever know a man named James Phinn?"

Terry's face went pale. "Uh, yes, I went to school with a James Phinn. Knew him from grade school through high school."

"Where is he now?"

"He died. A skiing accident years ago," Terry said weakly.

"Sir we have information that you were there with him when he died. That you witnessed the accident. Is that true?"

"Yes."

"How did he die? Can you describe the accident?" the officer asked.

"Why, that was so long ago..." Terry said. "I can't remember."

"Mr. Small, try to remember what happened."

"We were skiing and James fell. He hit his head. He died before they could get him to the hospital."

"Did you see him fall?"

"Yes. He was skiing and just lost his balance and fell over."

"Do you remember how he fell? Forwards? Backwards?"

"He fell to the side I think," Terry said. Terry decided to just answer the questions assertively enough to get rid of these guys.

"He was skiing when he fell?"

"Yes. We were skiing together and he lost his balance and fell to the side. Guess he caught an edge or something."

"Did you try to help him?"

"Yes, I sat him up and then I skied down to get the ski patrol."

"Was he conscious when you left him?"

"Yes. I told him I'd be right back. He seemed dazed but okay."

"Did he have any visible injuries?"

"Yes, he had a cut on his head. It was bleeding a little."

"Where on his head was the injury?

"It was on the right side just above his ear."

"Okay, Mr. Small. We're going to leave you now. We'll have this transcribed and someone will be back for you to read it over and sign it. Thanks for your help."

Terry said goodbye to them. He was sure he had handled the event successfully. Quick replies seemed to move the whole thing along. Good. He still wondered what it was about. Maybe James Phinn's family is after some insurance or something. Who knows. It was so long ago. He was sure it couldn't have anything to do with him.

## CHAPTER 37

FBI Special Agents Jackson Avery and Charlie Black found the casita listed as Oren Mackler's home address on the small side street behind the Taos plaza. No one was home. They went to the neighbors. The neighbors were very happy to talk to the FBI about that pot-head Oren. The lady who lived right across the narrow street had lots to say.

"Oren is a skinny gawky boy. He might be from the mid-east or somewhere. Has almost nappy hair. He keeps it cut real short so no one will notice. Wears hats, you know, backwards, like the young boys like to. But Oren isn't a teenager. Probably near thirty. He smokes pot like there's no tomorrow! Might not be many tomorrows for him if he doesn't stop. That pot, that's gotta be expensive. He rides his motorcycle most of the time, even though he has a car. He told me he works for that Northburn artist fellow who owns the house and casita. I don't see Northburn around here. The realtor lady told me he lives towards Angel Fire, up Taos Canyon. I do see the realtor lady pretty regularly. She handles the rentals. The house is like a hotel. Short-term rentals, she calls it. Oren lives in the casita all the time. I guess that's long term," the neighbor explained to Jackson and Charlie.

"Have you seen Oren today?" Jackson asked.

"No. Not today."

"Do you remember when you last saw him?"

"No."

They thanked her for her time, then went to the neighbor nearest the casita, on the same side of the street as Northburn's property. An old man occupied that house. He had a lot to say about Oren, too.

"Freaky kid! Never know if he's going to be friendly or accuse me of something. I think all that pot smoking has made him paranoid. I see him pacing around in front of his little house at night. I've seen him standing in the street with his flashlight at night. He just shines it up and down the street. Asked him what he was looking for, and he yelled at me to mind my own business. I told him it was my business. I don't want any crazy boy wondering near my house. He and his motorcycle come and go at all hours. He fancies himself a musician. He plays his drums and guitar at all hours. The guitar is electric. It's a mess of noise from his place. I think he's gay, too. He never has any women over. But, he has men over, different men, all ages, all the time. Maybe he's a whore."

Jackson thanked him for his time and information and asked when he last saw Oren. The man said he hadn't noticed Oren in a day or two.

Charlie also asked the man, "When did you last see Oren?"

"I don't know," the man responded as he hurriedly retreated into his house.

## CHAPTER 38

Gertie Small surprised Sherry Kroyton and Erlene Vigil at the office. "I am glad I caught you both here today. How's everything?" Gertie said.

Sherry said, "How nice to see you. Everything is great. How are you? How's Terry doing?"

"I feel bad I haven't had time to get over to the hospital," Erlene said.

Gertie said, "Don't worry about that. He's pretty doped up all of the time. I want to let you know that I'm divorcing him."

"Really? When?" Sherry asked.

"The papers have been filed. We're working on the details."

"Is Terry ever going to return to work?" Erlene asked.

"That's another reason I'm here. No, Terry isn't coming back here. He is being transferred to a rehab facility soon. I own this office and this company," Gertie said.

"So we work for you now? Right?" Erlene said.

"I don't want to own this business. I'm here to offer it to you both, if you want it. You have been the business. You are the business. You are the value."

Sherry asked, "You want to sell the business to us?"

"I want to give it to you...on one condition," Gertie said smiling.

"What condition?" Erlene asked.

"You have to reorganize and change the name! I'd love for you to stay in this office space. I'll rent it to you for ten dollars a month. You have to pick up the condo insurance and keep paying the utilities. What do you think?"

Sherry looked at Erlene and they nodded at each other. "Cool! Works for us," Sherry said.

"Good. I'll have my attorney draw up a simple document to finalize this. Oh, and you can't rehire the Duff!!" Gertie said laughing.

Sherry and Erlene laughed. Erlene said, "Duffy is not welcome here."

Sherry agreed, "It's been so nice without her!"

Gertie asked, "Has anyone seen her? Is she still in Taos?"

## CHAPTER 39

TJ was only going eighty miles an hour in a sixty-five zone when the New Mexico State Police officer stopped him.

"Hey officer. What'd I do?" TJ asked, trying his best to appear not-stoned.

The officer asked for license, registration, and proof of insurance. "You were speeding. The limit here is sixty-five. Do you know how fast you were going?" the officer asked him.

"Umm, I guess a little over sixty-five maybe," TJ replied.

"Umm, a lot over sixty-five. You were clocked at eighty-one."

"I didn't think this old car could go that fast. Not without self-destructing," TJ said trying to lighten the mood.

"Your license and this registration don't match. Whose car is this?" the officer asked.

"I borrowed it from my buddy. Oren Mackler. You can ask him. He said I could use it until my car is fixed," TJ answered.

"Okay. Just sit tight. I'll be right back."

The officer called in the info for the driver and the

vehicle. He was asked to call Mike Pelis. He did. Mike told him to hold the car and driver. Mike called Jackson Avery. He asked Jackson if he wanted Mackler's old Camry for anything. Jackson told him to ask the driver, TJ, if he'd meet him at the state police office in Taos in about an hour.

TJ agreed to the request. He was sure he'd be less stoned in an hour. Seemed like a good move to cooperate.

Jackson and Charlie were back at the state police office before TJ got there. Jackson called the FBI lab in Albuquerque and got them to send a picture of both sides of the Camry key that'd been jammed in the ignition of Karen Pilling's Camry.

When TJ arrived, Jackson compared the key TJ had for Mackler's Camry with the pictures of the key the lab had just sent him. It looked like a match. Jackson asked TJ, "You think you could leave this key with me?"

TJ replied, "Well, if I leave the key here, how can I start the car?"

Jackson said, "Let's call the owner of the car and see if he has a spare key."

TJ said, "Good idea but he doesn't. This is the spare key. He couldn't find his regular key."

Jackson suggested, "Let's ask the owner if it's okay to just leave the car here for a day or so. We'll give you a ride to wherever you were going."

"Uh, okay. His name is Oren Mackler. I've got his number right here in my phone."

TJ called Oren and told him that his Camry was at the Taos state police office, and that they wanted to use his key for something. Oren was sitting in his casita on the couch completely blitzed. He freaked.

"Don't let them have that key!" Oren screamed.

TJ replied, "Sorry, man, they have it."

Jackson asked if he could have a word with Mr. Mackler. TJ handed him the cell phone. "Mr. Mackler? This is FBI Special Agent Jackson Avery. I'm here with your friend TJ and..."

Oren hung up.

Jackson smiled at Charlie then handed the phone back to TJ. Jackson asked the officer who'd stopped TJ and then followed him back to the state police office to please give TJ a ride to wherever he needed to go.

After the officer and TJ drove away, Jackson said to Charlie, "I don't know what the hell Mackler and Northburn are up to, but I'm betting they shouldn't be doing it."

Charlie laughed, "Who are we going to talk to next?"

Jackson said, "Uncle Charles."

# CHAPTER 40

"Oh fuck fuck fuck!!!" Oren Mackler said as he paced manically around his casita. "I gotta get the fuck outta here!"

Oren grabbed his gallon zip lock bag of pot, a box of rolling papers, his coat, gloves, helmet, and the stack of cash that he kept in a plastic sandwich-sized box taped to the back underside of his kitchen sink. He ran out to his motorcycle, hopped on and headed out of town. Out of habit, he found himself going up Taos Canyon towards Peter Northburn's place. Oren was completely freaked out by the time he reached Peter's steep driveway. He almost skidded out of control as he turned into the driveway. He leaned forward and sped up the incline. At the top, he stopped in front of the stairs to the showroom's front door. He took off his helmet and found he was crying. He knew he was a mess. But he couldn't think of anywhere else to go.

Peter opened the front door. He looked down the stairs and said, "What the hell are you doing? You need to make a delivery to Fleeo. She wanted work a few days ago!"

Oren sobbed, "I fucked up. So bad!"

Peter stepped out on the landing and closed the door behind him. "What'd you do? Not pay your dealer?"

Oren replied, "You're going to kill me."

"Don't be so melodramatic!" Peter said with a laugh. "Park the bike and come in." Peter went back into the showroom. He was concerned, but knew he couldn't react yet.

Oren moved his motorcycle to the parking area then went up the stairs and in the front door of the showroom. Oren carried his helmet under one arm. Peter was sitting on a stool behind the display counter in the middle of the open room.

"Hang your helmet and coat there," Peter said pointing at the coat rack by the door. "Wipe your feet and sit down and tell me what has you so upset."

Still sobbing and manic, Oren said, "I can't sit down! I can't stop shaking! I really fucked up!"

Peter sighed audibly and said, "I'll wait here while you get a beer or something from the fridge in the studio."

Oren went to the studio, got a beer as instructed and returned to the showroom He sat on the couch that he'd slept on so many times. He guzzled the beer.

Peter waited patiently. "So, you better now?"

Oren was no longer sobbing. He seemed to have his emotions under control. He blurted out, "The FBI has my car key!"

Peter Northburn really didn't know what to make of the remark. "What? What do you mean?"

"TJ borrowed my car. He called from the state police office in Taos. Then some FBI agent got on his cell phone."

"What did the FBI agent say? What did he want?" Peter asked trying to stay calm.

"I don't know what he wanted. He had my key! I

hung up! What else could I do?" Oren said as he began to cry again. He held his head in his hands as he rocked back and forth on the couch.

Peter asked, "Who is TJ? Why did he have your car?"

"Huh?" Oren looked up confused by the question.

"Let's start with the easy questions first. Who is TJ?"

"He's a dude I've known for a while."

Peter said, "So TJ is a friend of yours?"

"Uh, kinda. We hang out together sometimes."

"So he's a pothead pal?"

"Yea, I guess.

"How old is TJ? Where does he live? What does TJ do? Does he have a job? What does TJ stand for? What's his full name?"

Oren replied, "I don't know. I don't know. I don't know."

Peter sighed, "You lent your car to someone who is unknown to you, except for his name? Or rather, his initials!?"

"Yea, I guess."

"Now the police, and someone claiming to be FBI, have your car key? Do they have your car?" Peter asked.

"I guess."

Peter said, "Perhaps TJ is the target of the police and the FBI. Perhaps he is a wanted man. Perhaps he was picked up on drug charges while in your car. So many unknowns. Have you called him back?"

"This just happened. I came right here. I can't call

him back. He's with the police."

"You came right over here?" Peter asked. "Hmmm. Tell me why you are so upset that the police have your car key and maybe your car. I'm not seeing the big picture yet."

"Ohhh. You're going to kill me!"

"You said that before. Why am I going to kill you?" Peter asked calmly.

"Okay. Okay. You know when you asked me to drive that tourist's car to Mora?"

"Yes, I remember."

"Well, you told me to lock the key in the car when I parked it."

"Yes. I recall you went back to do that just before we left the station."

"Well, I thought I did."

"What do you mean?" Peter asked sternly.

"I, uh, well when I got to the gas station and was, you know, getting out of the car, my key ring got hung-up on the door and busted open. When I was picking up my keys, I think I put the car key on my ring."

"Go on," Peter said.

"Then you reminded me to leave the car key in the car and lock it. When I did that, I musta left my car key in that car," Oren said. His eyes were filled with tears and open wide.

Peter Northburn asked quietly, "So if you left your car key in that car at the gas station, how did your pal TJ have it?"

Oren blinked and as the tears ran down his face, he

answered, "My extra key. TJ has my extra key."

Peter said, "So what is the problem?"

Oren said, "You're going to kill me."

"Am I? Why?"

"I went back to Mora. I went back to put the real key in the car parked by the gas station. I had that key on my ring. I had both keys on my ring. That's how I picked the wrong key, put it in the car, then locked it."

"And?"

"I thought I could just go back there, unlock it with the real key, get my key and..."

"And what?

"The car wasn't there anymore. It was gone."

"So you did what?"

"I asked the gas station guy if he knew what happened to the white Camry?"

"And?"

"He said it'd been stolen."

"How did he know it was stolen? Could have been picked up by the owner."

"It was found torn up in a field in Mora. The state police took it away."

"Let me see if I have the story right. The car was stolen from the gas station with your key in it."

"Yea."

"How did the thieves drive away with it?"

"I don't know. I don't know. Maybe they hotwired it."

"So, then maybe or maybe not your key was found with the car. If so, the state police now have both of your keys and your car. Sounds like you just need to get your car back."

"I can't."

"Why not?"

"Whose car was that? The one I drove to Mora? Was it stolen?"

"You just told me it was stolen."

Oren said quietly, "No. I mean was it a stolen car when it was here? Did I drive a stolen car to Mora?"

Peter laughed. "Not that I know of."

Oren said, "You have to help me."

"Help you what? Get your car back?" Peter asked with a laugh.

"You help me and I'll help you," Oren whispered.

"What? What exactly are you talking about? I don't need any pot," Peter said flippantly.

"Was that car one of your people's cars?"

"Oren, are you finally just too high?"

"No. You've been doing things to people since I first started working for you. I've seen stuff."

"Really? Like what? What do you mean?"

"I've seen the trash bags of clothes. I don't know what you do with them, but I've seen them. And the teeth and stuff."

Peter sighed dramatically and said, "Clothes for the trash. What teeth are you talking about?"

"From the ash pit, in the kiln. I've swept out teeth and bits of other dental stuff. I don't know what you do, but it is weird. I don't want to know. But I think the car had something to do with the whole thing."

"Oren, Oren. I think your brain has been scrambled by all the weed you've smoked. You are sounding a little crazy right now. How does TJ being picked up by the state police lead you to some paranoid story involving me?"

"I know you've taken a bag of clothes up into the woods. I've seen you with a bag on the ATV heading up that road at the end of the parking lot."

"Umm, and that indicates to you what??"

"That you've been doing things. Bad things."

"Like what?"

"I don't know. Robbing people? But I'll keep my mouth shut about what I've seen here if you'll keep the FBI away from me."

Peter cautioned Oren, "First of all, the FBI hasn't come for you. And you don't know if they care at all about you. Secondly, you don't have anything in your mouth that I am concerned about. So whether it is open or shut is of no matter to me."

"Does that mean you won't help me?"

"I don't see anything to help you do?"

"Take me to Albuquerque. To the airport. I need to leave before the FBI shows up."

"Oren, your paranoia has taken a seriously disturbing turn. Calm down. You don't have to run from anything."

"I don't want to be arrested as an accomplice to whatever you've been doing here!" Oren blurted out.

Peter stood and said, "Oren, this is ridiculous. Let's go into the studio, get more beer, calm down, and think this through."

Oren stood and followed Peter into the studio. Peter

got two beers from the refrigerator and handed one to Oren. "Sit down," Peter said pointing to a chair next to his drafting table. He sat on the chair behind the table.

"I don't know what I'm saying," Oren whimpered. "I'm just so…"

"What brought this on? Was it TJ being picked up by the police? Did he even say if he'd been arrested for anything?"

Oren drank half of his beer and replied, "I was just so freaked that I'd left my car key in that white Camry. I knew something wasn't right about leaving that car there. I didn't want anything to do with it. Then it was stolen with my key in it."

"What in the world wasn't right about that car?" Peter asked.

"You never do favors for anyone. Ever. You were working on the show, at the gallery. There was no way in hell you'd take your time to deliver a tourist's car to Mora for them!! Never ever," Oren said.

Smiling, Peter said, "But Oren, you said that white Camry belonged to a friend of yours. I followed you to Mora to leave it there for your friend. I was helping you help your friend."

Oren jumped up. "Oh no. That's not what happened! It was your idea, your plan to take it to Mora. I didn't know anything about that car."

Peter stood. He moved quickly towards Oren. Oren ran for the door that led to the kiln building. He dashed across the walkway and ducked inside the kiln building. Peter picked up a claw hammer as he followed Oren to the kiln building.

When Peter opened the door to the kiln building, he heard Oren on the far side of the kiln. Peter went around the kiln and saw Oren standing by the door. Oren was holding Peter's compound bow and an arrow.

"Really Oren! Do you know what you're holding?" Peter asked, setting down the hammer.

"I saw what you did to that woman. I was here that day you shot her over there across the creek. You thought I'd just gotten here when you heard me yelling. When I got here, I heard this door open and heard noises. I was at the back of the front wood pile. I saw her fall when you hit her with an arrow. You killed her. That must have been her car."

Peter said, "Do you know how to use a bow like that? It takes some practice to be as accurate as I am. It has a surprising range for such a basically simple weapon."

Oren was frantically struggling to use the compound bow. He couldn't right the assembly nor put the arrow in place. He threw it on the concrete floor. He turned and bolted out the door. He was outside exactly where Karen had been when she'd fled Peter. Oren ran for the back corner of the rear wood pile. He grasped the fencing that contained the wood and made his way around the cage. When he reached the far side of the tall cage filled with kiln wood, he let go of the fencing and ran into the forest.

Peter picked up his compound bow, slipped on his release, stepped outside, and then nocked the arrow. He saw Oren just as he slipped around the corner of the back wood pile. Peter went to the edge of the ravine drop-off and saw Oren jump from the fencing and run. Peter took a shot at him. The arrow was true but fell short. Oren was out of range.

"That didn't go well," Peter said aloud. "He'll be back. Where can he go? He'll need his weed."

Peter Northburn automatically clicked into damage control mode. He went to the parking lot. He pushed Oren's motorcycle into the shed and parked it next to the ATV. He went through the saddlebags on the bike. He found and took the bag of marijuana and the little box of cash. Then he went to the showroom and collected Oren's helmet and coat. Checking the pockets of Oren's coat reaped Oren's cell phone. Peter put that in his pocket. He took the coat and helmet to the studio and put them in a black plastic trash bag. He put the weed and cash in another black plastic trash bag and put the bags on a shelf in his studio between clay pieces wrapped for drying in black plastic trash bags.

## CHAPTER 41

Jackson and Charlie didn't have any trouble finding Uncle Charles' ranch. Michael had provided excellent directions. Uncle Charles was waiting for them.

"Can't imagine why the FBI wants to see where that crazy artist puts those clothes. Maybe it's some kind of art project," Uncle Charles remarked as he led the two FBI agents to the ATVs he readied for them. "Thought you'd prefer these four-wheelers...rather than horses!" he laughed.

Charlie said, "I love horses, but it would depend on how far we're going."

"It's a fair distance. Good thing you are bundled up," Uncle Charles said laughing.

Michael's Uncle Charles took Jackson Avery and Charlie Black on a long ATV trip through the snowy and cold forest to the site where he'd witnessed Peter Northburn disposing of clothing. As the men climbed off the vehicles, Charlie exclaimed, "What a beautiful place! This forest is magnificent. Look at these pine trees!"

Jackson remarked, "This is a nice spot. Kind of cold today, but remote and peaceful. So this is where Peter Northburn hung or discarded clothing? On these trees?"

Uncle Charles explained, "He always used the same couple of trees. See these with the low broken branches? He used these."

"How many articles of clothing did he usually leave?" Jackson asked.

"One full set. Pants, shirt, socks, shoes, underwear, sometimes an overcoat. The clothes seemed to be one person's outfit. He always hung them as if they were on a person. Looked like people from a distance."

Jackson asked, "Harry told us that you found the clothes arranged. Arranged like a scarecrow?"

Uncle Charles laughed, "Yes indeed. Weird. That guy hangs the clothes, from the underwear out to the overcoat just like someone would wear them. Then places the shoes on the ground at the bottom of the pants." Charles waved his hands and pointed to illustrate the scenario.

"And you collected the clothes?" Charlie asked.

"Yes. If there were clothes here, I took them. They're all in a box in my barn, back by the house. If he was here, you know, hanging the clothes, I'd wait until he left and take those."

"He ever see you?"

"Don't think he's ever noticed me. I was back in the trees. I'm not noisy in the forest like he is! I just stayed back and watched him those few times I happened to be here when he was."

"How long ago did you first find the clothes, or see him hanging them?"

"Been a couple of years now. I just happened to be up near here, heard his off-road vehicle roaring through the woods. So I eased over here to see what was happening. We're standing on my land right here. He came from his place through the National Forest property to get here. That first time I saw him was not any hunting season. Thought he might be a poacher. Anyway, I just wanted to know what was going on. That's when I saw his weird little ritual. There were older weathered clothes already hanging on the trees and kind of scattered around this area. He added to the collection that day with newer fresh clothes. Damndest thing. I didn't take the clothes that first time. I came back a couple of weeks after that and it looked like he'd added more clothes to the display. That's when I took them down. Trashy thing for him to be doing!"

"Harry told me you've also seen some light anomalies in this area. Can you show me where and describe them for me?" Charlie asked.

"Weird lights. Balls of light that bounce around in midair. I've never seen anything like it."

"Where?"

Uncle Charles went to the trees where the clothes had been hung. He waved his arms in the air near the trees. "All up in here," he said.

"Any color to the lights?" Charlie asked.

"Yes indeed. They changed color, each one was multiple colors. White, pink, blue, green, gold. Really very pretty."

Jackson asked, "How close could you get to them?"

"No closer than about fifteen feet. Any closer and they just shot straight up and disappeared. Poof."

"Did you hear anything while they were visible?"

"Nope. Quiet as can be. Forest was quiet when the lights were here."

"Which direction did Northburn come from?" Jackson asked.

"That trail right there," Uncle Charles said pointing at a break in the trees across the small clearing.

"Would you show us the box of clothes in your barn?" Jackson asked.

"You bet. Saddle up! Let's head back to the house."

The men road the ATVs back through the snow and tall pines to the ranch house. Once there, Uncle Charles circled around behind the big house to a steel building with a large sliding door. Jackson and Charlie followed him on the ATV they shared.

Uncle Charles opened the barn's big door and the men stepped inside. The barn was well lit and heated for the comfort of the five horses that occupied the palatial venue. Charles led Jackson and Charlie down the wide aisle between the stalls to a storage room at the back of the barn. When Uncle Charles opened the door to the storage room he snapped on the light in the same movement. But in that split second before the overhead lights came on, the three men saw a bright green glow coming from a large cardboard box set at the very back, down the left side wall of the room. The rest of the room was filled with horse tack, shovels, rakes, and other tools. Jackson reached out and turned off the room's overhead light. No glow.

"Did anyone else see that glow from the box back there?" Jackson asked.

"Sure did," Uncle Charles affirmed.

Charlie was already standing next to the box, looking all around and in it when he replied, "I know I saw it!"

The two FBI agents carried the big box out of the back room to the main area of the barn. They gloved up and gingerly went through the clothes without removing any from the box.

Charlie said, "These are not inexpensive brands. Charles, how do you know Peter Northburn? Seems you recognized him up there in the woods the first time you saw him...doing this."

Uncle Charles replied, "I've never officially met him face to face. But, he's a well-publicized artist. He's very tall and has thick blond hair. Easy to identify him. Also, he doesn't live far from that area. The trail he took to get up there goes right back towards Taos Canyon, very near his place. I just put two and two together."

"You ever take a picture of him up there putting the clothes out?"

"No. Now that would be especially weird," Uncle Charles replied with a laugh.

Jackson agreed with that thought. He said, "I'd like to take this box of clothes. Send it to our lab. See what we can find out about this little mystery. That okay with you?"

Uncle Charles said, "Sure. You bet. Please take them. I'll save any more if they show up."

"If you see him up there or find any more clothes up there, please call us right away!" Charlie said. "You have a cell phone?"

"I do. I haven't had it very long, but I'm learning how to use it."

Charlie said, "You can probably take pictures with it. Please try to get a picture of Northburn in the act of hanging the clothes. But, don't put yourself in any jeopardy. You have your phone on you?"

"Sure, here it is," Uncle Charles replied as he handed his phone to Charlie.

Charlie said, "Let's see how loud the shutter setting is." Charlie snapped a picture with Uncle Charles' phone. There was no shutter click at all. "Perfect," Charlie added. Then he showed Uncle Charles how to take a picture with it.

Jackson loaded the box of clothes into the back of the Suburban. They thanked Uncle Charles and headed back to Taos.

As they made their way down from Uncle Charles' ranch back to the highway, Jackson told Charlie, "I think I'm going to call in Sam and Carlos. We need to chase down all of the elements of this nonsense as soon as we can. Either Peter Northburn is a weirdo with some kind of strange clothes fetish, or he's a weirdo who is doing some bad stuff. Or both!"

"I don't think Sam or Carlos will mind leaving their current assignment to come to Taos," Charlie said. "Last I heard from them, they were totally frustrated with that mineral rights dispute."

Once back in at the rental house in Taos, Jackson called Dr. Watson in Dallas. Dr. Watson had been the Special Agent-in-Charge at the FBI center in Dallas for many years. He was Jackson and Charlie's boss and friend. Jackson said, "Hi, Dr. Watson. Would you please run a search in our files for anything related to Peter Northburn. Yes, the artist. He's a peculiar duck."

Jackson explained the clothes hanging and the light phenomenon.

Watson responded, "Northburn's name came up in the past couple of days. A woman in the Phoenix area has a ceramic sculpture that Northburn made. Recently the sculpture was damaged, cracked open, revealing a human femur bone inside the lower part of the sculpture. Both the Arizona Museum of Natural History and the medical examiner's office in Phoenix x-rayed the piece and found no other bones in it, but the femur was definitely human. Our agents there have sent the bone to Quantico for DNA testing."

"What? Do we know when the woman got the art? Did she buy it? Where?" Jackson asked.

"She bought it not long ago at all in Taos at the Fleeo Gallery. That's an art gallery," Watson explained.

"Would you pull Sam and Carlos off the Wyoming project and send them to Phoenix to interview that woman? Then have them come here to Taos. This Northburn thing is blossoming into a strange flower," Jackson said.

"Aren't you poetic today," Dr. Watson said. "No one has talked to the gallery owner yet. Her name is Marion Fleeo. You and Charlie should talk to her and her employees, and anyone who's had anything to do with Peter Northburn. We have to find out as much as possible about him and his art. We can't assume he does all of his work himself. Many artists, especially production artists, have minions who do a lot of the actual fabrication work."

Jackson said, "Ah. Perhaps his minion is named Oren Mackler."

## CHAPTER 42

Peter Northburn detested delivering his work to any gallery. It was demeaning for him to deliver. But, no Oren yet meant he'd have to take some pieces down to Marion Fleeo. She'd been waiting long enough. He loaded the van with some work. He didn't want to take too much to her. She might think he wasn't selling anywhere else. He loaded only a few platters and pots. No sculptures in this lot. He had the van loaded and was ready to go when an older Nissan pulled in and parked in front of his showroom. He saw a big woman climb out of the vehicle and trundle up the steps to his door. She was alone. He felt the familiar tingle at the base of his skull. He'd love to fire up his kiln again. He even had some artwork bisque fired and ready to go.

The big woman wondered into his compound at such an opportune moment. It'd been over a year since he'd had such a big body to fire. A year ago it had been a large man with ample fat. That vaporized fat had created very nice effects. Peter looked forward to this one. He wondered if female fat would create different effects than the male fat had. Long ago Peter had determined that there was basically no difference between male and female, young or old, or between one ethnic group and another in the effects created in his kiln. All people created the same intense surface finishes on his art. Excess fat was another matter. This woman had plenty of excess fat.

She'd been reluctant to admit that she didn't have anyone expecting her anywhere anytime soon. However, once she started talking, she droned on and on about her small life. Peter found her exceptionally tedious. Finally, she told Peter that she'd broken up with her married boyfriend, and she'd lost her job. Poor stupid woman was how Peter perceived her. She seemed to be a lazy, self-absorbed middle-aged idiot. Though in the current vernacular, he thought, she'd be termed chronically tired or some such crap. Maybe she was already on an array of prescription drugs for that very malady. She was easy.

He took her out to the kiln building, and told her he found her attractive. When she blushed and looked away coyly, he hit her across the forehead with the steel stoking rod. She didn't even go down. She stood there staring at him with her eyes wide open as blood ran down her face. He had to impale her with one of the arrows from his quiver hanging by the door. He jammed one of his aluminum shaft hunting arrows into her neck. He stabbed her with it twice. He was sure when he ripped it out of her neck after the first thrust, that it'd pulled her trachea out. But just to be sure, he did it a second time.

He thought it was a good thing she didn't run. She'd have been a hefty package to haul up from the ravine. She finally crumpled onto the concrete floor of the kiln building in a big blob heap. Her head and neck bled voraciously. He created a tourniquet at the base of her neck with her fashionable neck scarf. It didn't stop the bleeding, but it did absorb some of the blood. He threw a tarp under her as he loaded her body onto one of the four-wheeled carts used to move the larger sculptures. He rolled her into and through the studio then out to the shed behind.

As he rolled the cart, Peter again questioned himself about being so impulsive. Should he be taking another prize so soon? Was it dangerous for him to move so quickly? He concluded that whatever he did was right. He knew what he was doing. He had devised a very clever system. And anyway, she was already on the cart. No problem. There'd be no evidence.

Peter Northburn struggled a little bit to get the large woman's body into his freezer. He didn't want to cut her up unfrozen, because he'd lose essential body fluids that were important to the desired effects of the firing process. He stripped her, then twisted and folded her until she squeezed into his chest freezer. He tossed her clothes into a black plastic trash bag. He'd take those up to the forest soon enough.

He was happy that the forest had started decomposing the clothes more quickly than in prior years. The microorganisms in the forest must have developed a taste for human clothing, he thought. He'd left clothes hanging from the trees in his secluded clearing for years. However, only in recent years had the clothes disappeared altogether. Now when he took the latest set of clothing to his clearing, he no longer found any trace of the previous batches of clothes. Perfect. A big thank you to the forest.

Peter finally drove the load of art down to Marion Fleeo's gallery. She'd been emailing him every day for more work. He couldn't put it off. To his relief Marion wasn't at the gallery. That saved at least thirty minutes of idiotic banter time for Peter. He left the work with Sherman Kroyton, her fulltime salesperson. Peter liked Sherman. Sherman was a man of few words if words weren't needed. Peter wanted to get back to his compound. He was anxious to prepare for the firing.

Oren hadn't returned yet, so Peter would have to do everything, once again. Peter didn't really mind that Oren wasn't back yet. One less thing to deal with, he thought.

He left the new body in the freezer long enough for it freeze well enough for his purpose. He pulled the body out of the freezer and sectioned it in the usual way for the kiln. Using his sawzall, he cut the extremities from the torso, bisected the torso just below the rib cage, and cut the head off the top portion of the torso. The corpse was mostly frozen. Fat freezes fast. He was ready to begin another firing.

He put the unburned chips and fragments of bone and teeth from the last firing, retrieved from the ash pit and firing chamber floor, into the ball mill. He powdered everything and mixed it with the other ingredients of his special glaze mix. He painted his clayware with the glaze, and then began arranging everything in the firing chamber of his wood-fired kiln. He placed the arms, legs, and the two pieces of the bisected torso in the firing chamber exactly where he needed them to be. He put the two big pieces of the torso up near the ash pit.

The hottest spot is next to the firebox. When the firebox is roaring, the heat is sucked along the draft from the air intake ports then down from the firebox into the ash pit, and through the firing chamber, and then up and out the chimney. Between the firebox and the ash pit is a steel grate. The air rushing from the front air intake ports carries the heat and ash through the grate. The fierce oxygen hungry rampaging heat licks and swirls around within the firing chamber as it races to the chimney.

Peter put the head in a plastic bag. As always, he planned to pop the head into the firebox near the end of the forty-eight hour firing cycle. The head bursts, sometimes exploding, when it hits the extreme heat. Most of the fluids, the sinuses, eyes, and the brain immediately melt, boil, and shoot out the neck opening. The skull cracks apart as pieces fall through the grate into the ash pit. Peter will then later pulverize any remaining bits with any other un-vaporized bone fragments to add to his special glaze mixture. Future work will be specially flavored with the remnants of this firing. No waste. No evidence.

# CHAPTER 43

Quinton Quigley and Pokey took an early morning ride on their usual trails above Taos Canyon and the Rio de Fernando. The morning was cold, cloudy with no wind. There was a thick layer of snow on the ground, but no new snow forecasted for the day, so Quinton rode further than his ordinary route down the canyon towards Taos. From his vantage point up so high on the ridge, he could see down to the river and the series of National Forest picnic areas and campgrounds that edged the river. The river was mostly frozen, and the nights were so very cold that there were not many campers in the winter. In one picnic area, not an overnight camping spot, he saw a dark colored Nissan parked with the back hatch door open. He didn't see any people near it. No sign of a fire in the fire pit. The car had snow on it, so it'd been there at least a few days. He'd seen abandoned, usually stolen cars, left along the river. This looked abandoned. He made a mental note to call the Forest Service about it when he got back to his ranch.

Quinton and Pokey didn't get back to the ranch until lunchtime. After getting Pokey cleaned and in the barn, Quinton stood in front of his barn and made the cell phone call to the Forest Service office in Taos. He explained what he'd seen and where the car was. The ranger said he'd check it out.

The ranger wasn't busy, so anything to get out of the office seemed like a great idea. He responded to Quinton's call right away. The car was exactly as Quinton had described.

The older Nissan Xterra sat cold and open in the picnic area. The keys were in the ignition. The ranger sat in the car and turned the key. Nothing. He popped the hood. The battery was gone. He searched the vehicle for ID. In the glove box, he found the registration. The Nissan belonged to Duffy Dot, address in Taos. There were no personal belongings immediately visible in the car. The ranger called for a wrecker.

While waiting for the wrecker, he went through the vehicle looking for any clues that might help him determine why it had been left there. He found a gallon size zip lock bag of marijuana under the back seat. He found a small plastic sandwich box of cash, holding seven-hundred dollars in twenties and tens. He found a cell phone down in the crevice between the driver's seat and the center console. The cell phone was on and still had a little bit of its battery charge left, so he surmised it hadn't been abandoned too long.

He called the state police office in Taos. "This makes no sense. If someone stopped to steal the battery, why wouldn't they go through the car and at least clean out the drugs and cash?" he asked Criminal Investigations Officer Mike Pelis.

"Maybe the person was interrupted," Mike suggested. "So whose cell phone is it? What's the number?"

The ranger gave Mike the number. Almost immediately Mike said, "Oh really! The name on the cell phone account is Oren Mackler!"

"That's the guy everyone's been looking for," the ranger exclaimed.

"Stay with the vehicle, if you can. Have the wrecker bring it here to my office. We have Mackler's car. He's also linked to the Camry from Mora that belongs to the missing Texas woman. Now we have third car linked to him," Mike Pelis instructed.

The ranger said it'd be no problem to stay with the vehicle. He told Mike that he'd send him a copy of his written report as soon as he could.

## CHAPTER 44

After another week of one disappointing hospital meal after another, Terry received an unexpected visitor. "Mr. Small, I'm Robert Link, I'm here to serve you with a subpoena to testify at a grand jury hearing in Denver regarding the investigation into the death of Mr. James Phinn."

"What?" Terry exclaimed.

Mr. Link repeated himself and handed an envelope to Terry.

Terry asked, "What investigation? Why?"

Mr. Link said, "I'm not here to discuss the matter. Just here to serve the subpoena." Link looked at the traction harness and said, "Looks like you had a serious accident."

Terry responded weakly, "It was a hit and run."

## CHAPTER 45

FBI agents Sam Wester and Carlos Sanchez flew into the Phoenix Sky Harbor International Airport just before dinner. An agent from the FBI Phoenix Division met them at the airport. The young woman said, "Special Agent Chan O'Brien, at your service, agents."

Sam replied, "I'm Special Agent Sam Wester and this is my partner, Special Agent Carlos Sanchez. Chan, huh. O'Brien, huh. Interesting mix of ethnicity in your names, agent."

Carlos said, "Agent O'Brien, ignore my friend. He has so few manners and even less good sense."

O'Brien laughed, "Like I've never heard that before! I'm from San Francisco. My mom's family was of Chinese descent and my dad, Irish. Simple as that. Let's go out this exit. I left the car out there."

In the uniform FBI black Suburban, Sam asked Chan, "Where are we going?"

"I'm supposed to take you to your hotel first, then take you to eat dinner someplace, then we are going to the Arizona Museum of Natural History in Mesa."

"Oh good, a field trip!" Sam said excitedly.

"You'll like the special exhibit there. A human bone was extracted from a ceramic statue. A big bone, a femur that was perhaps used as an armature in the sculpture," Chan explained.

Agent Chan O'Brien took Sam and Carlos to a hotel in Mesa. She waited for them to check-in and drop their bags in their room. "What would you like for dinner? What kind of food?" Chan asked as the men were leaving the hotel lobby.

"I'm in the mood for steak. How about you?" Carlos replied.

"Great. I know just the place," Chan replied.

It was a short drive to the steakhouse restaurant. The place smelled wonderful to the agents as they made their way to a table. "Good choice, Chan!" Sam said. "If the food is half as good as it smells, we're in heaven. Steak heaven!"

"You'll love it."

When they were almost through the meal, Carlos asked Chan, "Tell us about the femur."

Chan smiled and said, "I have to admit, this is my first real case. Full disclosure! Well, the owner of the artwork, Lisa Mordant, discovered the femur. She lives here, but bought the piece while on a trip to New Mexico. Anyway, the piece was damaged when it was knocked over on her patio. It fell in the pool, but must have struck the side on the way in. When the piece cracked and part of the leg fell open or off, the bone was exposed. Ms. Mordant called someone at the Natural History Museum because it looked to her and her friends like a bone. They thought it might be a cow or dinosaur bone or something."

"But it's a human bone?" Carlos asked.

"Yes, it is human bone. It is the only bone in the sculpture. It was thoroughly x-rayed," Chan explained.

"Must be a sizable sculpture," Sam remarked.

"I haven't seen it yet," Chan O'Brien said.

"The FBI has the bone at Quantico?" Carlos asked.

"Yes, but I was instructed to take you to the Arizona Natural History Museum first. To talk to Mick Stevens who was the one who x-rayed and examined the piece. Then we're supposed to go talk to Lisa Mordant."

"We going to meet these people tonight?" Sam asked.

"We have an appointment with Mr. Stevens this evening. Then we'll go to Lisa Mordant's house in the morning," Chan explained.

"Ohhh, Museum of Natural History at night! Cool," Sam said.

They parked in the back of the Museum and Chan called Mick on his cell phone. Mick opened a rear door of the building. After introductions and credentials were shown, Mick Stevens led the FBI agents to the archeology lab. Mick had the x-rays of the sculpture out on a light table.

Pointing to a white linear shape on an x-ray, Mick said, "There she blows! That's the human bone, a femur in the sculpture."

"Is it a right or left femur?" Carlos asked.

"Right."

"Could you determine how long the bone had been encapsulated in the clay?" Sam asked.

"I understand your lab has ID'd the donor as a man from New Orleans who disappeared three or four years ago," Mick said. "But the bone looked older than that to me. I mean it looked like it'd been out of its original body for more than three or four years."

"How long?"

"Hard to tell without further investigation, but I would have put it at closer to ten years or more out in the desert sun and weather."

"The bone is at Quantico, but where is the sculpture?" Carlos asked.

"It's still at the Maricopa County Medical Examiner's office here in Phoenix, I was told. They also x-rayed it. They extracted the bone for your agency to test for DNA. I guess they kept the piece of art."

"Do you have any theory about the bone in the art?" Sam asked Mick.

Mick thought about it for a second and then replied, "I think whoever built the piece might have just thought it was clever to put a femur in the leg portion of the sculpture. Just for fun. It didn't seem a likely place to hide it. I mean, where is the rest of the skeleton?"

Sam said, "Yeah. Where is the rest of the skeleton?"

Carlos added, "And did the artist know it was a human bone? It looks like a plain old big bone. Could have been a cow. Any sign it had been glued in place, or was it held by the clay?"

Mick pointed to an x-ray and said, "No glue that I detected, at least in the x-ray, on the surface of the bone. Looked like it was helping to form the shape of that lower portion of the piece."

Sam asked Chan, "Would you please see if we can

visit the medical examiner's office tonight?"

Agent Chan O'Brien stepped away from the group and made some calls. She returned quickly to say, "Yes. We can go over there as soon as we leave here."

They thanked Mick for meeting with them. Then Chan drove them to the Forensic Science Center office of the Maricopa County Medical Examiner. When they got there, Chan took them straight to the office of the forensic pathologist who'd worked on the case.

"For a beginner, you seem to know your way around the OME labyrinth of labs!" Sam remarked.

Chan laughed and replied, "Yes. I've been in here numerous times, as a runner gopher for the FBI, before I became an agent."

Carlos said, "This is a nice and very large facility. Is it new?"

"Opened in 2002. It seemed larger then. The population of the Phoenix area is growing so fast, that..." Chan began, but was interrupted by an older man calling her name from the doorway.

Chan turned to see Dr. Whiteman. "Hi, doctor."

Whiteman smiled and said, "So these are the imported agents!"

"Yes, we are here to..." Chan began.

"Oh I know. Let's go look at the body," Dr. Whiteman said laughing. "Come on. Follow me."

Sam and Carlos had their badges and IDs in-hand but put them away and followed Chan and the doctor. They entered a large classroom. The narrow work tables were arranged in rows facing the main table and a white board on the wall behind it.

"There is the poor unfortunate woman," Dr. Whiteman said, pointing at the corpse of the sculpture lying on an examining table near the front of the room. The sculpture had been cut into from the midsection to the bottom, leaving a long gaping hole.

Sam and Carlos now introduced themselves and showed their IDs to Dr. Whiteman. "Yes, yes. You are FBI. You don't need IDs to prove that. You look the part you know! Those suits are very governmental!" Whiteman said laughing.

Sam responded, "Yikes! I will work on my presentation...immediately!" Sam whipped off his suit jacket.

Carlos Sanchez moved close to the sculpture. He said, "The finish on this clay is iridescent. So colorful."

Chan added, "It is beautiful. Wonder what makes it shimmer like that?"

"The glaze. It's all in the glaze," Sam remarked authoritatively. "I have done some ceramic work, though admittedly that was long long long ago. It is the glaze. I've never seen an effect like this. So, Doctor, what is your take on this bone thing?"

Dr. Whiteman replied, "I think it was a disrespectful way to inappropriately dispose of a human bone."

"But why did someone do this?" Chan asked.

"That I don't know. I've seen some peculiar and crazy stuff in my career, but this is a first," Dr. Whiteman remarked.

"Can you give an estimate of how long the bone was

in the sculpture, or how long it had been out of the, uh, the original body?" Sam asked.

"I'd say it looked pretty weathered. So maybe it had been many years out of its original body. Or, maybe when the sculpture was fired, it artificially weathered the bone. Your lab at Quantico should be able to provide more information," Dr. Whiteman said.

"Quantico matched the DNA to a man who went missing a few years ago. I don't have the details yet. But, that's only a few years ago. I am totally guessing if I say the man still had his femur when he went missing. No one has said otherwise, yet," Sam explained.

Chan said, "Quantico reported that the bone had been cooked thoroughly by the firing. Their timeline is vague at this time. They felt they'd done well to get good DNA samples."

Special Agent Sam Wester took photos of the sculpture. They thanked Dr. Whiteman for being available at the late hour. Then Chan O'Brien drove Sam and Carlos back to their hotel.

"See you at nine AM. We'll go see Lisa Mordant," Chan said as she dropped Sam and Carlos at the lobby door.

## CHAPTER 46

As promised, Chan and the Suburban were waiting in front of the hotel at nine AM. "Lisa Mordant lives nearby," Chan said as the agents climbed in the big SUV with their bags in hand.

Sam asked, "Have you met her?"

Chan O'Brien answered, "No. But I spoke with her on the phone just a little while ago. She's sounds like a straight-talking person."

Lisa met them at her front door. She took them through to the patio and pool area. "Y'all want some coffee?"

Sam said, "Yes ma'am. I'd love some. Can I help you with that?"

Lisa laughed, "Son, my housekeeper will see to it. Just have a seat."

They sat at one of the spacious poolside tables under the cabana. Lisa's housekeeper brought out a tray of coffee and pastries. Lisa explained what happened to the sculpture and how she'd rescued it from the pool.

"Tell us about when you got the piece. When you bought it, how you got it to Phoenix," Carlos asked her.

Lisa explained, "I bought it not too long ago, over in Taos, New Mexico. I went over there to see a friend. I just happened to wonder into an art gallery. There was an opening in progress. They had good snacks. The artist was there. I saw the sculpture, a tall stylized woman. She was perfect for my patio. I bought her to stand right here by the pool."

"Did you meet the artist at the opening?" Sam asked.

"Well I did indeed. What a pompous ass!"

"Why do you say that?"

"He gave a real hard time, rude as hell actually, to a nice older fellow who just asked about having a piece made special."

"Goodness, doesn't sound like good sales strategy," Sam remarked. "What did the artist do, specifically?"

"His name is Peter Northburn and he said some rude and uncalled-for things to the man. The man wanted a piece kinda like the one I bought, but he wanted a stylized likeness of his departed wife incorporated in the face."

"What happened?"

"Northburn and the man got into a fist fight. I broke it up," Lisa said. "I almost reneged on my purchase."

"Do you remember any other work in the show?" Carlos asked.

"There were three big pieces: my girl, a bear, and another figure but I don't remember what it was. And there were loads of plates and pots and shit like that. You know, ceramic stuff. Same old same old," Lisa explained.

"We saw your piece at the OME's last night. I have to say the finish on it is spectacular," Carlos said.

Lisa remarked, "That's part of what drew me to it.

My big girl was so pretty! Too bad she broke. Guess I'll have to see if that Northburn ass can repair her!"

"So you haven't talked to the gallery or the artist about the accident?" Sam asked.

"No, not yet. I emailed the gallery, but haven't heard back from them yet. Thought I should wait until I knew the full extent of the problem before pursuing the matter any further," Lisa Mordant replied.

"The problem is greater than the broken sculpture. Would you wait to contact the gallery or the artist? At this point in our investigation, we'd like to hold back this info about the bone as a surprise," Carlos said.

"What's the investigation? The bone thing?" Lisa asked.

Sam explained, "The bone and the artist, and maybe the gallery. We're off to Taos today. When I know more that I can share, I will."

"I'd not put anything past that asshole artist," Lisa remarked.

"How'd you get the sculpture here from Taos so quickly? I mean most things that large have to be packed and shipped. And artwork..." Carlos asked.

"I brought her back in my horse trailer. I took a horse to my friend in Taos, so no horse on the ride home. The gallery guy, nice fellow, wrapped her up real good in bubble wrap. Just laid her in the trailer and brought her home," Lisa said smiling.

"Can we take a look at the trailer?" Carlos asked.

"Sure, but why?"

"We just have to see everything we can that might

have anything to do with our assignment," Sam answered.

"Okay. Let's go to the barn," Lisa said.

"Where's that?" Chan asked.

"It's less than a quarter mile from here. Not far at all. We can walk," Lisa said.

"Great. A walk would be nice," Chan replied.

The three FBI agents and Lisa Mordant took a gravel path that ran from her back yard through a big gate to a field behind her house. The path took them to the barn. It was a large and fancy barn.

"Oh! This is a luxury barn!" Sam exclaimed.

Lisa said, "I love my horses! They have a good and safe life here."

The horse trailer was parked in a covered area to the side of the barn. They looked at and in the trailer.

"This trailer has an HVAC system of its own?" Sam asked as he took pictures of the trailer.

"Yes it does," Lisa replied. "In this area the heat would be critically devastating to the horses in a trailer. It could easily kill a horse to ride in a trailer without air conditioning."

"I'll bet it could. You have incredible heat here in Phoenix," Carlos remarked.

"Want to see the barn?" Lisa asked.

"I would!" Chan answered.

Lisa led them through a regular door into an office at the front of the building. The office was a nice room with normal office furniture. There was a large picture window looking into the main alleyway of the barn proper. They could see down the wide aisle to the far end of the building.

The far end of the aisle had a sliding barn door exactly like the front of the building next to the office. Lisa led them through another regular door into the wide aisle between the stalls. As soon as she opened the door, the horses began shifting and they all then stuck their heads out of their stalls to greet her.

"Good morning!" Lisa called out to her horses.

"How nice it is in here," Chan O'Brien remarked.

The center aisle was carpeted with a dense layer of crushed stone and a reddish colored bark. The stalls each had a wooden Dutch door with brass hardware. The lighting was mainly from clerestory windows above the stalls.

"Smells so nice in here!" Carlos remarked.

"I smell a little chocolate," Chan said.

"The building is climate controlled, of course. And you do smell chocolate. I get chocolate bean husks from my bark supplier. The chocolate husks are mixed in with the assorted bark and straw for the flooring. My horses seem to like the smell. My staff likes it, too."

"Me, too!" Sam said laughing. "This is the very nicest horse facility I have ever seen."

"Thanks. But it's not the fanciest in Phoenix! Not by a long shot," Lisa said.

"I hope your horses know what a great life they have here with you!" Carlos said.

"I think they do. They're all so sweet. I love 'em all," Lisa said as she stroked a horse face sticking out of the nearest stall.

"We better get going. Thank you for your time, the coffee, the tour, and your willingness to hold off contacting the artist and gallery," Carlos said to Lisa.

As they drove away from Lisa Mordant's house, Sam said to Chan, "Would you please take us to the airport. We're supposed to get a ride on a Bureau jet to New Mexico."

Chan remarked, "Ah, a Bureau jet. We'll see if it's really here. Or not!"

## CHAPTER 47

Uncle Charles took advantage of the beautiful morning to ride his big mare, Lomoto. There was no wind, and the temperature was promising to reach forty degrees by lunchtime. What an unusually fine February morning in the mountains. Charles headed due west from the barn. He slowly rode the ridgetop for an hour or so. As he turned Lomoto northward to dip through a little valley and then up to the next ridge, he saw something unexpected.

The low angle of the morning sun hit something that glinted kind of high up in a pine tree in the forest off to his left. He stopped Lomoto to look more closely at the anomaly. It looked like there was a set of clothes hanging in a pine tree about twenty feet back from the game trail he was riding. There was something long and shiny dangling with the clothes.

Uncle Charles got Lomoto as close to the tree with the clothes as he could. The clothes tree was in the middle of a pretty tight clump of pines and the snow was deep. Charles immediately thought it was more of Peter Northburn's shenanigans. But, these clothes were hung up much higher than Northburn ever hung them. The bottom of the pants was at least ten or twelve feet above the ground. It looked like there were boots sticking out of them. If Charles hadn't been riding Lomoto, and the sun hadn't hit the anomaly at just the right angle, he might not have even noticed the clothes. Now he could see clearly that the shiny dangling thing was a chain attached to the clothes.

Charles dismounted his horse to move closer to the clothes tree. He had to high-step carefully through the deep snow. When he got to the base of the clothes tree, he saw that there was a person in the clothes. The person was facing the trunk, straddling a stout branch, and had each arm hooked from the elbow to the armpit over branches on either side of the tree. The face of the person in the clothes wasn't visible from below. The head was slumped onto the right shoulder and upper arm. Looking up the tree, he called out to the person. No answer. Looking up at the body, Uncle Charles noticed the ravens circling above the trees. They'd found the unusual thing in the tree, too.

He carefully stepped on branches starting at the bottom of the tree trunk. He thought the person had probably used these branches as a ladder of sorts to climb up there. When he could just reach a boot, he shook it and called out again. No response.

He unlaced the boot and pulled it off. Still no response. He felt the ankle for a sign of a pulse or something. The ankle was cold. It felt kind of stiff, perhaps frozen.

Uncle Charles carefully climbed down the tree. He took out his cell phone, and found it didn't work. He surmised there was no cell service there. So he got back on Lomoto and hurried back to the ranch house and barn.

As soon as he was in the big clearing of the house and barn, he had cell service. He called 911. The dispatcher instructed him to wait at the house so he could take the responders to the site. Uncle Charles gave the dispatcher careful directions to his house. While he waited for the responders, he cleaned and put Lomoto in her stall in the barn. He gassed up his ATVs. Then he went inside the house to wait. His cell phone rang.

"Uncle Charles? Hi. This is Emma Spruce. You know, Harry's..."

"Sure, hi Emma," Uncle Charles replied.

"I just got a call from the Taos 911 dispatch that you found a body up there."

"That's true. I called it in a while ago. I'm waiting on the police or whoever," Charles said.

"I'm part of the whoever. I'm on my way. I'm a field deputy for the OMI, Office of the Medical Investigator. You have an unattended death! I'll be there in about half an hour or less. First responders will probably be Rio Fernando Volunteer Firefighters and a New Mexico State Police officer," Emma said.

"Well, the body is way up in a tree. They better bring some muscle and a ladder," Charles said.

"Up in a tree?"

"Yes indeed. It's hanging like a bear cub climbing up a tree trunk. Feet are at least ten or more feet from the ground."

"How far from your house is the site?" Emma asked.

"Oh, I'd say it's about two miles. I've got three ATVs ready to go."

"Great. I'll see you soon. If the firefighters get there

first, wait for me."

"Will do. It'll be nice to see you" Uncle Charles replied.

Two volunteer firefighters from the Rio Fernando Fire Station found Uncle Charles' place. "Hi, are you Charles McMarlin?" they asked.

"I am. You boys don't mind waiting on Emma Spruce, do you?"

"Not a bit. We have to wait for a state police officer, too. Dispatch said body in a tree," one of the firefighters said.

"Yes, sir! Looks like a young man, but I couldn't really see. The body is hugging the tree. Pretty far up. You'll need a ladder. I have ATVs ready to go. We can strap a ladder on one."

"We can't drive our pickup to the body?"

Uncle Charles replied, "No. No, the tree is deep in the woods. Only a horse or an ATV can get over there."

A firefighter asked, "How'd the deceased get there? You see a four-wheeler or anything?"

"Didn't see anything and didn't really look around for anything. The body up in the tree was pretty distracting," Uncle Charles explained.

## CHAPTER 48

Emma Spruce pulled up to Charles McMarlin's ranch house only minutes after the firefighters and the state police officer had arrived. "Hi. Are we ready to retrieve?" she asked the group standing by the ATVs.

Uncle Charles replied, "Hi Emma! Think we're all set except for the ladder."

The extension ladder on the firefighters' pickup was eight feet long not extended. One of the firefighters offered to hold the ladder if someone else would drive the ATV. "Ride with me," the other firefighter said as he gathered rope and bungee cords from their pickup.

"Okay then. You two take that ATV and the ladder, and Emma you take one, and officer, you ride with me. Remember, there'll be an additional passenger on the way back," Uncle Charles said. "Guess he'll ride with you, Emma."

Emma collected her death scene gear as well as a body bag and tarp from her car. She put them on the ATV with her and was ready to go.

The caravan of ATVs followed the horse trail into the pine forest. Near the ranch buildings, the ground was nearly devoid of snow. But, as they climbed higher, the woods were denser, and the snow was thicker and deeper.

It took a while to reach the tree with the body.

They parked the ATVs as close as they could to the body tree. The police officer and firefighters were the first to make their way through the deep snow to the base of the tree.

"Good God! What the hell?" a firefighter exclaimed looking up at the body.

Emma and the state police officer walked around the general area of the body tree. Both took pictures of anything and everything. She went back to the firefighters and said, "I don't see anything special out here except the body up there. Weird."

The officer said, "If this is a crime scene, there is no evidence of it on the ground. It is a weird one."

"You want us to get him or her down?" a firefighter asked Emma.

"Put the ladder up, I'll go up and inspect the body. Then you can take it down," she replied.

Uncle Charles just sat on his ATV and watched the goings-on. "You want me to do anything?" he asked.

Emma replied, "Don't think so. Someone will need to be ready to go for more help if we do something dumb."

A firefighter said, "We are too smart to do anything dumb!"

"Okay, please make sure the ladder is secure," Emma responded. The firefighters put a rope round Emma's waist and tossed the other end over a stout looking branch on the tree next to the body tree. "Oh this seems safe," she added facetiously.

"We'll hold the rope. It's just back-up," a firefighter

said. "You won't need it."

Emma laughed and climbed the ladder. Once up even with the body, she checked for vital signs she knew she wouldn't find. The face was swollen and red. The ravens had been pecking on the ears and neck. They tried to get to the face, but it was nestled in between the tree trunk and the right shoulder. The exposed ear and neck flesh showed signs of incidental raven nibbling. Emma called down to the officer and firefighters, "This appears to be a young man. No coat, no hat, no gloves. I don't see any wounds on his head or back, other than some minor damage done by the birds. I'll take a couple more pictures and then it is all yours."

When Emma was back on the ground, a firefighter removed the makeshift harness rope from her waist. He left the rope hanging over the branch of the other tree. He carried one end of the rope up the ladder, and then he looped it under the body's armpits and around the torso and tied it. His partner on the ground held the other end of the rope.

"Okay, put some tension on it," the firefighter on the ladder called down to his partner.

The firefighter on the ground pulled the rope tight, while the firefighter on the ladder struggled to release the body's frozen arms from their hooked position over the branches. Finally the arms were free of the branches that they'd been clinging to. "Okay, lift a little."

The firefighter on the ground pulled on the rope until the body lifted slightly off of the branch it was straddling. When the firefighter on the ladder was satisfied that the body could be lifted off the limb, he called down, "Okay, lift

233

it higher and I'll push it free."

The firefighter on the ground, with the officer's help, tugged on the rope until the body was high enough for the firefighter on the ladder to tilt one leg over the limb it had been hanging over. Then the body swung free. The firefighter quickly came down the ladder and helped lower the frozen body to the ground. Emma had spread a tarp to catch the body.

They looked at the body which lay in the climbing bear cub position on the tarp. "What do think happened to this guy?" a firefighter asked Emma.

Emma examined and photographed the body then replied, "No apparent external wounds. No ID in his clothing. This is strange. Why would he climb up in that tree way out here in such a remote area?"

The officer and firefighters assisted Emma with taking an inventory of the possessions. They found only boots, socks, jeans, a chain with keys on an attached ring, briefs, blue cotton work shirt, and a leather vest.

"Not a hunter or camper, that's for sure," a firefighter said.

"Let's bag him," Emma instructed.

With some difficulty, the firefighters straighten the crooked frozen arms and legs of the body. They rolled up the frozen body in the tarp and then put the bundle in the body bag.

The officer said, "We should look around this area for any sign of a vehicle."

"Or a horse," Uncle Charles added. "Could have come in on a horse."

"Would a horse stick around?" a firefighter asked.

"That depends. I'd like to think a horse could be that attached. You know, like Lassie," Uncle Charles suggested. "But I doubt even Lassie would freeze to death for Timmy."

They searched the woods finding nothing. Nothing at all. They loaded the full body bag on Emma's ATV and tied it securely. They gathered the ladder and rope, then headed back for the ranch house.

When they got there, Emma asked the firefighters to transport the body to the funeral home in Taos. Later, it would be picked up for transport down to the OMI center in Albuquerque for autopsy. They agreed to drive the body to Taos. The state police officer took Uncle Charles' statement then left. Uncle Charles asked Emma to stay for a cup of tea.

"I'd love to. I am cold to the bone!" Emma said.

They sat at the dining table in the ranch house. Uncle Charles put on a kettle of water. "Well today has certainly been out of my ordinary!" Uncle Charles remarked.

"I agree. It was an odd find. You know if you hadn't happened to see that body in the tree, it would eventually have been disposed of by the elements, insects, and animals. That body would have just vanished."

"Goodness! What was he doing there?"

"First guess is that he climbed up of his own accord and either couldn't get down or didn't want to get down. Really though, it just seems crazy. He wasn't dressed to be out there."

Uncle Charles asked, "How long do you think he was out there?"

Emma replied, "That's hard to say because he was frozen. I'd say he'd been in that tree only a couple of days at most because he hasn't desiccated."

"I wonder if anyone has been looking for him. I haven't heard of any missing persons reports on the news," Uncle Charles said.

"If it has been only a couple of days that he was in the tree, then how long has he been missing...if he was missing at all," Emma added. "We have no way of knowing, at this point, where he came from or when."

Uncle Charles served their tea. "Would you like a chocolate chip cookie? I made them myself."

Emma said, "You bet I would!"

As he put the plate of cookies on the table, Charles asked, "How are they going to identify that body?"

"It might have to be through DNA if the fingerprints aren't on file somewhere. And you never know, someone might recognize him. That always helps. These cookies are great!"

"So glad you like them. Please eat more, take some to Harry. I should not be left alone with them. These are my weakness."

"So don't make them."

"Oh Emma, that's so easy to say. You don't understand the intense pull of homemade chocolate chip cookies, do you? It is a pull like the gravitational pull of the moon on the oceans. Cannot be turned off," Uncle Charles said laughing heartily.

Emma responded laughing, "Harry will love some. Thanks!"

## CHAPTER 49

Mike Pelis called FBI Special Agent Jackson Avery with the news of the car found in the Taos Canyon with Oren Mackler's cell phone in it. Jackson asked Mike Pelis to meet him and Charlie Black at the site where the car was found. Half an hour later the men rendezvoused at the campsite in the canyon. Mike updated them on the car and everything he'd been able to find out about Ms. Dot. The men did a walk-around the campsite.

"Where is the car now?" Charlie Black asked.

"It's at my office. You want it to go to the FBI lab in Albuquerque I suppose," Mike Pelis replied.

Jackson told him that the flatbed from Albuquerque FBI office would pick it up as soon as they can get up here. "The car belongs to Duffy Dot? Who is she? Where is she?"

Mike said, "She lives in Taos. Works for a psychologist, Terry Small. Officers went to her home today after her car was found. She wasn't home. I have sent officers to her workplace. Haven't heard back on that."

"We did a drive-by of Peter Northburn's place. But, we haven't met him yet. His driveway is on this highway no more than a half mile from here. That seems close enough to walk to," Jackson said.

"You think he left the car here?" Mike asked. "Then

walked home? Why?"

"Could be. Or Oren Mackler left it here and walked back to Northburn's."

Mike said, "Oren wouldn't have left his weed and cash!"

"Probably not," Charlie agreed. "We don't know for sure if Oren works for Northburn."

Mike suggested that Jackson and Charlie check out the Fleeo Gallery before going to Northburn's place. "It's been my experience in Taos that the gallery staff will give you more info than you ask for. They love to dish on the artists," Mike explained.

"Okay then, we'll go to the Fleeo Gallery next," Charlie said.

Mike Pelis went back to his office. Jackson and Charlie went art shopping.

## CHAPTER 50

"Hello! Have you been in before?" Sherman asked the FBI agents when they stepped into the gallery.

"Hi. No, this is our first time in here. I'm FBI Special Agent Jackson Avery and this is Special Agent Charlie Black. Could we ask you some questions about Peter Northburn?" Jackson asked as he and Charlie showed their IDs and badges to Sherman.

"Sure. Want to sit down. We can go in the office," Sherman said.

"Do you own this gallery?" Charlie asked.

"No. My name is Sherman Kroyton. I'm a salesman. The owner, Marion Fleeo is out running errands. She ought to be back any time."

"This is all Peter Northburn's artwork?" Jackson asked as he began looking around the gallery.

"The one and only," Sherman replied.

"The finishes are pretty. Lots of iridescence," Charlie said.

"Yes, his shapes are nothing extraordinary. It's his glazes and surfaces that set him apart. He is one of the premier ceramists in the country because of those surface effects," Sherman explained.

"Hmm. Is he a nice guy?" Charlie asked.

Sherman laughed and replied, "He can be. He is a showman. He can also be a prima donna artist."

"Does his stuff sell well?" Charlie asked.

"Yes it does," Sherman affirmed.

Marion Fleeo stepped in the front door and greeted everyone with her best salesperson enthusiasm. Sherman introduced the FBI agents.

"Oh. FBI. About Peter?" she asked curiously.

"We are interested in learning more about Peter Northburn in connection with an on-going investigation," Jackson said vaguely.

"Oh. Ask away!" Marion said.

"Do you know Oren Mackler?" Charlie asked.

Marion said, "Oh, well Peter has a helper named Oren. But I don't think I ever heard his last name."

"Can you describe Oren," Jackson asked.

Sherman replied, "Sure. Oren is a skinny young man, probably in his early or mid-twenties. He's maybe five foot nine or ten. He has short black hair. And he smells like pot. All of the time."

Marion added, "Oh, and he bows and scrapes to Peter. Step and fetch-it."

Charlie laughed, "I know what you mean. Peter must be hard to work for."

Sherman said, "I know I wouldn't work for him. Ever."

"Do you know the name Karen Pilling?" Charlie asked.

Neither Sherman nor Marion had ever heard that name.

Then Charlie asked, "Have you been to Northburn's studio?"

"No. We were going there for a sales meeting just before this show opened. But Peter changed that. We met here instead," Sherman explained.

Jackson and Charlie were just about to leave when Jackson asked, "Does the name Duffy Dot sound familiar?"

Sherman immediately laughed and said, "Too familiar! She used to work for Terry Small."

"Used to?" Jackson asked.

Sherman explained his wife's connection to Small and to Duffy Dot. He explained Terry Small's accident and injury. "Small is out of the picture, as far as the firm is concerned. Gertie Small, his wife, has turned the practice over to my wife, Sherry, and the other psychologist, Erlene Vigil. Gertie instigated the firing of Ms. Dot."

"Why?" Charlie asked.

"I'm told it was because Ms. Dot is or was having an affair with Terry Small," Sherman replied.

"Do you know Ms. Dot?" Jackson asked Marion and Sherman.

"I don't think I've never met her. I have only heard my wife talk about her," Sherman said.

Marion Fleeo said, "Oh, I don't think so. But a lot of locals come in here, looking at art, and never give me their names."

Jackson said, "Let me get photos of Oren Mackler, and Duffy Dot. Perhaps you'll recognize one or the other."

Jackson called Mike Pelis and asked him to email the drivers' license photos of Mackler and Dot to him. Within a few minutes Jackson had the drivers' license photos of both on his phone. He showed the photos to Sherman and Marion.

"Oh. Yes, that's Peter helper. And the woman looks very familiar," Marion said.

Sherman said, "Yes that's Peter's Oren. And the woman...oh my god, Marion, that's the sad sack that came in looking for work!"

"Oh, you're right. Never got her name. She was such a pathetic one."

"When did she come in looking for work?" Charlie asked.

"It was not long ago. I don't remember the day. She seemed to be in a fog of some kind," Sherman said. "You know, the way people who take prescription drugs for depression and such seem out of it."

Marion added, "Oh. She liked Peter's work. I remember I gave her the brochure."

Marion gave Charlie a brochure. Charlie showed it to Jackson commenting, "It has a map to Northburn's showroom and studio."

Jackson asked, "One more thing. When did you last see Oren?"

Sherman and Marion looked at each other, then Sherman responded, "It's been a little while. We thought he'd deliver the additional work from Peter. Oren does all the deliveries. But Peter himself brought the work in the other day. Haven't seen Oren since probably right after the opening."

Jackson and Charlie thanked Sherman and Marion.

Left their cards and asked the gallery people to please call if they thought of anything to add or if they saw or heard from Oren or Ms. Dot.

## CHAPTER 51

Emma Spruce called Jackson, "So, having a good visit to Taos?"

Jackson laughed and said, "It is more interesting every day. What are you doing?"

"I had a very strange call, an unattended death in a tree in a very remote forested and mountainous area. In fact, it was discovered by Charles McMarlin, Uncle Charles!" Emma explained.

"What? We better get together and exchange info. Would you and Harry come to dinner tonight? I'll make Charlie cook!" Jackson asked.

"Love to. What time? Can I bring something?" Emma replied.

"Six-thirty. You remember where this vacation rental is?"

"I remember. You want me to bring something? Bread? Dessert?"

"Charlie likes to do it all. Just bring Harry," Jackson said.

Charlie overheard Jackson's end of the conversation. He said, "You pimping me out? I gather I am fixing a dinner tonight. How many people? Who?"

"Just Emma and Harry. I know you'll wow us, as

usual," Jackson said slapping Charlie on the shoulder.

The doorbell of the vacation rental rang. Jackson answered the door to find FBI Agents Sam Wester and Carlos Sanchez shivering on the doorstep. Neither of the young agents was wearing an overcoat.

"Hey! You're here. Didn't know when to expect you. Where are your coats?" Jackson said laughing.

The two young men hurried inside and closed the door. Sam said, "We left our coats in Wyoming! We were sent to Phoenix for goodness sakes."

Carlos added, "Then Dr. Watson informed us we were coming here."

Charlie said, "You are just in time. I'm fixing dinner for us all and Emma and Harry."

"Perfect timing, as always!" Sam said.

Jackson asked, "You drive or fly?"

"We drove. Just took the SUV that Chan O'Brien was driving. She said it was alright. We were supposed to fly. The FBI jet was going to bring us right here to Taos. But, without any notice to us, it was re-routed to San Francisco for some really important agent. So Chan said to take her car."

"Who's Chan O'Brien?" Charlie asked.

"FBI newbie agent in Phoenix. Good agent! She'll go far," Carlos explained.

"You took a Phoenix Division SUV?" Jackson asked.

"We did. She said we could!" Sam insisted.

"I'll call Watson. He'll smooth it out," Jackson said shaking his head.

Sam added, "What's to smooth out?"

"You kids!" Charlie said laughing. "I have to run. Gotta go to the grocery if we're going to have any kind of dinner at all. See you later."

Charlie left Jackson, Sam, and Carlos to exchange intel. He went to the grocery. It was early afternoon and the store was not busy at all. Charlie had formed a dinner menu in his head as he drove to the store. He grabbed a cart and began his sweep of the store looking for the ingredients he wanted. He made a quick turn into an aisle and bumped into a tall black-haired man wearing a black suit and tie, white shirt, and shiny black dress shoes.

Charlie did a double-take and almost screamed. It was Burkie. "Wha, wha, what are you doing here?" Charlie stammered.

"Hello to you Charlie!" Burkie said as he hugged Charlie. "Cooking tonight?"

"Uh, yes, dinner for six at six-thirty. What are you doing?" Charlie said.

"My dear friend, your sweetie, is so busy with tax work right now that I thought it would more efficient if I just came to see you," Burkie said. "By the way, Henry sends his love."

"Uh. Well what can I do for you?"

Burkie explained, "Since you need to get your shopping done, I'll get to the point. The spirits, the souls, of quite a few are in need of some justice, your kind of justice. These spirits are lost, restless right now. They were unexpectedly separated from their human form. The lights that were seen with the clothes were some of these spirits."

"How'd you know about the lights, the clothes?" Charlie asked.

"I just do. I am included in the information stream I guess is the best way to say it. But, what you need to know is that the lights are real and that you can identify who they are, or were, and how to stop the evil that unnecessarily intersected their lives. Don't discount anything you see. What's for dinner?" Burkie said as calmly as always.

"Uh, beef tenderloin steaks, sweet potato fries, orange slices, salad, and cake. Uh."

"What kind of cake? Ice cream?" Burkie asked.

"Chocolate cake, of course. Uh, no ice cream tonight. Too cold out."

"Good choice. This tangle of people and events that you and Jackson are dealing with is not as personally dangerous for you as some other cases you've been involved with, but it has some true evil sloshing around in it. If I can help you further, I will. This evil feels like it has been a long-running episode. Time to shut it down. Be careful, as always," Burkie said as he began to fade from view.

Charlie looked around to see if anyone witnessed the appearance. No one was in sight. With a final waft of the very comforting aroma that Burkie always emits, and a brief flash of cobalt blue light, Burkie was gone.

Charlie stood still for a few moments. He had to think about what Burkie had said to him. Then, when he felt ready, he finished his shopping and returned to the vacation rental.

As Charlie was preparing dinner, Jackson came in to uncharacteristically offer to help. Charlie gave Jackson the salad to assemble. While they worked on dinner, Sam and Carlos sat in the living room in front of the fireplace watching TV.

Charlie said to Jackson in a low voice, "You know that entity that comes out of the blue light? The one I've told you about before?"

Jackson replied, "Yes. I know who you mean."

"Well he was at the grocery store."

Jackson smiled and said, "Really? Like just at the store? Shopping?"

"No. Not like that. He just showed up to tell me the lights with the clothes are spirits of people, dead people, who we can identify. And that we should ID them. Also he said there is a person or persons who have been doing some evil stuff for a long time and that we have to stop them."

"That's what we do," Jackson assured Charlie.

"He said to keep our eyes open and believe what we see," Charlie continued.

"Glad to. I try to make that happen every day," Jackson said.

"This is real," Charlie insisted.

"I know. Your friend has helped us before. I know it is not easy to take in and believe what is in front of you when it is so horrifying and evil that you really don't want to know about it. Sometimes I want to turn away from information because it makes me sick. There have been people that we have stopped who were doing things so aberrant and hideous that it sorely tested my ability to continue with this work. I appreciate the support your friend gives us. Tell him thank you from me," Jackson said.

"Yes. I'll tell him," Charlie replied.

"Wait until you hear the incredible story of the Northburn sculpture in Phoenix. Emma has a story to tell us, too, a body in a tree that Uncle Charles found on his property. We really have to hurry up and put this entire picture puzzle together," Jackson said.

"Body in a tree?" Charlie asked.

"That's what she said. This is going to be a good dinner in so many ways," Jackson remarked.

## CHAPTER 52

Emma and Harry arrived at exactly six-thirty. Dinner was ready. The party sat down to eat and immediately began sharing information. FBI Agents Sam Wester and Carlos Sanchez were well acquainted with Emma and Harry. They had all met and worked together on previous FBI investigations in northern New Mexico. It was a pleasant reunion over dinner.

Harry said, "Emma has a very unusual unattended death to recount to you. Uncle Charles McMarlin discovered the body just a couple of days ago."

Jackson said, "That's what I am anxious to hear about."

Sam asked, "Who is Uncle Charles?"

Harry answered, "He is my old friend Michael McMarlin's uncle. I've known them both since Michael and I were in grade school. I think of them as family. Everyone calls Charles Uncle Charles. He has a large ranch in the mountains above and behind Peter Northburn's property."

Emma told the group, "Well, morning before last Uncle Charles called in a 911 on a body he found in a tree."

Sam interrupted, "In a tree?"

Emma responded, "Yep. In a tree. Uncle Charles was out riding his horse around on his property. He rides regularly: patrols his land, looks for signs of poachers, problems of any kind. He likes to ride. Well, it was early morning and the sun just happened to catch and glint off a silver chain hanging from the body's clothing."

Sam interrupted again, "A chain? Was the body bound up in the tree?"

Jackson said, "Let her finish..."

Sam said, "Okay okay. This is a great story so far."

Emma smiled and continued, "The chain was more of a fashion accessory than any kind of restraint. If Uncle Charles hadn't been up on his horse and riding on that very trail at that very time of the morning, he'd never have noticed the body in the tree. The body was up high in the tree and the tree was back in the woods about twenty or thirty feet from the trail. It was an odd set of circumstances.

"The snow was a couple of feet deep or more in most places. The wind can drift up the snow and if the sun doesn't hit it, it just gets deeper as the winter progresses. This discovery site was way up in the mountains about two miles from Charles' ranch house. It was inaccessible except by horse or ATV.

"Uncle Charles had three ATVs for us to use. The first responders were two volunteer firefighters from the Rio Fernando Fire District. That's a small station in the Taos Canyon. It is primarily supported by the people who live in or use the Taos Canyon. And the New Mexico State Police sent a young officer. I know most of the state police officers, but I'd never seen this guy before. He looked so young to me that it occurred to me he might be a new recruit. Anyway, I joined the officer, firefighters, and Uncle Charles, who led us out to the site.

"The body was hugging the tree while sitting on, or rather, straddling a limb. The feet were ten feet above the ground."

Sam interrupted again, "Ten feet! What kind of creature did you find?"

Everyone laughed. Emma picked up the story, "Just a skinny young man. What he wasn't wearing was interesting. He wasn't wearing a coat, or hat, or gloves. He just had on a shirt, leather vest, jeans, and boots. There were no external signs of injuries or wounds. He likely froze to death. The overnight temperatures up there this time of year drop to zero and below. The body is still in Albuquerque in autopsy."

"So, he was sitting high up in a tree in the cold, snowy forest without a hat or coat. How did he get to the site? How'd he get up in the tree?" Carlos asked.

"No signs of a vehicle or horse or anything in the area. If he hiked, then the snow or windblown snow covered his tracks. There was nothing to indicate how he got there. The tree was a good climbing tree. I think he just climbed up there. He was positioned the way you see bear cubs in trees. His arms hung over the branches and probably around the trunk until he died. Then they loosened their grip on the tree, but he froze in that position. When we took him down, his arms were hooked over the branches at his armpits. His legs were hanging down on either side of the branch he was straddling," Emma explained.

"I don't see a lot of bear cubs hugging trees," Sam quipped. "I live in Chicago."

Emma laughed, "Well, like in the cartoons. You've seen bear cubs in trees in cartoons haven't you?"

"Oh sure. Like in the cartoons!" Sam replied.

"Anything in his pockets?" Carlos asked.

"No ID, no wallet. A cigarette lighter was all there was."

"So he could have climbed down, built a campfire and survived," Carlos concluded.

Sam added, "Could have been a suicide."

Emma responded, "I've seen stranger suicides!"

Jackson asked, "Any reported missing person that matched the young man?"

Emma said, "Not that I know anything about. The ID will come from his fingerprints, dental, or DNA. The New Mexico State Police officer didn't seem to snap on any missing person. Maybe they have ID'd him by now. I haven't heard."

Jackson said, "I'll call Mike Pelis about this right now."

Since dinner had evolved to dessert by the fireplace, Jackson went back to the kitchen table to call Mike Pelis. "Sorry to call so late, Mike. But, Emma Spruce has filled us in on the body recovery from Charles McMarlin's ranch. Have you made any headway on an ID? Anyone know who he is?"

Jackson listened while Mike briefed him. Then Jackson thanked Mike and returned to the group by the fireplace.

"Any news?" Sam asked.

"Yes big news!" Jackson said. "Mike said the body in

the tree was Oren Mackler! Fingerprints were on file from a DUI arrest."

"Whaaaat?" Charlie exclaimed.

Sam asked, "Who is that?"

Jackson replied, "Oren is, or perhaps was, Peter Northburn's assistant! What the hell was he doing in that tree on Charles' ranch?"

"That Peter Northburn seems to be some kind of vortex for strange activity," Carlos said. "I want to meet him."

Jackson said, "You are going to. I think it is time to visit the artist's studio. You and Sam should go to Northburn's place tomorrow, in the morning perhaps. Go as art shoppers."

Charlie interjected, "First, maybe you should go to the Fleeo Gallery. Talk to Sherman Kroyton, the art salesman. Look at Northburn's work. Then when you get to Northburn's studio, you'll be able to appropriately gush about his work."

Jackson added, "That's a good idea, Northburn reportedly has a big ego. Feed it."

Charlie said, "We have so many lines in the water right now. We need to reel in some facts."

Harry asked, "What do you mean?"

"We sent the box of clothes from Charles McMarlin's barn to Quantico for DNA evaluation. Haven't got that info yet. Both Karen Pilling's car and Oren Mackler's car are being processed at the FBI lab in Albuquerque. No results from that yet. Now we just sent Duffy Dot's car to the lab, too. Plus, we are still looking for Dot," Charlie explained.

Jackson said, "Charlie, you and I are going to visit Terry Small's office tomorrow morning. According to Sherman Kroyton, Duffy Dot was recently fired from her job there. Maybe we can track her down."

Emma asked, "How are you going to determine Oren Mackler's sojourn to that tree?"

Charlie answered, "Good question. I don't know. First, we'll have to find out when Mackler was last seen, and who was the last person to see him."

Sam offered, "My money's on Peter Northburn."

## CHAPTER 53

Sam and Carlos began the morning clothes shopping in Taos. They bought coats and ensembles that they thought would be appropriate art tourist clothes. They both liked hip length leather overcoats. Sam went for jeans and a flannel shirt. While Carlos was sure sturdy khaki canvas pants with a cotton work shirt and fleece vest was best. The young FBI agents both opted for work boots.

So attired, they went to the Fleeo Gallery minutes after it opened. Sherman was there. He greeted them and showed them Northburn's artwork. The agents didn't reveal their FBI identities until after Sherman had given them the full sales spiel. When they did introduce themselves, Sherman was pleased to give them any other info they asked for.

Sam asked, "How often do you see Northburn? How often does he visit the gallery?"

"Hardly ever. He came to the opening, of course. And, he made one delivery of additional pieces. Marion just emails him," Sherman explained.

"You told Special Agent Avery that Oren Mackler usually made the deliveries. When was the last time he was here?" Carlos asked.

Sherman replied, "Not since right after the opening.

We didn't get additional work until Peter brought a load. Oren was here to deliver the couple of loads for the show, right before the opening. Then he was here for the opening... umm...and I guess maybe once after that. Northburn has a van that Oren drives. I know they left it here once or twice, and Oren always drove the van. Peter never drove the van that I saw, until this last delivery. He drives a Mercedes sedan. It's dark blue or black."

"What time is Peter's studio open for visitors?" Sam asked.

"I don't know that I've ever heard. I think since he lives there, that if he's up and about, he'll sell you some art."

"Okay. Thanks. We're going to visit him, as art buyers. If you hear from him don't tell him we're coming or who we are, okay?" Sam instructed.

"No problem, I won't mention anything about you, if by any long-shot I hear from him," Sherman said.

Sam and Carlos were still driving the FBI's Suburban that they'd taken from Phoenix. Sam thought maybe it was too big and governmental-looking to take to Northburn's place. Carlos insisted they would seem more like tourists in the Suburban. So, they drove up Taos Canyon towards Peter Northburn's studio.

"When they turned off the highway the big SUV took Northburn's steep driveway with a squeaky groan. "Uh oh, Chan's not going to like the sound of that," Sam noted.

Carlos responded, "I don't think Chan has any personal attachment to this big-ass car."

"Still, I hate to return it in sub-standard condition."

"You really should be more concerned about rolling up the cuffs of your jeans like that. Who, other than Marlon Brando, does that?" Carlos asked Sam.

"I think it makes me look more cosmopolitan!" Sam responded.

"What cosmopolitan metropolis are you thinking of? Okay, okay. How are we going to play this with Northburn?"

"Let's flirt with him. That'll either amuse him or anger him."

"Maybe neither. Maybe he'll flirt back and then what?"

"Yikes. He might. Okay, I'll flirt with him and you act jealous."

"Okay, those jean cuffs will authenticate your behavior!" Carlos said laughing.

They walked up the steps to the front door of the showroom. They rang the bell. No answer. They rang the bell again. Still no answer. They waited a few more minutes before wandering over to the adjacent metal building. They heard small noises from within the other building as they got closer to it. They stepped under the covered walkway and knocked on the door.

The tall handsome blonde-haired man who answered the door initially seemed highly annoyed, but quickly changed his demeanor to that of a welcoming salesperson. Peter Northburn said, "Oh, hello!"

Sam explained, "We rang the front door bell! Nobody there. Do you know if Mr. Northburn's showroom is open today?"

Peter replied, "I'm Peter Northburn, and my showroom is open! I didn't hear you drive up. Come in!"

Sam and Carlos stepped into the kiln building. Immediately they saw the source of the noises they'd heard. Peter was unloading the kiln. They'd heard the clay pieces being put on the carts and the carts being moved around on the concrete floor.

Northburn said, "If you have a moment, I need to complete the unloading of this batch. Then we can go into the showroom."

Carlos asked, "Oh, you've just fired these?"

"The firing ended several days ago. The work is just now cool enough to remove from the kiln," Peter replied.

"Oh, fresh baked! I love the smell of fresh baked," Sam said as he moved close to the firing chamber's wide opening. Sam took an exaggerated sniff.

"Careful not to breathe in ash! The wood-fire creates ash that can hang in the air in there," Peter warned.

Sam coughed and stepped back. "Uuww! That smells weird. What's that smell?"

Peter laughed, "Must be the wood and the glaze and the clay! I'm so used to it; guess I don't smell what you do."

Carlos stepped close to the open door of the kiln's firing chamber and took a sniff. "That is a peculiar smell!"

Northburn laughed again, "Not to me. It's the same old smell of every wood-fired kiln. Let's head in to the showroom."

"So this is your kiln? It's wood-fired?" Carlos asked.

"Yes. This is it," Peter replied.

"Wow, it's so big!" Sam exclaimed.

Peter smiled and said, "It is a magnificent wood-fired kiln."

"Where did you get it?" Carlos asked.

"I built it. I laid every fire brick, and built the steel skeleton!" Peter said with great pride.

Sam gushed, "You are so talented. This is a grand kiln!"

Peter smiled at Sam and said, "It's the best wood-fired kiln in the country."

"Ohhh, and these are beautiful!" Sam said as he looked at the work that had just come out of the kiln.

"Yes, this load fired perfectly!" Peter said.

Carlos added, "The surfaces are stunning. What color!"

"Yes. Let's go into the showroom. Gentlemen," Peter said motioning at the door Sam and Carlos had entered through. "Follow me."

Peter flipped off the overhead lights in the kiln building and led the way out to the covered walkway. Sam took a quick look back at the kiln. He saw a vivid green vaporous light cloud slide out of the firing chamber onto the concrete floor. It was a flat cloud of light that glided along the floor. Sam tapped Carlos on the arm, "Look!"

Carlos saw it. "That's just like we saw in Mexico! When José's brother's body was in that house. That green light was just like this. Light that moves like liquid."

Peter called out from the walkway, "What's keeping you boys? Come on. It's cold out here."

At the sound of Peter Northburn's voice, the green

light oozing out of the kiln vanished. Sam and Carlos looked at each other and nodded.

Sam and Carlos hurried out to the covered walkway and followed Peter into the studio space.

"Is this your storage room?" Carlos asked.

Peter sighed audibly and said, "This is my studio."

"I see. So, this is where you manufacture the art," Carlos remarked.

"I don't manufacture. I create," Peter corrected.

Sam asked, "Looks like a lot of work. A lot of time. Do you have a staff who do some of the production, or do you do it all?"

Peter Northburn said, "I do all of the creating, I make the work, I glaze the work, and I fire the work."

"Sounds like you do it all! Fantastic! You must work all of the time!" Sam said.

"It is my passion," Peter affirmed.

"I've read that you show all over the country. Who does your shipping?" Carlos asked.

Peter Northburn asked, "Are you looking for a job?"

"No. No. I am just fascinated with how you do all of this," Carlos replied.

"All of what?" Northburn asked coyly.

"Being the superstar artist!" Sam gushed.

"I do as much myself as I possibly can. I have a helper who drives my van and delivers to exhibitions. I try not to ship by freight companies. I've had too many losses with the freight companies."

"What kind of losses?" Carlos asked.

"Lost shipments! The freight never made it to

scheduled destinations," Peter explained.

"Ah. How horrible for you!" Sam exclaimed.

"Horrible and expensive!" Peter added.

"So your helper is more dependable that the freight companies?" Carlos said.

"Usually!" Peter said. "He has flaked out this week."

"What do you mean?" Carlos asked.

"He hasn't shown up," Peter Northburn said.

"Is he sick?" Sam asked compassionately.

"To tell you the truth, he's a stoner. He's probably off on an extended high."

"Well, can we see the showroom?" Sam asked.

"Yes, right this way," Peter said as he opened the door into the showroom.

Sam and Carlos looked around the spacious room at every piece of ceramic on display. Sam cooed over the work and Carlos remained appreciative but distant. Carlos made an obvious effort to quell Sam's apparent infatuation with Peter Northburn. Peter noticed the adoring attention that Sam was paying him. Peter's ego almost noticeably swelled.

"Sam, you are truly an art lover," Peter said.

"You don't need to spread that love beyond the work!" Carlos admonished Sam.

Sam blushed and said to Carlos, "I can't help it that Peter's work affects me so deeply."

Peter Northburn said to Sam, "I appreciate that. You are always welcome here. Come back any time. Is there any piece you are particularly fond of?"

"Ohhh, I love this plate," Sam said as he pointed to the platter closest to him. "Carlos, can we buy this?"

As Peter picked up the platter, he said, "Please! It is my gift to you."

Sam blushed for real. He said, "Peter! Thank you. We will treasure this."

After a few more rounds of Sam gushing and Peter casually reveling in the accolades, Sam and Carlos left the Northburn compound.

As they drove back to the vacation rental, Sam said, "Wow, what an ego that guy has! That was easier than I would have ever imagined."

Carlos said, "You were such a good flirt! My god. That was your best performance yet. And we got a sample of the work."

"We should send that plate thing on to Quantico for analysis. There is something very peculiar about the smell from that kiln. Maybe the lab can identify the stink factor," Sam said.

"And the green light! What about the green light? There is something so evil at that place!" Carlos said.

"I think the green light screams for investigation of that kiln."

"Then let's make sure that happens," Carlos agreed.

## CHAPTER 54

When Sam and Carlos recounted their trip to Northburn's place, Jackson agreed that the gift plate needed to go to Quantico lab ASAP. Charlie asked, "What did you smell in the kiln area?"

Carlos explained, "It had an acrid high note and a putrid low note."

Sam added, "It left a taste in my mouth. Really, it did. A very bad taste."

"Emma said that the smoke from the kiln smelled somewhat like a crematorium," Charlie said.

"Yuk. You think? You think Peter might be playing Hansel and Gretel up there?" Sam suggested. "Will the lab be able to get anything from the plate?"

"I don't know how the firing process in a kiln like that affects the chemical elements in the clay and glaze," Carlos said. "Something really smelled bad."

Sam said, "But there was something else...that we saw in the kiln building." Sam explained the vivid green light they saw crawling out of the firing chamber and along the floor in the kiln building, and recounted their experience in Mexico with a similar fluid green light.

Charlie said, "That's important. Northburn is up to something. We need to take some ash samples from the inside of that kiln."

Jackson responded, "Can't do that without a warrant. Unless we can encourage him to give us a sample."

Carlos suggested, "We need one of those fire bricks from the kiln. Maybe a brick that the green light slid over."

"Good plan. Jackson and I should visit Peter. See what he'll tell us. He doesn't know we found Karen Pilling's DNA on the items he discarded in the stream. He doesn't know Oren is dead. He doesn't know what we know."

"He might just give you a brick. He might give you a whole lot more than he knows he's giving you!" Carlos suggested.

Jackson said, "Watson is expediting the lab work on everything we've sent. So we should know about this plate thing and the clothes as soon as possible."

Charlie said, "Right now, Jackson and I are going to the Small Psychology office to talk to Sherman's wife about Duffy Dot. We still haven't found Ms. Dot."

"We're going to go get lunch. Have to get that nasty smell out of my sinuses!" Sam told Charlie and Jackson.

"You did a good job up there at Northburn's. We'll see you later," Jackson affirmed.

When Jackson and Charlie finally found Small's office, Sherry Kroyton and Erlene Vigil had just returned from lunch. "You don't have a sign," Charlie said to the two women as he and Jackson stepped into the office.

Sherry said, "We have a new name. A new sign is ready and should be installed this afternoon. How can we help you?"

Jackson asked, "New name? Is this Terry Small's

office?"

"It was. Terry was badly injured in a hit and run accident. He's not going to be returning to work. We are the new owners of this practice," Sherry explained. She then introduced herself and Erlene to the two men.

Jackson said, "Nice to meet you both. I met your husband, Sherman, at the Fleeo Gallery. He gave us your address here. I'm FBI Special Agent Jackson Avery and this is Special Agent Charlie Black. If you have time, we'd like to ask you a few questions?"

"Sure. Sherman said he'd talked to the FBI about Northburn and that you were interested in Duffy, too."

Charlie asked, "What happened to Terry Small?"

Erlene replied, "He was hit by a car in the parking lot here at the office. It was at night during a snow storm last month."

"Have the police found whoever hit him? Do they know what happened?" Charlie asked.

"No. Nothing. The police told me that they don't have any direction to go. No witness, other than Terry, and no information to follow up on. They probably never will identify the driver who hit him."

"There is no video surveillance on your building?" Jackson asked.

"No. We may have cameras soon though!" Sherry said.

"Well, we are here to find out what we can about Duffy Dot. She used to work here?" Charlie inquired.

Sherry and Erlene looked at each other, then Sherry said, "Duffy worked for Terry. We let her go when we took over. We don't need a receptionist."

"We can't locate her. She's not at her apartment. No one in the apartment complex has seen her lately. Her car was found abandoned in a campground in Taos Canyon."

"I don't know anything about her personal life," Erlene said.

"You might check the hospital. She could be over there with Terry," Sherry suggested.

"But she was fired," Charlie said.

"She and Terry are very close. Or they were," Sherry explained.

"Okay, we'll check in with Terry. We'll go over there next. If you talk to him, please don't announce us," Jackson said.

Sherry and Erlene both laughed. Sherry assured Jackson, "Don't worry. He doesn't talk to us."

The FBI agents found the hospital and Terry alone in his room. Jackson introduced himself and Charlie.

"Oh great. Now the FBI wants to talk to me! What about??" Terry whined.

Charlie ignored Terry's annoying tone and said with a smile, "Duffy Dot."

"Oh crap. What did she say?" Terry asked.

"Say about what?" Jackson inquired.

"I don't know! I am not really in touch with what's going on in the world. If you hadn't noticed, I am attached to this bed. Duffy is a crackpot."

Jackson asked, "What do you mean, crackpot? When did you see or talk to her last?"

"I don't know. She's delusional. I kicked her out of

here days ago. She hasn't darkened the door since. I don't think so anyway. I sleep a lot. They have me on serious pain meds!"

"What's she delusional about?"

"She thinks we're a couple or something," Terry said disgustedly. "As if! There's not enough tequila for that!"

"Are you involved with her? Personally?" Charlie posed.

"No! She's just crazy!" Terry insisted.

"Were you ever involved with her?" Jackson asked.

Terry Small hesitated, then said, "Women like me. A lot! They want me. Sometimes I give in to them."

"So you gave in to Duffy Dot, but no longer?" Charlie asked.

"Yes! That's it," Terry confirmed.

"Why did you cut off the relationship?"

"Duffy ruined my marriage. My wife is divorcing me because of Duffy."

"How'd she ruin your marriage?"

"She talked about our relationship. My wife found out!"

"If Duffy hadn't talked about your affair, would your marriage be okay?" Jackson asked.

"Duh?!" Terry exclaimed.

"Do you have any idea where she might be if she's not at her apartment? Where does she hang out?" Charlie asked.

That question sent Terry Small into a fit of laughing that threw him into a body-wide pain spasm. Jackson went out to the hall and called for a nurse.

Jackson and Charlie waited for the nurse to quiet Terry and make him as comfortable as possible. Then Jackson asked, "What was so amusing about that inquiry?"

Terry replied, "Duffy Dot has no life. She wouldn't be anywhere but the office or her apartment."

Jackson said, "She has no job that we know about, and she's not been to her apartment in at least a few days."

Terry responded in an angry voice, "Then I guess she's not anywhere."

Jackson and Charlie thanked Terry and left. On the way out of the hospital, Charlie noted, "Mr. Small is a very unhappy man!"

## CHAPTER 55

When Charlie and Jackson got back to the vacation rental it was time for dinner. Sam and Carlos were waiting for them at the house with pizzas on the table. "You read my mind!" Charlie exclaimed.

"And probably the minds of about seventy-five percent of America!" Sam said.

Jackson laid a healthy fire in the fireplace and suggested they eat dinner in the living room in front of the fire. Charlie threw together a salad. Jackson recounted for Sam and Carlos the weird reactions Terry Small had to their very simple questions about Duffy Dot. He reported that Sherry and Erlene had no ideas about where Ms. Dot might be.

Carlos said, "So, Dot's car is still being processed, and the only clue we have about the abandonment is the tie to Oren Mackler via his phone found in the car. Northburn told us that his assistant is a stoner. So the weed and money in Dot's car are likely to belong to Oren."

"We should have the results of Oren's autopsy by tomorrow. The New Mexico OMI sent Oren's personal effects, to the FBI in Dallas. There'll be a mountain of info coming as soon as the Bureau distills everything. The clothes, the vehicles, the femur," Charlie began.

"And my souvenir plate!" Sam interrupted.

"We really can't do much with Peter until we have something conclusive in-hand. If we just spook him, he might disappear," Jackson said.

"Let's all sleep on this. Maybe the morning will bring new ideas or new info," Charlie suggested.

## CHAPTER 56

Jackson's cell phone rang early the next morning. He was on the call for a long time. Charlie had made a rather elaborate breakfast of cinnamon rolls, eggs, and bacon, coffee, and cranberry juice. The breakfast was being put on the table as Sam and Carlos wandered in. They were all into the meal when Jackson joined them.

"Jackpot! What a breakfast spread. Nice work, Charlie," Jackson exclaimed as he sat at the table and loaded up a plate of food.

Charlie responded, "You are the happy special agent! What was that call?"

"Dr. Watson! He had all sorts of fantastic information for us." Between bites of cinnamon roll, egg, and bacon, Jackson explained, "Results from the DNA work with the big box of clothes matches six of the reported missing people to the clothes. Many of the clothes were too far gone to give up any DNA. But we do have six identified. All six came to the Taos area and vanished."

"When did they go missing?" Carlos asked.

"The dates range from a year ago back three years for the ID'd clothes from the missing persons reports."

"Six in three years," Charlie noted.

"If Karen Pilling is added to that, then there have

been seven that we can pinpoint," Carlos added.

"What about Duffy Dot?" Sam asked.

"We still don't know about her," Charlie said. "She may be off visiting her family or something."

"What else did Dr. Watson have?" Sam asked.

"The key that jammed in the ignition switch of Karen Pilling's Camry was the key for Oren's Camry."

"We all kind of knew that was the case," Charlie remarked.

"Now it is verified. And Duffy Dot's steering wheel, door handles, gear shift, mirror, etc. were all wiped clean of any prints. However the plastic sandwich box of cash had a couple of prints. They are still working on whose."

"Check the souvenir plate. I was oh-so-careful not to smear where Peter touched it when he handed it to me!" Sam said.

"They'll have that plate today. It is on its way," Charlie said.

"You took my plate? I hope you didn't take it out of the paper bag I had it in!" Sam exclaimed.

"It was picked up early this morning. It left here in the paper bag. The agent who came for it drove from Albuquerque in the snowstorm very very early."

"Snow? I hadn't even looked out. The smell of bacon is so intoxicating!!!" Sam said.

Sam and Carlos went to the kitchen window. It had snowed overnight. Taos was a wonderful white, quiet winter world. Charlie made a second pot of coffee. The men continued with breakfast.

"Somehow the snow here is more poetic than it is in

Chicago," Sam noted.

"Dry snow is fluffier," Carlos explained.

Jackson said, "The femur was ID'd as a Louisiana man who went missing in Taos just over a year ago."

"Now we're up to eight in three years! That is definitely serial killer territory," Sam exclaimed. "What was Oren's cause of death?"

"Oren died of exposure. He froze to death," Jackson explained.

"So we can't blame Peter for that. Hmmm. What if Peter isn't the serial killer here. What if it was Oren all along?" Carlos suggested.

"The adrenaline level in Oren's body was very high when he died according to the autopsy. That tells us he might have been afraid or stressed," Jackson said.

"I'm sure he was! He was up a tree! In the forest in the freezing weather! With no hat or coat or gloves! That is a stressful situation!" Charlie said.

Sam asked, "But why was he up in the tree? Why was he out there in the middle of nowhere? Freezing..."

"Maybe he was running from Duffy Dot. She's described by everyone as a large individual. Maybe Oren mistook her for Bigfoot," Carlos suggested. "Or, maybe he was running from himself in some existential crisis of conscience."

"Have another cinnamon roll!" Charlie laughed.

Jackson said, "We need to have a talk with Peter Northburn. Charlie and I will go up there after my stomach no longer requires so much of my body's available resources. Great breakfast, Mr. Black!"

"Thank you so much," Charlie replied.

Jackson's cell phone rang again. He got up and took the call in the living room. It was a short call. He returned to the dining table and said to Sam and Carlos, "You boys have to go up to Uncle Charles' ranch. He spied Peter Northburn hanging some clothes in the woods early this morning. Go get those clothes. Get tire impressions, too, if you can. At least get photos. New snow up there, and Uncle Charles said Northburn rode in on his ATV."

Charlie asked, "Did Uncle Charles get a photo?"

"Yes he did!" Jackson replied.

"Great! Hope the camera in his cell phone worked. Hope Peter wasn't out of range," Charlie said.

Sam and Carlos got directions to Charles McMarlin's ranch. The four FBI agents drove out. Sam and Carlos headed up Taos Canyon to Uncle Charles' and Jackson and Charlie to Northburn's.

## CHAPTER 57

Carlos easily found the turnoff to Charles McMarlin's ranch. Charles was waiting for them in front of the ranch house. He had two ATVs ready to go. After quick introductions, Charles mounted one of the ATVs to lead them to the clothes site. Carlos drove Sam on the other ATV. It was a long rough cold ride through the deep snow and dense forest to the clearing where Northburn had been displaying the clothes. When they reached the clearing, Sam and Carlos were stunned by the odd display.

From the dark-colored slipper shoes, the dark blue leggings, the orange tunic covered by an additional red cape-like tunic, all the way up to the red beret, the clothes were staged to look like a person standing.

"What the hell?" Carlos blurted.

Charles McMarlin said, "That artist is a freak!"

Sam was taking pictures of the clothes, the clearing, the ground, everything, with his cell phone as he carefully moved closer to the display.

Carlos hung back with Uncle Charles. "Jackson said you got a picture of Northburn doing this. May I see it?" Carlos asked.

"You bet. I took a few pictures, I think. I've never used the camera before. Only had the phone a few weeks,"

Uncle Charles explained as he handed his phone to Carlos.

Carlos brought up the images from the phone's camera function. There it was. Peter Northburn caught in the act of hanging and arranging the clothes on the tree. Charles had snapped Northburn taking the plastic trash bag off the four wheeler's rack behind the seat. The next shot was of Northburn at the base of the tree beginning to take the clothes out of the bag. Then four more pictures of Northburn hanging and arranging the clothes. Then two shots of Northburn standing back admiring his work. Two more shots of Peter Northburn returning to his ATV. One of those pictures had a peculiar and noteworthy element in it.

"Where were you when you took these pictures?" Carlos asked Uncle Charles.

Uncle Charles showed Carlos to a spot far back in the trees. "I rode up this way on Lomoto, my horse. We heard the ATV."

"We?"

"Lomoto and me. I left her way back there and walked or rather snuck up to this spot. It was very quiet up here after he turned off his ATV. He was humming while he was doing this whatever it is he's doing here. Hanging clothes. Charlie showed me how to take pictures. The camera was silent. I had no idea if I was supposed to focus or anything. I just took picture after picture. I hoped the camera would take care of the details."

"You did a great job! Look at this second to the last shot. There is a ball of light over the clothes. It covers the right shoulder, but you can see through it. It appears to be gold or yellow colored. Then in the next shot, from this exact same vantage, no change in the camera position, the light ball is gone. Interesting."

Uncle Charles said, "I've seen lots of those lights up here. I've been here evenings when it's looked like some kind of light show."

"Really?! Cool," Carlos remarked. "Did you see this one this morning?"

"Don't recall seeing it. But I was focused on the cell phone camera!" Charles said laughing. "I was sure I was going to drop the phone in the snow. Such an awkward thing to hold and take pictures with. Nothing to hold onto. I was so distracted while taking the pictures; I didn't even worry about him seeing me."

"You did a fine job! Thanks. May I email these pictures to Jackson and my own phone?"

"You can do whatever you want with them!"

Sam found Carlos and Charles in a thicket in the forest pretty far away from the clearing. "You guys hiding from me?"

"It's always about you! No. This is where Uncle Charles was hiding when he photographed Peter Northburn in the act of displaying the clothes!!"

Carlos showed Sam the photos on Uncle Charles' phone. "Wow. This is it for Northburn! If those very large women's clothes belong to the large woman I think they belong to, then we can probably make that at least nine people in three years," Sam said.

"What nine people?" Uncle Charles asked.

Sam explained, "Nine people who went missing in the past three years, who have now been linked to Peter

Northburn through DNA from their clothes. You have been a ginormous part of this investigation. Thank goodness you saved the clothes!"

Uncle Charles asked, "Do you mean you think Northburn, that artist, is a serial killer or kidnapper or something?"

"I do!" Sam replied.

"Me, too!" Carlos added.

"Holy Christmas! I knew I didn't like him. Did he kill that boy I found in the tree?" Charles asked.

"That was Northburn's helper, Oren Mackler. He died of exposure. But I personally think Northburn had some hand in it," Sam explained.

"Guess I'll keep up my patrols of the ranch! Never know what's lurking out in the forest," Uncle Charles said shaking his head.

"Let's gather those clothes and get back to Taos. We need to send them on to Quantico immediately," Carlos said.

## CHAPTER 58

Jackson and Charlie were standing in Peter Northburn's showroom chatting away with the artist about how lovely his work is, when the email with Uncle Charles' photos from earlier that morning came through to Jackson's cell.

Jackson noticed that in the pictures of Northburn, returning to his ATV after hanging the clothes, his coat was open and the plaid flannel shirt he was wearing that morning is the same one he was still wearing, right there in front of them. Jackson handed his phone to Charlie. "Take a look," Jackson directed Charlie.

Jackson addressed Peter Northburn, "Mr. Northburn, we are FBI Special Agents. We'd like to talk with you about your operation here." Jackson and Charlie showed Northburn their IDs and badges.

Peter Northburn didn't flinch, "You sure can. What's up?"

"You have an assistant, Oren Mackler?" Charlie asked.

"I do. Though he hasn't shown up for work in days! What's he done now? He's a serious stoner. I imagine he'll wander in sometime. He'll need money," Peter said casually.

"Let me start at the beginning. What brought us to New Mexico? A woman named Karen Pilling was reported missing. Does that name mean anything to you?" Jackson said.

"Not that comes to mind. She's missing?" Northburn said pensively.

"Yes. She's missing. But we found her car and some items from her clothing."

"Her car! That sounds like you're on the right track then. Where did you find her car?" Peter responded.

"Mora, New Mexico. It was stolen from a gas station and then left in a field. We found the key to Oren Mackler's car in Pilling's stolen car."

"Oh my god! Oren??! What has he been doing? Did he steal her car?" Peter asked.

"Pilling's car was same make as Oren's car, but a newer model," Jackson clarified.

"I can't imagine why Oren would...," Peter began.

"But then we also have notions, buttons, zippers, rivets, from Pilling's clothes that you put in the ice in a stream just across the highway from here. What should we make of that?" Jackson asked.

"What?? That I put somewhere? Not possible. No. Not me. Maybe Oren, but not me," Peter insisted.

"But you were seen doing it. We have an eyewitness," Charlie mentioned.

"I don't remember ever even being across the highway. What's over there?"

"The Carson National Forest land specifically," Charlie said.

"Your eyewitness is mistaken. That's all there is to it," Peter said flatly.

"Moving on. We have surveillance footage of Oren at the gas station in Mora asking about Pilling's car. The owner of the station said the car was left there and then stolen and later abandoned in a field in Mora," Jackson said.

"Oren, again. He must have been involved in something..." Peter began.

"There is also surveillance footage of your Mercedes at that gas station from the previous week. Your Mercedes pulled in at the edge of the station parking lot and Oren got in and then out and then back in your car."

"Not my Mercedes!" Peter insisted.

"The license plate image captured by the station's camera as you drove out, says it is your car. Same model and color."

"Oren must have taken my license plate. You know he associates with drug people, and Mora is a known drug haven," Peter informed them.

"And Karen Pilling's cell phone pinged the tower that phones in Mora ping. It pinged at that same day and time that your car is seen in the gas station. Where is Karen Pilling?" Jackson continued.

"I have no idea. I think you need to talk to Oren Mackler," Peter said casually.

"Does the name Duffy Dot mean anything to you?" Charlie asked Peter.

"Not a thing," Peter replied.

"Okay. Within the hour we will have a warrant to search your property. So in the meantime, why don't we sit down here on your sofa? I have a few more questions for you," Jackson said.

"I should call my attorney," Peter suggested.

"If you like. You're not under arrest. We just need some things cleared up. You've been helpful, and we appreciate that," Jackson said.

"Okay. Let's sit. You boys want a beer or coffee or something?" Northburn asked.

"I'm fine." Charlie said.

"I have my water," Jackson said. "But you get whatever you need. We'll wait."

Peter took a bottle of water from behind the showroom reception desk and display counter. "I'm fine," he said as he sat on the stool behind the desk.

Jackson and Charlie sat at either end of the couch. "You sold a sculpture to a woman named Lisa Mordant."

"Did I? I sell a lot of art," Peter said smiling.

"This particular piece was in your show at the Fleeo Gallery. Ms. Mordant lives in Phoenix. Does that ring a bell?" Charlie asked.

"Oh yes, the old cowgirl from Phoenix!" Peter said with a laugh.

"Yes, well, the sculpture fell and broke. It broke open and do you know what was inside of it?" Charlie asked.

"I imagine it had a steel armature inside. That's how I build them," Peter replied.

"There was some steel inside. But, there was also a human bone," Jackson said.

"What are you talking about?" Peter Northburn said with a measure of defiance in his voice.

"Yes, a human bone. A femur. A man's femur. A Louisiana man who went missing on a visit to Taos," Jackson continued.

"That could only have been put there by me or Oren. And it wasn't me!"

"Really. You let Oren build your sculptures?"

"He is my assistant. He assists me in all sorts of ways. He can build an armature and begin putting the clay over it."

"What else does he do?"

"He moves wood. He stokes the kiln during firings. He delivers. He is an assistant."

"Where do you think he got the femur?" Charlie asked.

"I have no idea. Like I said, he consorts with drug people," Peter replied.

"So you don't really do everything here. What are your responsibilities?"

"Don't be ridiculous! I am the creator. I am the artist."

"But you don't make everything that has your name on it?"

"I do! If it has my name on it, I conceived it and made it."

"You just told us Oren does some of the fabrication," Charlie insisted.

"Just the basics. He never does any real artwork," Peter said offhandedly.

"Just to be clear, you create the work. Do you glaze it and put it in the kiln?" Jackson asked.

"Exactly. I do everything. Oren is just here to help me, if I ask him to. Ask him yourself," Northburn explained.

"Can't ask him. Oren Mackler is dead," Charlie told Peter.

"What?! He's just off on a drug thing," Peter said with a laugh.

"He really is dead, Peter," Jackson affirmed.

"Where? How?" Peter asked, genuinely surprised.

"He died in the forest, probably six to eight miles from here," Jackson said.

"How?" Peter asked.

"He froze to death," Jackson answered.

"That's too bad," Peter said.

"Peter, do you have an ATV? A four-wheeler?"

"Yes. Everyone in this area has one."

"Where is yours?"

"It's in a storage shed at the far end of my parking lot. Why do you ask?"

"We have pictures of you on an ATV this morning. You were photographed on property owned by a man named McMarlin. You were hanging clothing in a tree. What was that about?" Jackson inquired.

"What? This morning?"

"Yes, fairly early this morning, just after daylight. You hung a full woman's outfit in a tree."

"That's just something a shaman told me to do. Hang clothes in the trees, you know," Peter said casually.

"I don't know. Why would you do that? What's the point? Where do you get the clothes?" Charlie asked.

"I do it to bring good luck. I get the clothes from the

used clothing store in town."

"What's the name of that store? What's your shaman's name?" Jackson asked.

"I don't remember. It's on the highway in town. It is one of the shamans at the pueblo. I don't know his name."

"Do you have receipts for any of the clothing? We know you've been hanging clothes in the forest for a long time."

"I have not! What are you talking about?" Peter said.

"When did your shaman tell you to do this?" Charlie asked.

"Not long ago. I don't remember. He stopped by here one day. We got to talking. He told me to hang the clothes for good luck. I thought, what could it hurt?" Northburn explained.

"You know something Peter, I don't believe you," Jackson said. "I think we probably have a couple of agents outside by now. They're going to come in and sit with you until the warrant gets here. Then we're going to have more agents here to search your property. So at this point, consider calling your attorney."

"Are you arresting me?" Peter asked.

"What a good idea," Charlie said to Jackson.

Jackson said, "Peter Northburn you are under arrest for conspiracy to commit murder. How's that?"

"Murder?? Who?" Peter said indignantly.

"Maybe Karen Pilling," Charlie suggested.

"Where's the body?" Peter said smiling.

"Why do you ask?" Charlie said.

"Well, you haven't mentioned finding anything but her car and a zipper or something!" Peter said quickly. "What makes you think she's dead?"

"Where is she? Where is her body, Peter?" Jackson asked.

Peter didn't answer.

Jackson read Peter his Miranda rights and told him to sit on the couch. Jackson called in the two agents who'd come up from Albuquerque. They babysat Peter Northburn who was on the phone with his attorney.

Charlie asked one of the agents, "Did you bring the warrant?"

The FBI agent replied, "It's on the way. Dr. Watson told us to fly it up here as soon as we have it. It should be here very soon. The CSI van should be coming right behind us."

"Don't let him out of your sight," Jackson instructed the agents.

## CHAPTER 59

Jackson and Charlie waited at the highway end of Peter Northburn's driveway for the FBI crime scene team. The big van rolled slowly around the last curve before the driveway. Jackson stepped out in the road and waved them in. It was not an easy thing to maneuver the large vehicle off the highway and up the steep driveway. Once at the top of the driveway in Peter's parking lot, the van backed up to the kiln building. The FBI agent driving the van hopped out and said to Jackson, "We're going to start with the kiln unless you have other instructions for us."

"Go ahead. You do what you do as you think best," Jackson Avery replied.

"Oh and here's the warrant. Should I serve it or do you want to?" the driver said as he handed Jackson an envelope.

Jackson smiled at Charlie and said to the driver, "Thanks. We'll serve it."

Charlie said, "Let's go inside and make sure Peter is comfortable."

Jackson and Charlie found Peter Northburn sitting in the same place they'd left him, on the couch. One FBI agent was sitting behind the reception desk and the other was walking around the room. When Jackson entered, both agents stood more or less at attention.

Jackson said to the two agents, "Thanks. The CSI agents are here. Can you stay a bit longer?"

Both agents said they'd be happy to stay as long as needed.

Jackson then turned his attention to Peter. "Peter Northburn, this is the search warrant we've all been waiting on. I know you must be relieved. Your innocence in this matter finally can be verified."

Charlie asked, "Where is your attorney?"

Peter spoke, "He's on his way. I expect him within the hour."

"Excellent," Jackson said.

Charlie commented to Jackson, "They're starting the search with the kiln aren't they?"

Peter stood and said, "I have to be there if they are touching my kiln!"

Jackson said, "Fine, let's go out to the kiln."

The FBI crime scene investigators were already at work within the kiln building. Jackson and Charlie accompanied Peter Northburn through the studio and across the covered walkway to the kiln building.

"This kiln is huge!" Charlie remarked.

Peter easily slipped into his salesperson persona and said, "Yes, this is one of the largest wood-fired kilns in New Mexico. It certainly is one of the finest in the country."

"You can heat this up hot enough, with wood, to fire pottery?" Charlie asked.

Peter chuckled and replied, "Yes. This kiln fires at a high temperature of at least twenty-four hundred degrees

Fahrenheit. That's just over thirteen-hundred Celsius."

"That must take a lot of wood!" Charlie said.

"It does."

"Peter, where do you load that much wood?" Charlie asked.

"On the other side of the kiln is the firebox door. The fire is in there and takes continuous stoking throughout the firing process. The heat builds during the firing," Peter explained.

"Oh…show me the firebox," Charlie requested.

Charlie and Jackson followed Peter around to the other side of the kiln. The FBI CSI technicians were all around them taking samples from surfaces, as well as bagging and tagging various items. Peter was visibly annoyed at the intrusion.

"This steel door slides up, and the wood is fed into the fire through the opening," Peter said as he lifted up the sliding guillotine door of the firebox. "The fire sits on that grate, and the hot embers and ashes drop down into the ash box as the fire burns. The heat builds. It is pulled through the firing chamber towards the chimney. It is an ancient process," Peter explained.

"What pulls the heat through the chamber?" Charlie asked as if he was a student asking the master.

"The air in the kiln, starting at the firebox, grows hot and oxygen hungry. The fire pulls oxygen in through the air intake ports at the firebox. The chimney provides the heated air's way out, its path to more oxygen. The hot fired air in the kiln wants desperately to survive. It needs oxygen. It runs for the chimney and rides its own heat up and out. That creates the draft. Simply put, air enters the kiln at the air intake ports in front of the firebox and out at the chimney," Peter explained.

"Yes. Hot air rises," Jackson confirmed.

Peter glared at Jackson. Jackson laughed.

"You are not a centered sort of man, are you, Agent Avery?" Peter said to Jackson.

"I have no idea what you mean by 'centered sort,'" Jackson replied.

"You don't use the right side of your brain enough to balance the heavier use of the left side," Peter said.

"I use my entire brain all of the time. Nice of you to inquire though," Jackson responded.

Charlie interrupted the brewing argument with another question. "If this firebox is where the wood goes, it seems you'd have to add wood continuously to get the temperature up to twenty-four hundred degrees and hold it there long enough to fire the pottery. How do you do that?"

Peter answered, "You stoke the fire. By putting fast or slow burning wood in, the fire can be regulated as needed."

"But how often are you stoking it? For how long?"

"Depends on what you are firing, and the kiln. This kiln requires stoking about every three or four minutes during the two day firing cycle," Peter said.

Charlie exclaimed, "Good Lord! Every four minutes for two days!! That's seven hundred and twenty rounds of stoking! Or, worse yet, if every three minutes, then nine hundred and sixty rounds of stoking! That's crazy! Wouldn't a gas fueled setup be easier?"

Peter laughed, "Gas kiln results are not the same at all! Wood-fired kilns create a visibly visceral different kind of surface on the fired objects. As wood ash flies into the chamber, it lands on the ceramic work and fuses to it. Only wood-firing can mark, color, and blush the surface in such a way."

Jackson asked, "How are the surfaces different? What do you mean by visceral?"

Peter sighed and replied, "Visceral means from within the human gut, an emotive and intuitively perceived difference. You can feel it. You know and relate to the art at a base, visceral level, rather than at an intellectual level."

"I was told you're famous for the surfaces on your pottery. Does that come from the wood-fired process?" Jackson asked.

Peter Northburn replied, "The magnificent surfaces that I achieve on my fired art pieces come from the entirety of the work and the process: the clay, the glaze, and the wood firing. All of the elements work in concert with each other."

A crime scene technician interrupted, "Agent Avery, we are going to take the firebricks from the bottom of the big part, the firing chamber. So, I have to ask you all to move out now. We need the space to work."

"What?? You're not going to dismantle my kiln! No you're not!" Peter said emphatically.

"Yes. Yes. They are," Jackson said.

"I have spent decades perfecting the design and operation of my kiln. You are going to destroy it! Why??"

Peter lamented forcefully.

"You explain it to him," Jackson asked of the crime scene technician.

The tech told Peter, "The bricks, especially on the floor of the firing chamber absorb and hold certain oils, residue if you will, from items fired. That's one of the reasons crematoriums don't resell their fire bricks for any subsequent use or purpose that might be ill-affected by the smell or release of human oils and secretions. The bricks will give us an indisputable history of their use. We'll tag every brick. It'll be possible to reassemble the kiln exactly as it is now."

Peter had nothing to say to that. Jackson and Charlie led him back to the showroom. They turned him over to the two agents who were still waiting there.

## CHAPTER 60

"Love that gate, Quinton!" Charlie exclaimed. "Opens by itself."

"You have a beautiful ranch," Jackson said.

Quinton said, "Thanks. Actually I opened the gate with my cell phone. There's an app for the gate mechanism. I can see who's at the gate and open it."

Charlie said, "You've just taken the last bit of magic out of my life."

Harry and Emma called hello from the porch. Quinton escorted the FBI Special Agents to the porch.

"Where are Sam and Carlos?" Emma asked.

"They're waiting on the FBI CSI people to finish up at the Fleeo Gallery. The techs are taking everything connected to Northburn into custody. Even the packing materials Peter brought with the artwork to the gallery. There is so much stuff!" Charlie said.

"Sam and Carlos will be here after they pick up Uncle Charles," Jackson added.

"Uncle Charles was..." Charlie began but was interrupted by incessant honking from the road.

Quinton Quigley looked at his cell phone and said, "They're here." He tapped the phone.

Sam and Carlos came barreling up from the gate in

the purloined Suburban from Phoenix. Uncle Charles was the first one out. He called out, "Who taught these boys to drive??"

"They're from Chicago!" Harry commented.

"Enough said," Uncle Charles replied laughing.

The group of now close friends gathered in Quinton's great room. Everyone sat in the area near the fireplace. A large friendly fire heated the room.

"This has been quite the unexpected investigation," Charlie commented.

Jackson said, "So happy Emma called me."

Emma added, "So happy Quinton and Uncle Charles like to ride their horses."

"Yeah, if Pokey and I see anything else, we'll call it in!" Quinton remarked.

"Roger that! If Lomoto and I see any strange lights or clothes or bodies or anything strange on the ranch, I'll definitely call it in!" Uncle Charles affirmed.

Harry asked, "Has there been an ID on the last load of laundry Uncle Charles saw old Peter Northburn hanging in the woods?"

"Yes. It was as we thought; those were Duffy Dot's clothes. We got DNA from her apartment. Matched it up," Jackson said.

"What about Oren Mackler? How'd he get that far into the forest? Any way to tell why he was up the tree?" Uncle Charles asked.

Jackson replied, "Not really any way to know for sure. As far as we can determine, he walked into the woods. Perhaps he was just scared or spooked into hiding up there.

Or maybe he was lost, looking for a place with a sightline vantage. Remember he was a long-time drug user. No telling what he was thinking."

"What has happened with the evidence and everything taken from Northburn's place?" Quinton asked.

"The techs found all sorts of stuff there. They found Oren's helmet, jacket, and his motorcycle. They found a huge chest freezer in a locked shed behind the studio. There was immediately visible blood residue in the freezer. The whole chest went to the lab. The folks at Quantico were inundated with objects to test for DNA. Initially, they've ID'd Duffy Dot's and Karen Pilling's DNA in the freezer. But they report there is also additional DNA in the freezer. The firebricks from the kiln's firing chamber floor are riddled with human DNA from many different subjects. It's going to take a while to sort that out. But, it does verify that Peter fired some humans or parts of humans in the kiln."

Emma interjected, "Ah, my nose still works! Good news. I've been afraid after all of the dead bodies, in various stages of decomposition that I've dealt with, perhaps my nose had lost its keen abilities!"

Quinton asked Emma, "Can your nose tell what we are having for dinner?"

"Elk!" Emma responded.

"Correct!" Quinton Quigley exclaimed.

"It wasn't my nose. It was my intuition. We usually have elk here," Emma said laughing.

Sam said, "Carlos and I have never had elk. This is a dinner we've been looking forward to!"

"You guys should stay a few more days and go

hunting with me," Quinton suggested. "Get an elk for yourself!"

Sam looked at Carlos. They both smiled big. Sam asked Jackson, "Okay if we stay over and hunt? You don't have to send us back to Wyoming right away do you?"

Jackson replied smiling, "You can stay if you take the Suburban back to Agent O'Brien in Phoenix when you're finished here. Then you have to fly on back to Wyoming!"

"Can do! Hunters! We're going to be hunters!" Sam said laughing.

"Hunters hunting!" Carlos added excitedly.

# CHAPTER 61

Terry Small was still in the county hospital, and still in traction. He was still a prisoner of his injuries. It was early morning so he was listening for the breakfast cart noises. The door to his room opened. He opened his eyes to see an attractive fortyish looking woman rolling a gurney into the room. She was followed by a tall burly young man. Both were wearing jeans and blue-green colored uniform shirts and jackets decorated with patches and badges. The woman had a stethoscope around her neck.

"Who are you?" Terry asked. He wasn't wearing either his contacts or his glasses. He couldn't read the badges and patches, though he could make out that one of the patches on their right shoulders was a red cross on white.

The woman replied, "We're here to transport you to Denver for the grand jury hearing. We're going to take you to the rehab center at the Presbyterian Hospital in Denver. That's where you'll be staying while in Denver."

"What? No one told me about this?" Terry said. Then he remembered. His attorney and one of the doctors had told him that he was going to Denver for the grand jury hearing. They told him that he'd be transferred back to New Mexico once the hearing was over. At that time he'd be going to a rehab facility in Albuquerque. The doctor told him, he'd be up and walking either while he was in Colorado or soon after coming back to New Mexico. The doctor told him he was healing nicely. "Oh, yeah I remember now. Okay."

The medical personnel were joined by a male nurse to lift Terry from the bed to the gurney. In order to do that, they had to disconnect Terry's legs from the traction harness. He'd only been out of traction to exchange the plaster casts for the high-tech aluminum, nylon, Velcro clamp-on braces, and to begin limited therapy. The leg braces were locked at the knee joints to keep the legs from bending. The medical personnel carefully slid Terry onto the gurney. They strapped him securely in place. The nurse gave him a form to sign. And Terry was wheeled out to the waiting ambulance.

The woman and man wearing the jeans and uniform shirts slid the gurney into the back of the ambulance. They locked the gurney in place. The woman climbed in the back with Terry. The man hopped in the cab to drive.

Terry looked over at the woman. She was buckling into her seat. Terry was close enough to read her nametag. He read it aloud, "Phinn."

She looked at him. She stared at him. "Yes?" she said.

Terry had been off the morphine drip for days. His pain medication was now delivered by injection. He hadn't had an injection this morning before they came for him. He asked, "Are you going to give me my pain meds before we hit the road?"

"No. What meds? They didn't give us any medications for you."

"Will you go ask that nurse for my pain med? It's a shot."

"No. You are in our custody now. I cannot administer medications to you without your doctor's instruction and consent."

"Well go ask him? Before we go!" Terry insisted. He could feel the ambulance moving already. "Please!"

"Mr. Small. Settle down."

"Phinn. Where are you from?" Terry asked as he realized the connection of the last name.

"Colorado."

"I knew I guy in school in Colorado named Phinn," Terry said.

"I know."

"You know? Did you know James Phinn?" Terry asked.

"James was my big brother," she said.

"Small world. He was my best friend," Terry said as he tried desperately to form a bond of some kind with the woman. He needed her help. He needed pain medication. He needed some relief from the excruciating pain in his legs and pelvis. His body was screaming in pain from the transfer.

She said, "I know all about you, Mr. Small."

Terry said impatiently, "Surely you have some pain meds in this tub."

She smiled at him and said, "No, we don't carry drugs. It is five hours to Denver. No stops. This 'tub' has a very stiff suspension. It's liable to be a bumpy ride. This might hurt a little. Enjoy."

ONCE before

*Keep reading for an excerpt from the next novel by Lucinda Johnson*

A Novel

## CHAPTER 1

He ordered the equipment weeks ago. Where was it? The delivery was scheduled for this morning. He wasn't going to wait forever. Just as he climbed back into his pickup, he saw the cloud of dust at least a quarter mile down the farm road. He stood in front of his pickup and watched both the dust cloud and the flatbed truck get bigger and bigger as they got closer. He could see the yellow eighteen-ton 318E CAT excavator peeking over the flatbed's cab.

Finally. He waved the flatbed driver off the farm road onto his property, through a wide gap in the fencing that he'd made just that morning. When the full length of the truck was off the farm road, he ran up to the cab to talk to the driver.

"You get lost?" he asked.

The driver answered, "Yep! Couple of times. This is way the hell out in the middle of nowhere!"

"Yeah, it is. Glad you found me."

"Where do you want it?" the driver asked.

"See that red post? Straight in front of you?"

"In the middle of this field?"

"Yes. If you'd drop it by that post," he requested.

"Sure can." The driver slowly maneuvered the flatbed across the open field that was defined only by ghosts of old plow rows. Time and the elements had rendered the field almost flat. The field was transitioning into a pasture. When the driver reached the red post, he stopped. He got out and lowered the ramp at the rear of the flatbed. He climbed up and drove the big CAT excavator off the truck. The driver parked the excavator next to the red post.

After all the paperwork was signed, the delivery was complete. The driver climbed back into the cab of the flatbed, made a wide turn, and went back towards the farm road. He waved as he passed Leo.

Leo got back in his pickup, and followed the flatbed to his fence. He pulled the fencing across the gap then tied it securely to the post it'd been attached to. His field was once again defined. He drove out to the red post. He got in the cab of the big excavator and fired it up. He'd driven lots of heavy equipment over the years, so he knew this was a sweet machine. He began the dig.

He'd marked the rectangle with bright pink spray paint on the dirt. The entire pit was going to be forty by forty feet by ten or more feet deep. It was going to be his new water tank. His simple plan was to dig the hole, line the hole, then divert the stream on the far side of the field to the new water tank.

The first scoop of the earth was very satisfying for Leo. He smiled through a couple of hours of digging. He made smooth steady progress.

As he began another run up the forty foot length, the scoop hit something more unforgiving than any of the rocks he'd already found. He stopped to see what he'd hit. When he climbed down into the pit, he saw he'd scraped what looked like a concrete platform or slab that was hiding about five feet from the surface of the field. He got a shovel from his pickup to find the top edge of the concrete slab so he could dig down to determine how thick it was.

He found the top edge of the flat concrete not four feet from where the scoop had scratched it. But it didn't seem to be a platform, or slab, or a foundation for anything because he couldn't find the bottom edge of it. He dug straight down the newly discovered side about three feet without finding any bottom edge.

Leo got back in excavator and gingerly scooped along the side where he'd dug with his shovel. He dug a trench alongside the concrete that was ten feet deep before he found the bottom edge. Now he had a top and a side and not a complete length of either. This was a big something made of concrete.

He continued excavating the concrete until he had exposed part of the top and all of one side. The side measured fifteen feet across. Leo had two of the dimensions: ten feet deep and a side that was fifteen feet long.

"What the hell?" Leo said out loud.

It was time to get back to the house; his wife would have dinner ready soon. He dropped the scoop and locked up the big excavator. He got in his pickup and headed across the field towards a large stand of tall pines and his home.

Leo told his wife what he'd found. She asked him if it might be an old cistern, or maybe an old root cellar. He didn't think there'd ever been a house anywhere near the middle of that field. Seemed like an odd place for a cistern or a root cellar. She agreed.

"Yes, you're right. And there's no rise there. Flat as the rest of the field," Sally said.

"You come with me in the morning. Maybe you'll figure it out as I unearth it," Leo said.

The two older people ate dinner, watched some TV, then went to bed. They habitually got up at five-thirty every morning. No need for any alarm clock after all of these years. This time of year it was daylight at five-thirty. Still hours away from the heat of the day. Early summer in northern New Mexico.

After breakfast, Leo and Sally drove out to the excavator. Sally liked the beginning of the new water tank. "The cows will love this," she remarked.

"Here's the concrete mystery box," Leo said pointing to the flat gray surfaces juxtaposed the tan textures of the hole.

"I love the new excavator!!" Sally exclaimed. "It's beautiful!"

Leo had been so intrigued by the concrete box that he'd failed to show Sally the CAT. "Honey, get up in the cab.

You'll love it even more! Wanna operate it?"

"Yes, I do. Anything special about it?" she asked.

"Nope, you'll figure it out," Leo said.

Sally started up the excavator, positioned the machine, lifted the long arm with the scoop, and expertly began to dig along the side of the concrete object. She worked on revealing the side that was at a right angle to the already exposed side. Leo watched. Suddenly he yelled for her to stop.

"Holy moly, Sally! Come look at what you uncovered," Leo said excitedly.

Sally cut the engine and jumped down from the CAT. Leo had grabbed his shovel and was already scrambling down into the hole. Sally followed him.

"What is that?" Sally asked.

"What's it doing here?" Leo asked.

Leo used his shovel to clear the dirt and rocks away from the concrete structure until the anomaly in the concrete side was unobstructed.

Sally said, "It looks like a metal door."

"It sure does. What'll we do now?" Leo asked his wife.

"Open it," she replied.

Leo pushed and pulled on the metal handle. The door didn't give at all. He put his ear to the metal door, but didn't hear anything.

"Should we continue uncovering the box? Or should we blast this door open?" he asked Sally.

"Let's dig until lunch," Sally suggested. "Maybe there are more doors."